PRAISE FOR A

THE TWILIGHT WIFE

"An aura of suspense hangs over every page of this well-plotted psychological thriller . . . Don't plan to sleep until the last word has been read."

—RT Book Reviews, 4.5 stars, Top Pick

"You may often have the deep urge to flip straight to the last page— but don't do it. A. J. Banner sets up her mystery perfectly."

—*National Post*

"A canny premise and an intense follow-through."

—*Seattle Times*

"Banner milks every ounce of suspense out of this harrowing plot that reveals memory to be both unreliable and impossible to fully wash away . . . Kyra is a believable, empathetic protagonist, and Banner's ability to maintain tension while teasing out the truth of her hazy past will keep readers engaged."

—*Publishers Weekly*

"This taut psychological thriller ticks all the requisite boxes with a compelling plotline, lovely young heroine, gorgeous seaside setting, and seemingly supportive spouse."

—*Library Journal*

"Tautly written."

—*BookRiot*

THE GOOD NEIGHBOR

"Thrilling."

—*First for Women*

"Breathtaking and suspenseful . . . unique and highly entertaining."

—*Fresh Fiction*

"Packed with mystery and suspense . . . the final destination is a total surprise. Well done."

—*New York Journal of Books*

AFTER NIGHTFALL

AFTER NIGHTFALL

A. J. BANNER

LAKE UNION
PUBLISHING

Text copyright © 2018 by Anjali Writes LLC
All rights reserved.

Published by Lake Union Publishing, Seattle

www.apub.com

Amazon, the Amazon logo, and Lake Union Publishing are trademarks of Amazon.com, Inc., or its affiliates.

ISBN-13: 9781503900813 (hardcover)
ISBN-10: 1503900819 (hardcover)
ISBN-13: 9781503949249 (paperback)
ISBN-10: 1503949249 (paperback)

Cover design by Rex Bonomelli

Printed in the United States of America

First edition

For Janine Donoho, a great friend,
with gratitude

CHAPTER ONE

Lauren is flirting with my fiancé over the dinner I spent hours preparing. She gets this way when she's had too much wine. I'm not far behind her; I'm already into my second glass of merlot. I'm not even sure why I'm drinking—I usually don't. But tonight, Nathan and I are planning to announce our engagement. Our shared future shimmers on a single fragile thread—his daughter's approval. Anna is only nine years old and fiercely loyal to her mother. He promised he'd broken the news to her earlier today, but she hasn't said anything to me. At the moment she's busy hiding olives in her lap. I forgot that she hates them in pasta.

And now Lauren. I can't even. Her husband, Jensen, pretends not to notice. But his eyelid twitches as she flaps her lashes at Nathan, who keeps his cool, while most men fall over themselves in her presence. Never mind that her right eye wanders and her nose meanders to the left. She exudes a strange, hypnotic allure. Her little black sheath dress clings to her curves as she leans over Nathan to refill his wineglass. Her left breast touches his arm, and my face heats. I bet she hovers over her patients this way, everyone's fantasy nurse.

Compared to her, I feel frumpy in my lavender dress, although the silk flatters my hips and the color brings out the brown in my eyes. I dab at my mouth with a cloth napkin, gaze out at the November dusk, at the ocean glimmering through the trees. A distant freighter winks on the horizon, perhaps en route to Seattle. The darkness etches our reflections in the window. Anna, blond and birdlike. Nathan, charmingly unkempt. Jensen, the Viking, enraptured by his voluptuous wife, Lauren, who flirts like an insecure adolescent. And I, the nervous hostess, teeter on the edge of my seat, wavy hair frizzy to my shoulders, my face an indistinct oval, except for luminous eyes. At the round dining table, beneath a rustic wood chandelier, we resemble a happy gathering, but Lauren's behavior pulls us all taut. Perhaps I should not have invited her, but I've known her forever. I long for our childhood friendship, two girls giggling under the covers, sharing secrets at sleepovers. But those days are gone.

Anna watches Lauren surreptitiously, copying her movements, gripping her glass of sparkling apple juice between forefinger and thumb. She's been mimicking Lauren all evening. "Where are Uncle Keith and Aunt Hedra?" Anna glances at the clock on the wall. It's just after seven.

"They probably hit traffic," Nathan says tightly. He gulps his wine.

"Again? They're an hour late." Anna pushes a strand of fine blond hair behind her ear. "Auntie Hedra promised to show me how to put on lipstick—"

"You want a lesson?" Lauren says, smoothing the napkin draped across her lap. "I'm happy to teach you—"

"Anna's too young for makeup," Nathan says sharply, turning to his daughter. "Be patient, Sugarplum. They'll be here soon."

But like Anna, my patience is wearing thin. I need a buffer to keep me from throttling Lauren. I wish my best friend, Julie, had not flown off to a teachers' conference. I need her reassurance.

"That's all you're having?" Lauren's gaze slides to Nathan's half-empty wineglass. "What does it take to get you sloshed?"

You'll never know, I want to tell her. *Back off.*

"I'm not a big drinker," Nathan replies, reaching for another helping of pasta.

2

"Come on, have a little fun. Maybe Marissa can convince you." She throws me an ambiguous smile. I could convince Nathan to kick her out, but I'm better than that, and Jensen should be the one to rein her in. He's staring out the window, his mind a mile away.

"How long have you and Lauren known each other again?" Nathan says, resting his hand on mine. The warmth of his touch gives me temporary comfort.

"Since we were five," Lauren says, slurring slightly. "Marissa moved in next door, just before school started in September."

"Up in Silverwood," Nathan says.

She waves her spoon back and forth, as if conducting an orchestra. "You should've seen her on the swing set. I thought she would flip over the top. Right then, I knew we would be best buddies. We used to pretend to be sisters."

"Marissa didn't tell me that little detail," Nathan says, throwing me a quizzical look. "The sister thing."

"Slipped my mind," I say, putting it mildly. My insides pull together in self-protection. I can't imagine pretending to be related to Lauren, although as kids, we did wear similar clothes, and we both spritzed on her mother's heavy perfume. *We smell the same now*, Lauren said. *Like twins.* As a grown-up, she has taken to wearing the same cloying fragrance.

She reaches for her wineglass. "We lost touch, eventually. You know how it goes. But last year, we ran into each other, and well . . . it's been great to catch up."

Great. Not a word I would use to describe our friendship this evening.

"I'm glad you're talking again." Nathan kisses my cheek, a light touch meant to pacify. He can read my emotions.

"Serendipity," Lauren says, patting his arm.

Her fingers linger too long. Jensen stares at his plate, holding his knife in a death grip.

I look away, forcing deep breaths. One, two, three. Give her the benefit of the doubt. Blame the wine. Or maybe her perfume is poisoning her brain.

Jensen slathers butter on his dinner roll, takes one bite, then another, stuffing the whole thing down his throat. Anna watches him with a slight sneer of disgust. She's into manners these days.

"Here's to neighbors." Nathan raises his glass and gives me a brief, sidelong smile, calming my frayed nerves. He slipped me the same irresistible smile when we first met at Anna's school. Although I sat across from her, his shy, stuttering child, I could only stare at him. At those intense, dark eyes, rough-hewn features. He looked haphazard, lopsided, unfinished. His hair is never completely combed, his shirt never buttoned to the top.

No wonder Lauren is drawn to him. But she needs to back off. Her husband stiffens with suppressed resentment.

"Come on," she says, still leaning into Nathan. "It's not like you have to drive home. Or are you working a night shift?"

"Not this time," Nathan says smoothly.

"No daring rescues?" She waves her hand through the air, fluttering her bejeweled fingers.

"That's not usually how it goes." He stabs a spiral of pasta with his fork.

"You don't give yourself enough credit. You're in such a romantic profession."

She reaches for the wine bottle, but Jensen stays her hand.

"Lauren, take it easy." His voice is clipped, a warning.

Yeah, take it way the hell easy. Maybe he'll yank her to her feet, drag her home, call her out for her outrageous conduct. But he only moves the wine bottle out of her reach.

What happened to the Lauren I once knew? The girl who linked arms with me, who promised we would be best friends until our hair turned gray and our teeth fell out? She must still be in there somewhere, drowning in a gallon of merlot.

"Why should I take anything easy?" She raises her glass. "Life is short. We need to celebrate friendship." A touch of bitterness creeps into her voice. She holds her glass suspended in the air, swaying a little. Her fingernails, normally manicured, are bitten to the quick.

"Yeah, let's celebrate," Anna says, raising her glass, too. But uncertainty darkens her eyes. Did Nathan give her our news?

"Thanks, Sugarplum." He smiles at her.

I pass the plate of dinner rolls to Lauren. The bread will help absorb the alcohol in her system, or so I hope. "Two more courses to go," I say. "This is only an appetizer."

"You've outdone yourself with this dinner." Jensen looks at me, admiration brightening his eyes.

"Surprise, I learned to cook." I grin at him over my wineglass.

Lauren throws him a glare that could freeze the room.

Jensen shifts his gaze to Nathan. "When we were undergrads," he says, "Marissa made a religion of ordering takeout, whenever I was at their place."

Nathan pats my hand. "Is that true?" He's not surprised that I hung out with Jensen in college. The three of us—Lauren, Jensen, and I— were friends long before I met him.

"I wasn't the greatest cook," I say, smiling ruefully.

"You nearly set the kitchen on fire," Lauren cuts in, dropping her fork on her plate.

My cheeks heat. Maybe I should have burned down the whole apartment with Lauren inside. Why did I ever agree to be her roommate? She ended up ruining my life. But I pull back on vindictive thoughts. I only wish the best for her now, don't I?

"You've come a long way, baby," Nathan is saying, lifting my hand and kissing my fingers. "Now you're the world's best chef."

"I wouldn't go that far," I say.

Lauren picks up her fork. "Let's not talk about those days anymore. Makes me feel old."

"We are seventeen years older now," I say. Hard to believe we are both thirty-six. We felt grown-up at nineteen, but we were naive.

"You're only as old as you feel," Nathan says. "Right, honey?"

Before I can answer, the doorbell rings. I leap to my feet, grateful for any excuse to leave the table. I rush to open the front door.

Keith steps inside, bringing a blast of cold autumn air. He drops his bag in the foyer. "Sorry we're late, but my brother here lives out in Timbuktu." Impeccably dressed and groomed, he's a taller, polished version of Nathan but with a narrower face, eyes the color of a rainy sky, and not a hair out of place.

"You know Timbuktu is a real place," I say. "How was the drive?"

"Not bad once we left the city."

"I've always loved the quiet out here." Hedra follows in his wake, a fairy-tale princess flitting in from another world. Her features are sculpted to perfection, strands of silvery hair blowing about her face. But shadows lurk beneath her eyes. She reminds me of an exhausted Gwyneth Paltrow. She hands me a bottle of wine.

I admire the label. "Prosecco. Nathan will be thrilled."

"Nathan doesn't know prosecco from prosciutto," Keith says, whipping off his trench coat. He's in a gray cashmere pullover and pressed black slacks, one step short of a tux.

"Oh, Keith. Don't start." Hedra unwraps her tailored shawl, revealing a long-sleeved, emerald dress that matches her eyes. The satin fabric hugs her willowy shape. But Keith isn't looking at her. He's already striding into the dining room, his gaze drifting to Lauren. She flashes him a grin. My stomach turns. To attract men, she has only to breathe. Even with that gap between her teeth. Or maybe because of the gap.

Hedra must have noticed. Two pinpoints of color appear on her cheeks as we all arrange ourselves in chairs around the table.

"Good to see you again," Jensen says, keeping his gaze on Keith. "When was the last time we all had dinner together?"

"Neighborhood barbecue, August," Nathan says, gesturing with his fork.

"Right." Jensen swigs his wine. "The four of you don't get together more often?" A Southern twang creeps into his voice, a remnant of his Houston childhood.

"Keith and I live in Bellevue," Hedra says politely, as if this explains everything.

Lauren spears an olive with her fork. "But it's not like you're in New York or Europe. You could pop over after rush hour. Couldn't you?"

"Just like that," Hedra says with a mocking smile. She and Nathan trade a quick look, as if to agree on Lauren's stupidity. I feel a flash of protectiveness toward her.

"I work six days a week," Keith explains. "And I'm on call a lot."

Hedra rests her hand on his forearm. "His team is in high demand. His surgeries—"

"Let's not get into the details," Keith says. "We're all here together now. Let's be happy."

"Yes, happy!" Anna says, but she's the only one smiling.

Keith loses his gaze down Lauren's dress. If looks could kill, Hedra would be slaying him. She will probably admonish him in the guest room later. If they fight, they'd better do it quietly. Anna's a light sleeper. She's gazing down at the cell phone in her lap, texting again. Strictly speaking, she's too young to own a mobile phone, but she needs one to keep track of where she goes each week—here to Nathan's place or off to her mother's.

Lauren leans into Nathan again, and he politely pulls away, sips his wine, and looks at Hedra. "What happened to your arm?"

She lifts her right hand, and her sleeve slips down her arm, revealing a dark bruise on her wrist. "Photo shoot last week. I fell off the platform. My heel got caught in the carpet."

7

"Looks painful," I say, wincing. "Must've been a hard fall."

She nods, the color draining from her cheeks.

Lauren reaches over to touch Hedra's delicate wrist. "The bruise is still red," she says. "The hemoglobin hasn't broken down yet."

I look at Lauren, unable to hide my surprise. The haze of inebriation has partially cleared from her eyes—and evidently from her brain, too.

"Really? What does that mean?" Hedra glances anxiously at Keith.

He takes her arm and examines her wrist. "The photo shoot was only two days ago. Not last week. Remember?" He lets her arm drop.

Hedra blinks, her eyes stricken with confusion. "I don't know where my mind is. You're right. It was only two days ago."

"The shoot for the winter clothing catalog, right?" Nathan says.

Darkness flickers in her eyes, then she smiles. "You're the man with the photographic memory." She casts another fleeting look at Keith, but he's staring at Nathan, his eyes glittering stones.

"Remembering things is part of my job," Nathan says, avoiding Keith's gaze. "Can't forget a procedure. Or a dosage. I could get in some serious shit."

"Such high stakes," Keith says derisively.

"I carry thirty-three essential drugs. I could shoot you up with any one of them."

Keith's right eyebrow rises. "Are you a paramedic, or a drug pusher?"

"Are you a surgeon, or an asshole?" Nathan says.

"Nathan!" I say in mock horror.

Keith laughs. "This asshole gives dying patients a second chance at life. It's gratifying to know I'm the one who made it happen."

"It's clearly humbling, too," Nathan says.

Keith's face clouds over, and an awkward silence follows. Hedra rubs her wrist, her eyes vacant. Anna makes a show of slurping her juice; Lauren's face turns the pale-eggshell color of the walls.

Jensen clears his throat. "How about Marissa's cooking? *Molto bene.*"

"I made a Ligurian minestrone for the next course," I say, trying to sound upbeat.

"What's that?" Anna says, wrinkling her nose.

"It's a soup made with vegetables and garlic—"

"Before we move on to the next course," Nathan says, "we have an announcement to make." He pulls me to my feet, looking down at me with such love in his eyes, I lose my breath. My heart thrums; I feel giddy. I'm sure I'll faint. He's going to do this—now, in front of everyone.

He drops down on one knee. My face flushes hot. He pulls a small, black velvet box from his pocket and gazes up at me. "When I first saw you at Anna's school, I fell in love. At first sight."

"Me too," I say, tears springing to my eyes. "When I first saw *you,* I mean." He told me only much later that he watched Anna and me through my office window. When he strode inside, pretending he had only just arrived, our gazes locked, and that night, I dreamed of him. He entered my head and never left. Even now, as he takes my hand, I feel an ethereal connection between us. The first time he touched me, the first time he kissed me, the first time he wrapped his arms around me. Our first romantic dinner here, in this very room. All the firsts compress into this startling moment of intensity. Even though he has already whispered in my ear *Marry me,* somehow our engagement didn't feel real until now.

"Marissa Parlette, will you spend the rest of your life with me?" he asks, his voice hoarse with emotion. "Will you marry me?"

A hush falls through the room, everyone holding their breath. Then someone lets out a gasp. Lauren. I'm aware of Anna furiously texting on her cell phone. I smile at Nathan, then I'm laughing. I've wanted this, although it seems like such a cliché. The proposal on one knee, the declaration of love. Still, it's a perfect moment. "Yes, I will marry you," I say. "Yes."

He slides a filigreed gold engagement ring onto my finger, stands and swings me around while the guests cheer and whistle. He puts me down, and I hold up my hand to the light, proudly displaying my new ring. Out of the corner of my eye, I see Lauren hunched forward, the color leaching from her cheeks.

"Congratulations, bro," Keith says, raising his glass. "You're marrying a therapist. Maybe she can fix what's wrong in your head."

Does he think he's making a joke? I glance at Nathan as we both sit down again, but he's still smiling, not letting his brother ruin the evening. "Marissa can fix everything," he says.

"I'm not a therapist, per se. I'm a speech language pathologist," I say. "SLP for short. I help kids with speech and language disorders."

"You're not a shrink," Keith says, his gaze piercing me. "I knew that. Too bad. Nathan needs therapy."

"Keith!" Hedra gives me an apologetic look. "We're happy for you both."

"Yeah, way to go," Jensen says, patting Nathan on the back. "When's the wedding?"

Nathan looks at me. "We're thinking . . . late spring?"

"We went on our first date in May; we'll get married in May," I say, grinning at him. The first thing I noticed when I showed up at his front door was his T-shirt on inside out, his hair a mess. The look of shock on his face. I was early. But the shock instantly turned to delight. The salty ocean air drifted in, his subtle cologne blending with the scent of pine from the forest. *I'm trying to cook,* he said, ushering me inside. *I hope you don't end up with a stomachache.*

Lucky for me, I have a medic at my fingertips, I said.

I don't know how to do this anymore. The whole dating thing. I've just been Anna's dad for so long.

You cook for her, don't you?

Macaroni and cheese, sandwiches. If you call that cooking.

But he did know. The *dating thing* came to him naturally—his easy laughter, the way he wooed me with that smile and his funny stories.

"No summer wedding for Nathan," Hedra is saying now. "A rebel as always. What are you going to wear? Your uniform?"

"I'll opt for a tux," he says, winking at me.

"But I'm thinking I'll go unconventional." I show her a photo on my iPhone of me in a full-length, elegant silk dress in pale blue. The gathered waist, flowing skirt, and scooped neckline flatter my figure. "Lauren gave it to me in college." Her last true gift of friendship.

"It's exquisite," Hedra says.

Lauren's eyes light up. "Marissa and I—we used to go junking together. You know, thrift shopping."

"You found that dress in a thrift shop?" Hedra says, leaning in.

"It's a rare find from the eighties," Lauren says.

"Wow," Anna says, furiously texting with her thumbs. "That's a movie-star gown. My mom sells dresses like that in her shop."

Hedra draws in a breath. "It's gorgeous."

"We both fit into it," Lauren says. "But it looked better on Marissa."

She's lying; the dress fit her perfectly, and she wore it twice before giving it to me. She loved the shiny blue, the designer stitching. She stares at the photograph, a look of longing in her eyes. A long-dormant feeling of betrayal awakens in me, slowing the blood in my veins. If she asks me to return the dress after all this time, I will refuse. She has already stolen enough from me.

"Why didn't you wear something like that at our wedding?" Keith says to Hedra.

"You picked out my gown, or don't you remember?" Her cheeks redden.

"It was perfect for you." He reaches for her hand, but she scrapes back her chair and stands abruptly.

"Will you all excuse me?" She strides down the hall toward the bathroom.

"Well, cheers," Jensen says, raising his glass.

The air buzzes with Hedra's absence, despite the clinking and toasts that follow. Anna's thumbs tap her cell phone screen, and Keith appears to be texting, too. He looks up at her and grins, and she grins back. He tucks his phone into his pocket.

I get up to carry plates to the kitchen, and when I turn toward the hallway, I see Hedra stepping out of the bathroom, the mascara smudged beneath her eyes. Nathan walks toward her and whispers something briefly. She nods and frowns. He keeps going into our bedroom. Hedra returns to the dining room. A dark feeling floats up inside me, but I push it down.

I leave the dishes in the sink, and when I sit at the table again, Nathan is back in his seat, watching Anna devour her minestrone. How did we make it to the main course? I vaguely remember retrieving the serving bowl from the kitchen, placing it on a trivet in the center of the table.

Anna pushes back her chair and bounces to her feet. "May I go to my room now? I'm done. I'm so full."

"Are you okay?" Nathan's brow furrows. "It's still early."

"I have things to do. Homework and stuff."

"Shooting more squirrel videos?" Keith says.

"Wildlife documentaries. But I'm not allowed out after dark." She dashes around the table to kiss her dad on the cheek before rushing off down the hall. No complaint about our announcement. But I wonder about all the texting and her abrupt exit.

"She's a regular Jane Goodall," Keith says. "Next she'll be off to Tanzania to live with the chimpanzees."

"Don't say that aloud," Nathan says. "She just might try. That whole sitting still in the forest thing. She's always done that. Caught her following a line of ants when she was three. Fascinated by them."

"Where does she get her focus?" Hedra says.

Nathan spreads butter on a roll. "From her mom. They can both obsess over one thing for hours."

Hedra lowers her voice. "When she used to stutter. Was that inherited too?"

"It can be genetic," I say. "Stuttering is a neurological condition. It could be a problem with speech motor control."

"She was upset about her parents' divorce, too," Hedra goes on. "She probably—"

"Stuttering from emotional trauma is rare," I say.

Hedra nods, her face flushing a little as she stirs her minestrone. Keith keeps glancing at her bowl, as if monitoring its contents.

Lauren looks down at her cell phone, then up at us. Her face is white. "Oh, uh, emergency. I'm afraid I have to run." She is up in an instant.

Jensen grabs her wrist. "What's going on?"

She grimaces and yanks her arm away from him. "It's Brynn. I have to pick her up from a party in town."

"I'll go," he says.

"No, you stay."

"Lauren," he says. "You shouldn't drive."

"Yeah, stay a while," Nathan says.

"I'll be fine. Congratulations, both of you, on your engagement."

I get up and follow her to the foyer. "Is everything okay?" I pull her raincoat from the closet.

"I need some air. Come see me out."

I go outside with her, into the cold. The rain has stopped. We move a few yards away from the house. The night flings up the scents of kelp and salt and fir. "Is Brynn okay?"

"She's sixteen. Everything feels like the end of the world to her." Lauren glances over my shoulder toward our house. The rising moon defines her features, pulling them out of the darkness and shaping them within its beam. "Thank you for dinner. Marissa—I really am happy for you and Nathan."

"You could've fooled me. What were you doing, coming on to him?"

"I know I had a bit too much to drink. I didn't mean to—"

"No, you never do." I cross my arms over my chest in the cold. "I thought you and I could be friends again, but—"

"We can. There's more going on than you know. I need to explain—"

"What is there to explain?" I'm struck by the image of Lauren falling all over Nathan. I'm not feeling charitable toward her right now. "I should get back inside—"

"I know you have guests. But . . ." She steps toward me, her voice urgent as she grips my arm. Her fingernails dig into my skin. I shrug off her hand. "I need to talk to you."

"Marissa?" Nathan calls from the doorway. He steps out beneath the porch light. "Are you coming back?"

"I have to go inside," I say.

Lauren glances toward him, then she looks at me. "Could we talk tomorrow? Alone?"

"Tell me now. What is it?"

"Marissa?" he calls out.

"I'll be right there!"

He hesitates, then goes back inside.

"Tomorrow," Lauren says, watching him retreat. "It's important. You'll want to hear this. It's about Nathan."

"What about him?"

"In the morning," she says, turning on her heel. "First thing."

"Wait!"

But she is already hurrying home.

CHAPTER TWO

I consider running after her, but there's nothing she can tell me about Nathan that I don't already know. But as she crosses the fifty-odd yards between the houses, she has already set me off-kilter. The mist swallows her, and I hear the distant slap of the screen door. I linger outside to quiet my thoughts.

Anna's silhouette appears at her bedroom window, the soft song from her jewelry box wafting toward me. The theme from *Swan Lake*. The haunting melody gives me the energy to go back inside and play the gracious host, newly engaged to a man who swept me off my feet. While I was treating Anna, I never imagined he would walk into my office and throw me for such a loop. He was in his blue uniform, just off afternoon shift. He said something like, *Cool decor*. His deep voice mesmerized me. That was it. Anna flew into his arms. Her problem was more difficult than most—she stammered midsentence and often lapsed into silence. But I worked with her on fluency shaping, focusing her breathing, alleviating anxiety, and slowly, over nearly a year, she improved. I hope she will accept me into her home. I hope she loves me as much as I love her. As much as I want to love her, if she will let me.

For now, I savor a few more minutes in the fresh air. I follow the stepping stones back through the garden to the edge of a dense forest. Past these woods, the hillside drops gently to the beach, with a wooden staircase leading down—I've counted 115 steps. A great cardio workout. No staircase exists on the Eklunds' property next door. The bluff rises there, the cliff much steeper, treacherous. Beyond the Eklunds lives Arthur Nguyen, a sixtysomething, divorced family-law attorney. The irony does not escape me. His much younger ex-wife and three daughters left him and moved to California. He consoles himself by walking his cairn terrier, Bert, and pretending to fish in the large man-made pond in his backyard. More of a mini lake. Nathan invited him to join us for dinner tonight, but he declined the invitation.

I inhale the salty air, listen to the soft rush of the sea. We're fifteen minutes beyond the outskirts of Tranquil Cove, a sleepy town of ten thousand residents, west of Seattle on the shores of Enchanted Bay, on the Olympic Peninsula—a protected, curved inlet meandering in from the Pacific Ocean. Idyllic, peaceful. I didn't anticipate that Lauren and Jensen would buy the house next door to Nathan, but the dominoes fell in quick succession—a house up for sale with a view, a shortage of homes on the market, and the Northwest architecture about which Lauren had dreamed when we were kids. *Exposed cedar beams, log cabin, vaulted ceilings, to die for,* she told me. *I want this house.* The same architect built both homes—Nathan's and the Eklunds'. Arthur Nguyen's squarish, modern bungalow stands out on the corner, an incongruous anomaly.

Jensen's voice drifts through the air as the kitchen door opens. "Thanks, man—say thanks to Marissa." He doesn't see me out here in the dark. Hunched in his overcoat, he rushes home to join Lauren. He couldn't stay away from her, after all.

I head back inside and take off my coat. I put on a smile and bring out homemade chocolate cake for dessert, and later, after Keith and Hedra have gone to bed, I'm exhausted but can't close my eyes. I see Lauren's troubled face in the moonlight. Maybe I should have followed her home. But I didn't want her to usurp the evening.

I reach back for better memories of her, from a long time ago. When we were maybe eight years old, she helped me build sand sculptures at the beach. Together, we created two mermaids, fishtails intertwined in the sand. *We'll come out of the sea,* Lauren said. *And marry humans. And live happily ever after. Mermaid sisters.*

We were best buddies then, sharing hopes and dreams. Exactly when did our friendship crack apart? Was it years later, when we were young adults in college, driven by hormones and ambition? Or did a rift form between us earlier? After all this time, my memory blurs.

In the master bathroom, I reach into the back of the medicine cabinet, find the sleeping pills hidden there. My doctor prescribed them three months ago for a bout of unexplained insomnia. But I only took one pill—it knocked me out cold. I shouldn't take another one. I should be able to turn off my worries, and these last several years, I've mostly succeeded. I've excelled at my profession, treating over fifty students a week at the elementary school. I've helped thousands of kids overcome speech and language disorders. I've fallen in love with a loyal, caring man. My history does not rule me.

I down the tiny pill with a glass of water, and in the living room, I kick off my shoes and collapse on the couch. I'm not ready for bed just yet. The house sings a soft lullaby in the breaths of heat from the ceiling vents, in the distant hiss of running water. Nathan must be brushing his teeth. The sounds relax me, and my eyelids grow heavy.

A few minutes later, Nathan saunters into the living room in his blue-and-white-striped pajamas.

"You're clothed," I say. "What a disappointment." Usually, he sleeps in the buff.

"Regretfully. We have company." He sits next to me and pulls me into his arms.

"They're right down the hall," I whisper, pressing a finger to my lips.

"They can't hear. Keith sleeps like a log, when he's not acting like an asshole."

"He's your brother.'

Nathan lowers his voice. "In DNA only."

"What, you don't love your family?"

"*Love*. Such a strong word."

"I know he was cruel to you, but kids are like that."

"You don't have any brothers or sisters," he whispers. "You have no idea. You know what he did once? Locked me in the shed when he was supposed to be watching me. He wanted to go to some skate park with his friends. He threatened me with death if I told on him."

"Did you?"

"Hell no. I was only seven and he was thirteen. I thought for sure he could kill me."

"We didn't have to invite him—or any of them," I whisper.

"Let's ditch them and get married tomorrow."

I interlock my fingers with his. "But we need time to plan . . ."

"What's there to plan? Let's get married on the lawn."

"You don't have a lawn. You have moss and trees."

"So, we'll get married in the moss and trees."

"What should I wear? The blue dress I showed everyone? It's daring . . . blue instead of white."

"I prefer you in nothing. It's what I thought the day I met you."

"You were in that sexy uniform. But I mainly noticed your eyes. You were wearing those amazing eyes."

"I chose them just for you."

"You mean you have others?"

"Take your pick. You were in your gorgeous body. And some gauzy fabric."

"Linen."

"Whatever. You had painted your toenails bright pink. I wanted to kiss your toes."

"I didn't know you had a foot fetish," I say, slapping his arm playfully.

"I have a Marissa fetish," he says.

"And Lauren has a Nathan fetish."

He tilts his head back and groans. "Oh no, let's not go there."

"She was fawning all over you."

He looks at me, his brows drawing together. "What do you mean? I didn't notice—"

"Stop it. You loved the attention."

He laughs. "She did go a bit overboard."

"When she left, she said she needed to talk to me alone. Something about you."

"Oh? What about me?" He kisses my neck. I feel my body waking up.

"She wants to tell me tomorrow."

"Let me know how it goes. I'm eager to hear my secrets."

I pull away a little. "What could she tell me about you?"

He shrugs, his eyes half-closed. "No idea. Who cares? Let's go to bed."

"I promised Julie I would try to call." I pick up my cell phone. "But it's late now. Weird getting engaged without her."

"We were already engaged. She kept our secret."

"But she would have danced with me tonight." I keep my voice low. "She would've been a breath of fresh air."

"We'll make sure she comes to the wedding. Have you heard from her?"

"She texted from her last conference session. Training young art prodigies in the modern age or something."

"The jet-setting life of an elementary school art teacher."

"And I live the domestic life of an SLP." I nestle into his arms. "I want to stay like this forever."

He tightens his hold on me. "I never want to go back to work."

"Then don't. Stay here so I can keep smelling you." I sniff his neck, inhaling the faint soapy aroma and his indefinable male scent.

"That's all you love about me? My smell?"

"Yup, that's all." I tap his abs, firm but with a comfortable layer of insulation.

"Aw, you're killing me." He kisses me again, passionately this time. "I love you like crazy."

"I love you crazier," I say, my signature line. "I love Anna, too."

"And she loves you."

"She seemed upset. I thought you were going to tell her—"

"I did, in a gentle way. But I guess it didn't sink in until I proposed to you formally at dinner, in front of everyone."

"She was upset. She ran off."

"She's okay. She was fast asleep last time I checked. Come on." He gets up, gently tugging my arm, and I see Lauren years ago, yanking my arm in our shared apartment. *Come on, let's go to the party. You can study later.* Stupidly, I went with her, and she ditched me. Nothing like a dark memory to kill the mood.

"I'll be there in a minute," I say, pulling away.

"Don't be long." He heads to bed, and I close my eyes. I'm dozing off, drifting through a grassy field, the sky darkening, the ocean crashing against a distant shore. The field dissolves into the classroom. I'm helping Anna relax her diaphragm, and she smiles at me, but she is not Anna. She is Lauren, her grin malevolent, her teeth sharp. She's going to drain me. I look around for a weapon. But there is nothing. Lauren lunges for me, and I shove her, knocking the wind out of her. I can feel the cold night air on my skin. She tips backward, and we're both tumbling through space. Time passes, minutes, maybe hours.

I wake with a start, my throat parched. I sit up quickly, gasping in the dimness. I'm cold, groggy. I stagger to my feet. What time is it? I can't think straight. The clock in the kitchen reads 12:15 a.m. The full moon climbs high in the sky. I can hear the rhythm of the surf in the distance.

My black flats sit on the floor next to the couch. I pick them up, tiptoe down the hall to the bedroom. I change into pajamas in the darkness, slip into bed beside Nathan. He's snoring softly. I drift off again, lost in a deep slumber until a noise awakens me. Perhaps it is the box spring creaking, the shifting of the mattress as Nathan gets out of bed. The digital clock on the nightstand reads 2:05 a.m. He's trying to be quiet, but I hear his breathing, watch his dark silhouette through the haze of my lashes, my body heavy with medicated sleep. Through the slightly open window, night sounds seep in—crinkles in the underbrush, the drip of residual rain from the downspouts. The air smells cold and clean. At first, I'm sure he's going to the bathroom, but he's moving in stealth, pulling on pants, sweater, and shoes. Does he have a night shift? He said he didn't. *Not this time.*

I want to reach out to him, to say something, but my mind is foggy. I keep my breathing even, as if I am asleep. He's looking at me in the darkness, I think. I can't tell. He turns his back to me and bends his head down, his face faintly illuminated by his cell phone. Is he sending a text? Reading one? If there is some emergency, he would say so. He would wake me. But he doesn't. He slips out into the hall and pulls the door shut behind him.

Cotton clouds drift through my brain, and I hear the distant yapping of Arthur Nguyen's dog, two doors down. When I wake again, a floorboard creaks in the hall—a door shuts softly nearby. Someone must be up, but this time it's not Nathan. He's in bed beside me, his breathing soft and regular. It's as if he never left. Next thing I know, it's 6:45 a.m. Perhaps everything—the door closing, the creaking floor, and Lauren—was all a dream.

I get up quietly and change into jeans, sweater, socks. Nathan doesn't move. I need to get out of here. In the foyer, I bundle up in my overcoat, put on my sneakers. They're still damp, probably from yesterday's walk, a few blades of grass clinging to the soles.

Out in the crisp dimness, I take the path back through the garden. My faint shoeprints lead me through the dirt. Also from yesterday—must be—but it rained last night. Strange. I shiver and glance over my shoulder, half expecting to see a shadow of myself racing up behind me.

I descend the long staircase to the beach. When I reach the bottom, I turn right, heading north along the rocky, detritus-strewn shoreline. My legs are shaky, but the farther I walk, the stronger I feel. The more alert I become. When I reach the headland, I turn back, leaning into the wind. The madrone and fir trees at the top of the bluff lean dangerously. Nathan's disappearance in the night now seems almost ordinary. Almost. He went out for some air. Or to talk to someone at work. No need to worry. We'll live happily ever after. Nothing will stand in our way.

And I won't take that medication again; I'm fuzzy-headed. I've got too much to do putting up my little house for sale, choosing furniture to bring to Nathan's place. This is real, my decision to move in here. The future is already in motion.

I lean into the wind with renewed resolve. I'm nearly back to the wooden steps up the cliff when I spot a pile of clothing—or a large clump of kelp—several yards south of the steps. I pick up my pace. A dull headache pushes at my temples. I duck my chin against the gale, my running shoes pumping below me. My toes go numb. The cold claws at my bones. I should've worn the new silk long johns Nathan bought me for winter.

As I round the promontory toward the dark heap in the sand, the beach widens ahead of me, and I come upon a broken umbrella lying askew at the bottom of the bluff, the handle embedded in the sand. Like an exotic bird that has tumbled down from the clifftop. I recognize the bright-blue pattern of Laurel Burch cats, and my pulse quickens.

I can't move fast enough. Pebbles sneak into my shoes and slow me down, but I'm close enough now to see. The pile of kelp is not kelp at all, and it's not a clump of clothing. It's a woman in a long, black coat. She's lying on her stomach, her head turned to the side, her legs at a peculiar angle, one bent backward. She's barefoot. Her dark hair blows across her face.

I rush toward her, kneel next to her. I'm light-headed, afraid I might faint. I try to shake her, but she doesn't respond. A part of me pulls back, suspended outside my body, watching from a distance. Behind her, a rockslide has left a large pile of debris at the bottom of the cliff. She must have fallen. All the way down. Time slows. The world backtracks. I see her the way she was only yesterday, her magnetic smile, the black sheath dress clinging to her curves. I'm leaning over her now, shouting at her to *Wake up, say something*, but she doesn't move. Her cheek feels cold to the touch. Her lips are blue; her eyes have turned to clouded marble.

CHAPTER THREE

I focus on a spot on the living room wall, on the watercolor painting of a great blue heron perched in the shallows. I'm cold, so cold, even with Nathan sitting next to me on the couch. Nausea rises in my throat—I haven't had breakfast. I need to vomit, but there's nothing in my stomach. Nothing but acid. The living room window is open, letting in brisk, salty air. I can hardly believe we're sitting here while the police swarm the beach and the house next door. It took them ten minutes to get here from town.

I turn my hands palms upward in my lap. They hardly seem like my own appendages, trembling and faintly stained with dirt. Or is it dried blood? I tuck my hands under my thighs, out of sight.

"Should we go down to the beach?" I say.

Nathan pulls me closer to him. "They've cordoned off the area. They have to examine the body."

I flinch at his words, *the body. Come on,* Lauren says, grinning over her shoulder at me. *Let's go to the beach. I saw a purple sea star . . .*

"What are they going to do with her?"

Nathan pulls my hand out from beneath me and holds on. "They might take her for an autopsy."

The word *autopsy* punches me beneath the ribs.

There's a knock on the front door. Nathan gets up to answer, comes back with a tall man in a black trench coat and slacks. He's slim, with slender fingers, a narrow face, and intense, dark eyes. That bit of a mustache seems like a mistake.

Nathan sits next to me again, rests a protective arm around my waist. The detective folds into the armchair across from us and pulls out an old-fashioned notepad and pencil. "I'm Dan Harding. I've been assigned to this case." He hands me a business card.

"You're a detective," I say. "Does that mean she was killed?" Lauren is not a case. She is a person. Was. She lived and breathed, loved and hated, laughed and cried.

"We're trying to figure out what happened." He jots down our personal information. He's not wearing a wedding band. His jacket hangs from his shoulders, and he hasn't ironed his slacks. He looks at me again. "Tell me about this morning."

My tongue ties itself into knots. I'm floating above myself again.

"She's in shock," Nathan says. "Is it necessary to do this now?"

"Memory tends to degrade over time. We should talk now, while your recall is still fresh."

Fresh, as if my memory has an expiration date. *Best before . . .*

"I'm fine," I say, although I'm trembling, my mind wandering away.

The detective taps the eraser end of his pencil on his notepad. "Why were you on the beach so early?"

"I was out for a walk," I say faintly. "I go every morning, early, when I'm staying here, a few nights a week . . . I live across town on Juniper Lane. I walk to get my blood moving, to wake up. We had a dinner party last night and my brain was fuzzy."

"Fuzzy because . . . ?"

"I had a glass of wine," I say. Or two. And a sleeping pill. "It was a special occasion. I hardly ever drink. I'm sort of . . . allergic. When I drink wine, especially red wine, my nose stuffs up and my brain turns to mush. I had to get outside to clear my head."

"Did you see anyone else out there?"

"I wasn't looking. The houses were dark. I saw a freighter in the distance, on the water. But no people."

"Did you see any other boats nearby?"

"Not that I remember. Why?"

"You didn't see Lauren when you first got to the beach."

"No." I squint out at the day, awash in light and shadow. I want to burst out of myself. "I walked in the other direction, north. I only saw her when I got back. I thought it was a pile of kelp or . . . Sometimes things wash up here. But . . . I had a worried feeling. Then I saw the umbrella. She borrowed it from me last week."

"The umbrella belongs to you?" The detective's pencil scratches across the notepad, grating at my eardrums.

"I recognized the pattern of Laurel Burch cats . . . and the small rip on one side. The umbrella was upside down." I make a motion with my hand. "Embedded in the sand, like she'd let go of it. I got on her case about umbrellas."

His brows rise. "Oh? How's that?"

A tear trickles off my nose. I hastily wipe it away. I didn't know I was crying. "She took them everywhere and then forgot them." *Why can't I catch my breath? Why can't I stop the tears?*

The detective nods slightly. "Did you notice anything else unusual nearby? Scuffed sand, objects? Footprints?"

"No, I don't know. The tide was on its way out. I remember thinking—I know it sounds weird—that the ocean had left her alone. The tide came up almost to her coat and then receded, as if the sea respected her." It returns to me now, the image of her black raincoat billowing in the wind. She was barefoot. Her shoes must've fallen off on the way down.

The detective scratches away at his notepad, and I imagine he's writing, *Marissa Parlette, looney tunes, heading for the mental hospital.* "You went up to her and—?"

"I spoke to her, but she didn't answer. I tried to shake her."

"You touched her?"

"I didn't realize I wasn't supposed to . . ."

"There's no law against trying to revive a friend."

I nod, the word *friend* reverberating in my brain. Does the detective even understand the complexity of the term, especially when it came to Lauren and me?

"Ms. Parlette? Did you try to resuscitate her?" He waves his pencil through the air. "Did you perform CPR, or . . . ?"

"What? No." I swallow the dryness in my throat. "I knew it wouldn't help."

"How did you know?" His voice sharpens.

"Her eyes were open, and they looked . . . cloudy." Now I see her in my memory, the way she really looked, the way I couldn't bear to think of her—dried blood on her forehead, her misshapen skull. Bruises on her face.

"Potassium," the detective says. "The cloudiness comes from potassium released into the vitreous humor, the liquid in the eye."

"Oh," I say faintly. How quickly Lauren has been reduced to a collection of chemicals and body parts. And eventually, she will dissolve into dust and blow away, forgotten—the fate for all of us. I bite my lip, fighting back more tears.

"You don't have to talk about this," Nathan says. He tightens his hold, his heartbeat thudding into me.

"I need to say what I saw . . . It helps me make sense of it. But there's no sense in it, is there?" Lauren parades through my mind, hips swaying, dark hair shining in the sun. I see her at age five, her hair already luxurious, singing in a breathy voice as we played hopscotch on the sidewalk.

"She wouldn't have gone to the edge of the cliff," Nathan says.

I reach for his free hand, grip his fingers tightly. The dream somersaults into my memory. Lauren tips backward, plunging into an abyss.

"Oh?" The detective's brows rise. He leans forward. "Was she afraid of heights?"

"More than afraid," Nathan says. "Terrified. She never went past the gazebo."

The detective jots a note, turns to me. "What's your take on that? Did you have the same impression?"

"Uh, yes," I say. "She wouldn't take the stairs if she could see down through the steps. She never dove off the high board at the pool. At the Space Needle, she stayed at the bottom while the rest of us rode the glass elevator to the top."

Detective Harding sits back, runs the palms of his hands along his thighs, as if his hands are sweating. "But she lived near a cliff."

"Great view from there," Nathan says. "And she and Jensen loved the house. They've been there almost a year."

The detective looks out toward the bluff. "She never went all the way back there—at any time?"

"Well, she could have gone for a smoke," I say, grasping on to this possibility. "Jensen thought she'd quit a long time ago. But she took it up again recently. The occasional cigarette to calm her nerves. That's what she told me, anyway. She asked me not to mention it to Jensen, so I didn't."

"Did her nerves need calming for any particular reason?" the detective says.

"She didn't give me a reason," I say. "But smoking seemed to help her. She could have gone back to the gazebo to keep the smell away from the house."

The detective is nodding thoughtfully. "Did she drink alcohol last night?"

"Wine," Nathan says. "A few glasses."

"A lot of wine," I say.

"But she did leave early," Nathan says, looking at the detective. "She had to pick up her daughter from a party in town."

"She probably drove drunk," I say. "Now that I think of it. Or maybe Jensen drove. He left soon after she did."

"All right," the detective says, writing on his notepad again. He looks at me. "After you found her, what did you do next?"

I let go of Nathan's hand and flex my cramped fingers. A gust of wind slaps at the window, tossing cold air into the room. "I rushed back up here. Everyone ran outside. Nathan called 911. I brought Anna back inside. I tried to pretend everything was okay. I didn't want her to know what was going on. But I couldn't keep it from her . . . She asked me what happened . . . I told her Brynn's mom fell." I look down at the dirt and sand clinging to my clothes. The crime scene followed me back to the house. I'm aware of the ticking of the wall clock, and far in the distance, a boat's foghorn.

The detective tugs at his thin mustache. "What was Lauren's state of mind? Did she seem depressed to you? Did she ever talk about suicide?"

"I don't think so," Nathan says, looking at me. "Did she?"

"Suicide? No, but the last few times I saw her, something seemed off."

"Off how?" the detective says.

"When we went for coffee, she stared out the window. Sometimes she didn't seem to be listening. I used to be able to read her, but we weren't close anymore. We had fallen out of touch for a while."

"How's that?"

"In college, we went our separate ways. We got back in touch just over a year ago," I say, feeling a need to explain. "She'd gotten a job at the hospital. We had lunch now and then, coffee, that kind of thing . . ."

"Thank you." Detective Harding gets up, tucks his notebook and pencil back into his jacket pocket. "I'll need to speak briefly with the others in the house."

"My brother and his wife are in my daughter's room," Nathan says.

"What about the neighbor on the corner, on the other side of the Eklunds?"

"Arthur Nguyen," I say. "I heard his dog barking sometime in the night . . . I don't know what time it was. Usually, I don't hear the dog making noise so late."

"I'll pay him a visit. I may be in touch again if I have further questions."

As Nathan leads the detective down the hall, my mind whirls with questions—did Lauren fall? Was she pushed? Or did she walk to the edge of the cliff and take a deliberate step into the darkness?

CHAPTER FOUR

In the hall bathroom, I wash my hands. A cloud passes over the skylight, plunging the small space into shadows. I keep washing and washing, scrubbing and scrubbing, but I need a wire brush to scrape off my skin. The molecules of Lauren sank deep into the pores. I wish I could erase the image of her lying there, her cheek pressed into the sand. Her half-closed eyes—filmy, looking past me. No, looking at nothing. I still feel the salty breeze on my skin, her voice in my head. *I need to talk to you.* But she won't speak to me ever again. I sink to my knees, grief exploding inside me. I can't stand this tiny room, this house, the voices murmuring down the hall. The detective must be interrogating Keith, Hedra, and maybe even Anna. She's only a child, but we can't protect her from the news, from the internet. From violence, from death.

Lauren was alive only last night, and now here I am, sobbing in a tiny bathroom. She rushed to my rescue in a similar bathroom many years ago, when a boy had cornered me at a fraternity party. I don't know why he picked me—I was so shy, a wallflower type. Maybe he found me an easy target. He pressed himself against me, and my throat constricted; my body trembled. His breath stank of beer, and the sheer weight of him paralyzed me. Then instantly, the weight lifted. Someone wrenched him away. Lauren. *Get off her, asshole!* she yelled, and suddenly he was on the floor, his nose bloody. Lauren grabbed my arm. *Come on, Marissa. Let's go.*

Usually I was the one doing the saving. How many nights did I waste coaching her for tests she failed? How many hours did I spend taking meticulous notes, while she skipped class and copied mine later? *I'll make it up to you.*

But I don't care anymore about who saved whom. I only want her to walk through the door and say this was all a mistake, a nightmare. I'll wake up in bed, not in this bathroom.

I'm drying my hands on a towel as someone knocks on the door.

"Marissa," Nathan says on the other side. "Are you okay?"

I yank open the door, look at him, and collapse into his arms. He strokes my hair. "They're gone," he says. "They took her. It's over."

"It's over. What's over? Nothing's over."

"I mean—there's nothing more we can do for her now. We wait for the police to do their job."

"It's my fault. I was rude to her last night. She wanted to talk. But I let her go."

"You can't think that way." He pulls back, his hands heavy on my shoulders. "You couldn't have stopped her—"

"But what if I could have? What if I'd followed her home and insisted?"

"We could all say the same thing. Nobody could be with her every second of every day. Most likely, she still would have fallen."

"But would an autopsy show if she was pushed?"

Nathan rubs my arms. "I'm not an expert. But it should show what kind of injury killed her, whether it was from the fall. They have sophisticated methods of figuring things out, including the estimated time of death."

Time of death—an unknown moment lurking around the corner, waiting to pounce on each of us. I see her applying bright-red lipstick in the mirror, puckering her lips. *How do I look now that I'm dead?*

I brush past Nathan to the master bedroom. The house feels stifling. Suffocating. The air congeals in my lungs. I can hardly breathe.

Muffled voices drift from Anna's room. I go to the closet and start pulling shirts and pants off the hangers.

"What are you doing?" Nathan says.

"I should go home for a while," I say, my voice shaky. If I don't, I will lose my mind.

"You just got here. I thought you were staying—"

"I was planning on it, but . . . I'm in shock. We all are. I need some time to myself."

He sits heavily on the bed. "Don't go. We can work through this."

"I need a little space to breathe." I throw my suitcase on the bed. I'm sick of living out of this weathered blue Samsonite.

"There's something you're not telling me."

I look at him, my uncertainty rising to the surface. I take in his tousled hair, those eyes, so sincere and steady. That intense look of concern. A flash comes back to me, of his face lit by his cell phone screen in the night. And I wonder.

"Something's been nagging at me, yes. Last night, you went out. Where did you go?"

"Nowhere. What do you mean?" He loosens his shirt, although the top buttons are undone as usual.

"I mean, around two in the morning, you went somewhere." I toss a soft black turtleneck into my suitcase. I planned to wear the sweater for a romantic dinner, but I can't imagine going on a date now or ever again.

He scratches his chin. "What are you talking about?"

"I woke up for a minute . . . I had a headache, a foggy mind . . . I looked at the clock. You were trying to be quiet . . ."

"I wasn't." His face pales. A bead of sweat glistens on his forehead.

"You pulled on clothes and left the room. You went somewhere in the middle of the night, Nathan. Are you going to tell me where you went?"

He runs the flat of his hand across his forehead, wiping off the sweat. "What's this about? You don't think—"

"You didn't, I mean you wouldn't—"

"What the hell are you saying?" He lowers his voice. "I know you're upset about Lauren. You're trying to get your mind around what happened."

"You're right, I am. You got up and you were looking at your phone, and you left. I don't know for how long. Where did you go? Don't tell me you were called in to work. I know you weren't."

His face flushes. I'm not sure why I'm pushing him. I trust this man who loves his daughter so much, who fell in love with me in the classroom.

"I went outside," he says. "But I had nothing to do with what happened to Lauren."

"Really?" I look at him.

"You don't believe me? Jesus, we're . . ."

"Engaged? We are, but that doesn't mean—"

"You really think I would lie to you? I got a text from Rianne—I went out for some air."

"From Rianne. In the middle of the night." My insides twist into knots. His ex-wife's name has been popping up in conversation recently, but I can't reasonably complain. She's Anna's mother.

"It was about Anna. When I proposed to you, she started texting her mom like crazy. Rianne was concerned." His jaw twitches, as if he's holding something back.

"Concerned about what? That Anna's head might explode, because you're marrying someone else?"

"Look, it's the way things are. Families are complicated."

"The three of you aren't a family anymore."

"I still need to deal with Rianne, much as I hate doing so."

"I heard you get up. I watched you get dressed."

"I didn't think . . . I thought you were asleep," he says.

"Why? Because I didn't move?"

"You woke up when I got back. At least, I thought you did. You sat up and mumbled something, then you went back to sleep. I thought you were awake."

"I wasn't," I say. Was I? Did I wake again? I don't remember. In the morning, I saw my shoeprints outside. "I woke up later, when you were already back. You didn't tell me you were going anywhere."

"I went out for some air. That's all, like I said."

"Are you sure there isn't anything else going on? Something I should know about?" I try to keep my voice to a loud whisper.

"Like what? What the hell is this, Marissa?"

I sit on the bed next to my suitcase. "You're right, I don't know what this is. But everything about last night wasn't right." My heart is hammering, fast and loud in my ears.

"Wasn't right how?"

"Like, Lauren was all over you, but you didn't complain. You didn't tell her to back off."

"I was trying to be polite."

"Was that all it was?" I rearrange the clothes in my suitcase, folding and flattening my shirts, a vain attempt to restore order. But life, everything, is spinning wildly out of control.

"What else would it be? Did you want me to make a scene on our special night?"

I look up at him. "It didn't turn out to be so special, did it?" Lauren ruined everything—but how can I think about myself? She is the one who suffered. She is the one who is gone.

"We couldn't know what would happen. We couldn't know that Lauren would—"

"Did she text you last night?"

"What?" He looks incredulous.

"Did she send you a text?"

"This is coming out of the blue. One minute, you love me, you trust me. The next minute, this interrogation."

He's right, but I can't help myself. I'm treading water in an endless ocean, trying to stay afloat. "I'm only asking—"

"Why would she text me? I barely knew her."

"You obviously got to know her after they moved in." I gesture toward the Eklunds' house, my fingers trembling. We watched the moving van unload their furniture. A week later, they invited Nathan over for dinner while I was at my place. "Lauren always did like to move quickly." Even as I say the words aloud, I regret them. He looks stunned.

"What? It was just dinner. One dinner. And I go jogging with Jensen sometimes. Share a beer. You knew Lauren half your life."

"She flirted with you at dinner, and in college she did things . . ."

"Like what? You think Lauren seduced me?"

"I wouldn't have put it past her."

"And what about me? You think I would let that happen?"

"No, I don't. I don't know what I think. Lauren and I . . . we seemed to be . . . friends again. But it was a mistake to invite her. She didn't behave herself. I thought maybe she was in touch with you when you went out."

He tosses his cell phone on the bed. "You want to check my texts? Be my guest. Read my email while you're at it. Listen to my voice mail."

"Nathan, stop—"

"No, you stop." He presses his fingers to his temples. "You have to trust me."

I take a deep breath, slowly exhale. "You're right. My mind is in a weird place."

He wraps his arms around me. "It's okay. Nothing makes sense right now. We need to let it all sink in. Don't run away just yet. Stay a little longer. I need you."

"I need you, too." He doesn't know how much. I lean into him, his heartbeat strong and steady against my ear. Lauren steps out of the shadows, an apparition at the edge of my vision. *I'm not supposed to be gone yet,* she says to me, staring with milky eyes.

CHAPTER FIVE

We find Hedra watching over Anna in her room. They're both on the bed, propped on pillows, pretending to read. Pale morning light fogs in through the window. Anna resembles her mother—delicate boned, with translucent blond hair and a haunting of freckles across her nose. I've known her just shy of two years, but she has grown a few inches, her body elongating, her face maturing, losing its softness. Before long, she'll demand a purse, a training bra. She'll want to learn how to drive. Nathan says it scares him to imagine her behind the wheel. Or dating. *Nobody will ever be good enough for my little girl.* She inherited his pronounced jaw and his love of nature. Of saving things. He once helped her capture an injured towhee to transport to the wildlife shelter in Port Gamble. Later she plastered stickers on the windows to prevent any more birds from hitting the glass. *Birds.* Her bird-print pajamas. I could've sworn she went to bed in them last night, but now she's in her turquoise pair.

On her desk, a photograph of the family's distant, happy past smiles out at us—Rianne, Nathan, and Anna at their mountain cabin near Olympic National Park, a forest darkening in the background, smoke pluming from the stone chimney. A selfie from Anna's iPhone. She sits on a mossy log between her parents, grinning into the lens. Rianne's radiant smile reflects infinite patience. Nathan ducks his head to fit into the photo frame, sticking out his tongue. Anna's suppressed laugh bursts out all over her face. She shares a secret with her dad.

I shift my gaze to the windowsill, on which a glass bottle catches the sun, sending a rainbow across the floor—an array of colors and light that Lauren will never see again. Never a sunrise, never a sunset. A dusting of dry soil spreads across the sill, maybe from Anna's dirty hands. She's forever playing on the ground, crouching to shoot videos of ants, squirrels, birds. Her backpack sticks halfway out of the closet—bulging with clothes.

Hedra unfolds from the bed, languid in her leanness. She ushers us out into the hall. "Anna seems traumatized." Her eyes are dark ringed, but I'm still struck by their cinematic green. "Is Rianne picking her up soon?" she whispers, stepping close to Nathan. She stands only an inch or two shorter than him, her face close to his.

"Not until tomorrow afternoon," he says, glancing at Anna. "Why?"

"She needs to get away from here," Hedra whispers.

Nathan brushes past into Anna's room. "Sugarplum—"

"Leave me alone," Anna says.

"Let's just talk."

"Go away." Her voice is snippy, almost hostile. She's either angry or frightened, but I can't tell which. Maybe both.

Nathan comes out and gently shuts the door. "Leave her for now. I'm going to take a shower. Let's give her some time."

Hedra and I head to the kitchen, where Keith stands at the window, hands shoved in his pockets. The light defines his sharp features in profile. Nathan's face forms rougher planes. And yet, the two brothers still look remarkably alike—same prominent jawline, and they both stand with their legs shoulder width apart.

But Nathan tolerates disorder, throwing spoons into the drawer in a jumble, while Keith straightens his cutlery at right angles, laying his life in symmetrical lines. At dinner, he tucked Hedra's bra strap under the shoulder of her dress and kept an eye on her bowl. Does she suffer from an eating disorder? Maybe that's why she went down the hall to the bathroom when Nathan followed her. I wonder what he whispered to her, before she returned to the dinner table. He probably asked her if she was all right.

Hedra slides into the breakfast nook, her knees drawn up, gazing out across the backyard. Her face has a stark quality without makeup.

I keep my hands moving, pouring coffee into the basket, filling the chamber with filtered water.

Hedra gestures toward the house next door. "Their lives will never be the same."

"I know, it's surreal," I say, my voice shaking. "I still can't believe it." I open the fridge, bring out a carton of creamer for the coffee.

"What was Lauren even doing out there?" Hedra shivers, rubs her shoulders. "Why was she wandering around in the middle of the night?"

"We don't know that it happened in the night," Keith says.

"When else would it have happened?" she says, picking at her fingernails.

"Maybe early this morning?"

"Anyone want breakfast?" I stare at the shelves in the fridge. "We have leftover pasta. Or eggs. We have organic eggs from free-range chickens."

"At least the hens are happy," Hedra says.

The coffee bubbles and drips into the glass carafe.

"I'll make an omelet," Keith says, reaching past me into the fridge. He smells faintly of sweat and sleep. He brings out eggs, onion, tomatoes.

"Thank you," I say, pulling my sweater close around me. The loosely knit cotton unravels at my wrists, as if the whole thing might come apart.

"She must've jumped," Hedra says, looking at me. "Don't you think?"

"What?" I say faintly. "No." I wash the tomatoes in the sink. They're soft, the skins beginning to wrinkle.

"She seemed unhappy."

"Exactly how?" Keith says, laying a cutting board on the counter. "What made you think she was unhappy?"

She twists her hair around her finger, an oddly adolescent gesture. "At the last barbecue, I saw her go off for a smoke. She took that trail to the beach stairs, where she thought nobody could see her, and she lit a cigarette. Her eyes were all red, and she wiped them when she saw me coming up to talk to her. She said she had allergies."

"Maybe she did have allergies," Keith says. "Or she had smoke in her eyes."

"I could tell she was crying," Hedra says. "She asked me if I've ever wanted something more than anything in the world. I said yeah . . . freedom."

Silence follows, and then Keith laughs. "Freedom from what exactly? From me? You want to leave our marriage?"

I open the drawer, make myself busy putting spoons and forks on the countertop. *Please don't let them get into a fight, right here in front of me. I won't be able to take it.*

"I didn't say that," Hedra says, the color rising in her cheeks. "Freedom meaning . . . any modeling gig I want. Freedom to travel."

"You do have freedom to travel," Keith says.

"Well, you know what I mean," Hedra says. "She asked me what I would do if I finally got what I wanted, but then, it gets ripped away, and you'll never have it back."

I tear off a thread hanging from my sweater sleeve, throw it away. Try not to look at Keith's expression.

"What did you say?" he says.

"I said I don't know. I asked her if this had happened to her. She didn't answer."

"What did she want that got ripped away?" I say. Lauren had everything—a caring husband, a beautiful house, a job she loved, a daughter.

"She never said. She just stamped out her cigarette and went back to the party. But I could tell she had struggles. She could have thought about suicide. Although she didn't act like it at dinner. She acted like—"

"Stop speculating." Keith drops the knife on the counter with a clatter. He picks up the knife and resumes chopping an onion. "None of us know what happened. We're only guessing."

"All those rocks on the way down," Hedra says. "It's got to be a two-hundred-foot drop."

"Closer to one hundred," I say.

"There should be a railing. There shouldn't be a way anyone can fall."

"We can't cordon off our coastlines," Keith says.

"They're adding a suicide guard to the Golden Gate Bridge," she says.

"This isn't the damned Golden Gate Bridge," he says.

I'm watching the coffee percolate. I hear the shower running in the master bathroom. A helicopter passes overhead, its blades spinning in a deep, pulsing roar.

"This will all be on the news, no doubt," Hedra says. "All the sordid details. They should leave her in peace. Her family deserves privacy."

"Not if they could be responsible," Keith says. "Everyone needs to be questioned. Not by the paparazzi, of course. But by the police."

Hedra makes a sour face. "Responsible? What's that supposed to mean?"

"Take Jensen. We all saw the way Lauren was acting toward Nathan and me, right in front of him."

"You think he would kill her for flirting?" Hedra stares at him in disbelief.

Keith smirks. "The way she acted. Who would blame him?"

Hedra's mouth drops open. "So, he would be justified in pushing her off a cliff?"

"I'm only saying—"

"I know what you're saying." She gets up and strides off toward the guest room.

"Excuse me," Keith says. He goes after her, leaving me to gaze at the knife in my hand, at the cutting board on which the chopped tomatoes are bleeding out. But I don't feel like cutting any more vegetables, or cooking an omelet, or eating anything at all.

I hear the shower turn off in Nathan's bathroom. Cold air wafts into the kitchen, as if a window is open somewhere. The house is too quiet. Motionless. Waiting to exhale. It takes me a minute to put the pieces together in my mind. Anna's full backpack in the closet. *Leave me alone.* The frightened look on her face.

"Anna!" I call out, running down the hall. "Anna?"

Her door stands ajar, the window gaping, cool air blowing in, rumpling the sheets. The photograph of Anna, her mom, and Nathan perches at the edge of the desk, about to fall off. Behind the photograph, on the shelf, Anna usually keeps her jewelry box, her precious gift from Nathan. Only last night, the melody of *Swan Lake* wafted out across the garden. Now the box is gone. A strand of her sweater snagged on a sliver of wood on the windowsill. There's a note on the bed, weighted down by a rock. I snatch up the paper. It reads, in Anna's childlike cursive: *I'm okay. I ran away. Don't look for me. Love, Anna.*

CHAPTER SIX

"What's going on?" Nathan says, striding into Anna's room in his jeans, toweling his hair. "I heard you yelling."

"Could she be any more direct?" I show him the note and point to the open window, lacking a screen.

"She ran away? What the hell?" He crumples the note, throws it on the ground.

I gesture to the turquoise pajamas on the bed. "She was wearing those . . ."

He peers out the window. "Anna! Get back here!"

"Like that's going to help. You yell, and she comes running home?"

"This is not the time," he says, his face dark with anger. He picks up a grain of uncooked rice from the nightstand. More grains of rice are scattered on the floor. "What is this? Anna!" He checks the closet, dashes down the hall, calling for her.

Keith and Hedra emerge from the guest room, following us, white faced.

"She did it again," Hedra says. "Took off?"

"What do you mean, again?" I say, alarmed.

"She ran away when her rabbit died three years ago," Hedra says.

Nathan glares at her. "She came back. Keep looking."

"Get dressed," I tell him. "You'll catch cold. I'll look for her out-side." I can't slow down my breathing.

"We'll check next door," Hedra says.

I pull on my boots and dash outside. After throwing on clothes, Nathan's not far behind me, calling for Anna. No sign of her in the garden. But she could be crouching behind a tree. We both look toward the tangle of forest at the back of the property, between the garden and the bluff.

"Anna!" Nathan calls, cupping his mouth with his hands. We check every corner of the yard, behind a rock, an old wheelbarrow, in the toolshed. Nothing. Keith and Hedra have come out in their coats. They head next door.

"I'll check the front," I shout. But she's not in the yard or on the road.

Arthur Nguyen emerges from a forest trail at the end of the cul-de-sac, the entrance to the wildlife refuge. Bert trots ahead of him, a mop of white fur straining at the leash. Arthur waves, his beret falling over his eyes. I've never seen him without the hat, maybe to cover his bald spot.

I dash up the road to meet him. He's only slightly taller than me and square all over—square face, square shoulders, square shoes. He's all dressed in wool and tweed, grays and browns, to match his hair. "Oh, my word, you found Lauren, didn't you?" he says.

"I did," I say, light-headed.

"How awful, my dear—"

"Thank you. Listen. Anna took off. She ran away."

"Ran away!" He picks up Bert, tucks him beneath his armpit, as if Anna ran out to steal his dog.

"Have you seen her?"

"Nope," he says, shielding his eyes with a gloved hand. Faint scents of woodsmoke and wet dog hair emanate from him. "She didn't come my way, but then, I wasn't looking. Last night I was out, though. That detective came by asking questions, and I realized I did see something."

"You did," I say, shifting from foot to foot.

Nathan calls for Anna in the distance.

"I was out with Bert. Sometime after two. I heard voices, and that sensor light went on in the Eklunds' back porch. I saw someone rushing out toward the gazebo, and somebody else was out there. It was just a shadow. Couldn't see who it was without my glasses. I didn't pay much attention, thought you were all still partying. Wish I could've made it for dinner."

"You think you saw two people?" I say, a ripple of apprehension traveling down my spine.

He nods, petting Bert, who's quivering with cold. "But I can't be sure. Couldn't tell who they were."

"You told the detective."

"I did. Told him every word."

"Anna!" Nathan calls.

"I have to look for Anna," I say. "If you see her, could you let us know?"

"Did you check the tree house?" Arthur says, walking me back up the road.

"What tree house?"

"In the woods behind Nathan's place. My daughters used to play in there all the time." His voice drips with sadness.

"Where is this tree house, exactly?" I say, my heart skipping a beat.

He points back into the woods. "Over there—where it's all tangled up and overgrown. The people before Nathan built it for their kids. Pretty broken down now, but I bet it's still there."

CHAPTER SEVEN

As Nathan and I trample through the backyard, Arthur's recollection races through my mind. *Two people. Sensor light.* Was someone else out there with Lauren? Someone who pushed her? Or without his glasses, did Arthur simply see moving shadows?

"Look," Nathan says, pointing at the ground. Sure enough, someone has worn a narrow path into the woods. We follow the trail, pushing branches out of the way, burrs sticking to our clothes. We keep calling for Anna, no answer.

"I didn't know there were so many trees back here," I say, sprinting to keep up.

"The Eklunds' property was logged, but not on this side." He stops at a clearing, and there it is, a small, dilapidated structure, perched maybe ten feet off the ground between two firs. A slanted ladder curves around the trunk of the biggest fir, missing a couple of rungs.

"Anna, are you up there?" he shouts up. "Anna!" No answer. He starts to climb the ladder, but I yank his arm.

"You're too heavy," I say. "Stand here in case I fall. I'll go up."

He frowns but stands back. I climb up and peer inside the tree house, light leaking through holes in the roof. The smells of old wood and damp mold waft toward me. Candles and books crowd into a corner of the sagging floor, and there is Anna, sitting cross-legged on a tattered sleeping bag, her backpack in her lap. I exhale with relief.

"She's here!" I shout down.

"Go away," she says. "Leave me alone."

"We were worried about you," I say.

"I'm good. I'm staying here."

"Anna!" Nathan says. "What are you doing up there?"

"I'm not coming down," Anna says.

"But all your stuff is in your bedroom," I say, not daring to crawl inside. The whole thing might collapse.

"I have all the stuff I need."

"But you've got a nice room—"

"I don't like my room anymore."

"It gets cold up here."

"I have a sleeping bag. I love it up here. I can see everything."

I motion to Nathan to stay at the bottom. "You're going to stay up here forever then?"

"I don't know about forever," she says. "This is my first stop."

"Where else would you go?"

"I don't know yet."

"So, this is like a hotel?"

"More like camping."

"Anna?" Nathan calls from the bottom of the ladder. "Come down. Now."

I reach for her hand. "We're coming down. Aren't we?"

"I'm staying up here," Anna says, tucking her hands under her armpits. "I don't know why everyone is making a big deal. I've only been up here for like, five minutes."

"It's not that," I say. "It's just . . . with everything that's happened, we're all a bit spooked. And we want you safe."

"With everything that's happened? It's one thing. Brynn's mom died."

"One terrible thing," I say. "Do you have food for forever in your backpack?"

"I'll get more later."

"Shouldn't you talk to your dad about this?" Taking a chance, I cautiously crawl inside and sit cross-legged next to Anna. A plank groans under my weight.

She shrugs, looking at her ragged fingernails. "He can come but he has to knock. You didn't knock. Nobody ever knocks."

"I'll knock next time," I say. "If you live up here, you would miss the view from your room."

"No, I won't."

"I'm coming up!" Nathan says.

"Just wait!" I call down. I look at her. "If you stay up here, you'll need double pajamas. There's no heating system. Where are your bird pajamas? The ones you wore to bed last night."

She says nothing.

"Did they get wet?"

"Yeah."

So, she did go to sleep in them, then changed out of them. "Look, I know things have been crazy," I say. "But—"

"Anna!" Nathan calls up. "Please come down."

I look at her. "Let's go down and talk about all this."

She looks at me, her eyes wide. "We could go somewhere, right? We could go away?"

"Where would we go?"

"Somewhere like a palace or a fortress or . . ."

"Is that why you're up here? You don't feel safe in the house?"

She doesn't reply.

"We're safe in the house with your dad."

She glares at me. "No, we're not. You don't get it. People can be bad."

"Who, exactly? Who can be bad?"

"Just people."

"Which people?"

She shrugs again. "Brynn's mom is in heaven, if she was good. But what if you're both? Good and bad?"

"That's a difficult question," I say, stopping short of *for someone your age.* "Who's good and bad, Anna?"

"Nobody."

"What's going on up there?" Nathan says.

"We're all human," I say to Anna. "Everyone has elements of good and bad in them."

She narrows her eyes at me. "Even me? Even you? Even—?"

"What?" Her questions throw me off. "What is this about?"

"Nothing." She looks down at her hands again.

"Anna—"

"I was just asking, that's all." She's shivering.

"You're cold. Let's go inside the house. Come on." I reach over and grab her backpack. "Ready?"

The wind blows; the tree house creaks. Leaves rustle around us, and not far from here, the ocean rushes up across the sand. I can sense Nathan at the bottom of the ladder, losing his patience.

"I don't want my mom to know I'm up here," Anna says.

"She doesn't," I say, although I'm not sure.

"Dad probably called her again. He left her a message this morning."

"Look, I'll speak for you. You'll be fine," I say, but I may be wrong. It's not up to me. But right now, I'll say anything to get both of us out of this rickety contraption.

"I'm still planning to leave," she says. "After breakfast."

"Sure, you need to eat."

"I can't cook up here."

"No, it would be a fire hazard. Shall we go down?"

She nods with resignation. As we descend the ladder, a woman rushes toward us through the brambles, translucent blond hair flying.

"That's my mom," Anna says softly. "I'm in big trouble now."

49

CHAPTER EIGHT

Rianne rushes to Anna and envelops her in a hug. I'm struck by her singular focus. She's in a vintage coat, boots—she must've ripped herself away from her shop. Her expression instantly shifts from worry to anger. "Oh, Anna, what were you thinking? You scared us all half to death." Then she grabs Anna's hand and drags her back through the rain toward the house.

"I was in the tree fort," Anna says. "I'm allowed to go up there!"

Nathan and I follow, Nathan giving me a look that says *Now we're all in big trouble.*

"Up where? What are you talking about?" Rianne's voice cuts through the wind. "Where is your phone? I tried to call a hundred times!"

"I don't know—I lost it."

"Where did you lose it? Is it in your room somewhere?"

"I don't know."

Nathan grabs Anna's backpack from my arms as we speed up. "What did she put in this thing? A ton of rocks?"

"Food for forever," I say.

Back at the house, Keith and Hedra are waiting in the kitchen, dressed and ready to go. Nathan hoists Anna's backpack onto the counter. She dashes off to her bedroom and slams the door, still in her coat and boots.

"You could have completely lost her in those woods," Rianne says, glaring at Nathan.

"I didn't," he says.

"But you could have. You know how she gets. When she's upset, she takes off. What were you doing?"

"I was occupied."

Keith motions to Hedra, and they move into the living room.

"Not occupied watching your daughter, obviously," Rianne says, ignoring the rest of us. I stand back, but I don't leave the kitchen.

"It's been crazy here with the police," Nathan says.

"They weren't interrogating Anna, I hope."

"Look, you didn't get back to me. I called you. You were working or whatever."

"Yes, I run a business." Rianne looks at me as if seeing me for the first time, her face etched with worry. But she found time to call Anna more than once.

I take my cue to disappear into the living room, stripping off my wet coat. Nathan and Rianne head down the hall to Anna's room.

"Just like old times," Keith says, sighing. He is standing at the window. Hedra is sitting on the couch.

"What's that supposed to mean?" I say. I feel shut out, the former family of three together again in Anna's room. But at least she is safe.

Hedra pats the cushion next to her, but I don't want to sit. "Rianne wants Nathan to keep an eye on Anna 24-7," she says. "Didn't I tell you? She's looking for a reason to call him a bad dad."

"But that's ridiculous," I say. "He's a great dad."

"We know that. But does she?" Hedra nods toward the hallway.

We're quiet, listening to the murmur of voices. Soon, Rianne comes back down the hall, Nathan in tow. "I've got to get back to the shop," she says, stepping out on the porch. Nathan follows her out. Her voice drifts in through the open kitchen window. "What the hell were you thinking? . . . Don't want to leave her . . . Lauren . . ."

"Traumatic day . . . ," Nathan says. "She'll be fine."

"Get to the bottom of this . . . family." Her door slams; the SUV revs up and screeches off.

Nathan comes back inside, shoulders slumped. He hugs me. "Thank you for your help . . . in the tree house."

Keith goes to the foyer, picks up the overnight bag. "We should get out of your hair. I'll load the car. See you two out there?"

Nathan nods, distracted. Hedra gets up from the couch and follows Keith outside, leaving Nathan and me alone. "What happened out there?" he says. "What did she say in the tree house?"

"She asked me if people can be both good and bad." Her words dig into my brain. *Even me? Even you?*

"What's gotten into her?" He scratches at his chin with the back of his hand. I pull a few burrs from his hair.

"Something has her spooked." I unzip her backpack on the counter, bring out squished bananas and bread, a bottle of water, socks, underwear, jeans, a shirt. And her damp bird-print pajamas. No jewelry box. "She went to bed in these," I say, holding up the pajamas. "But they got wet. She changed into the other ones in the night."

"What, you think she's wetting the bed again?"

I sniff the pajamas. I smell only the outdoors—moss and cedar and the salty sea. "No, but look at the mud on the cuffs and knees. She went outside."

Nathan frowns. "At night?"

"I don't know. Arthur Nguyen said he saw two shadows last night when he went out with Bert. But he wasn't wearing his glasses."

Nathan stands perfectly still, looking at me. "You think . . . you still think it was me. It wasn't. Arthur can't see beyond the end of his nose without his glasses."

"He could see well enough to walk his dog."

"He could navigate that yard with his eyes closed." In the driveway, Keith starts up the Mercedes.

"I'm not arguing with you," I say. "But I'm worried about Anna. Maybe she needs a break somewhere away from here."

"We can't," he says. "Rianne's rigid about her schedule."

"Talk to her. She can't dictate our lives."

"She can dictate Anna's life. She's her mother."

"And you're her father. You have as much of a say."

"Rianne wants my hide. Maybe she should have it."

"No, it's not your fault that Anna ran to the tree house."

"Maybe it is," he says, opening the front door. The engine noise and smell of exhaust waft in.

"How is she?" Keith says, rolling down the driver's-side window.

"She'll survive into adulthood, I hope," Nathan says. "But I should get back inside. Thanks for coming, you two." He goes back in the house, leaving me standing awkwardly in the driveway.

"Drive safely," I say to Keith.

"Will you be all right?" he says.

"I'm okay—it's Anna I'm worried about."

"She has always been troubled. This is nothing new."

"Only in the last few years," Hedra says. "Since Nathan and Rianne started fighting. She's an only child—"

"We shouldn't keep you from her," Keith cuts in. "We have to head out. I've got to go into the hospital. Surgery."

Hedra casts her gaze downward.

"I hope it goes smoothly," I say.

Keith adjusts the rearview mirror. "Hedra. Your seat belt."

She pulls the seat belt across her shoulder and clips it into place.

I wave as Keith pulls out of the driveway a little too fast. Hedra waves back at me, a false smile pulling at her lips. Her green eyes have gone dark. Keith reaches an arm around the back of her headrest, but as his hand touches her shoulder, she shrugs away.

CHAPTER NINE

As Nathan and I unload the dishwasher, I imagine hurling each bowl against the wall, stomping on the glasses, smashing them. Who cares about piling the plates just so, arranging cups in the cabinet? I can't concentrate on ordinary tasks, when each moment becomes an exercise in endurance, haunted by Lauren's urgent voice. By everything she wanted to say. Last night will always be our final dinner with her. The evidence lines up on the countertop—the wineglasses too delicate to run through the dishwasher.

I wash a glass beneath the faucet, washing and washing over and over until Nathan gently takes the wineglass from my hand.

"Don't worry about it," he says, placing the glass on the counter. "We can do this later."

I grip the sponge, feeling untethered, my feet barely touching the floor. If it weren't for gravity, I would have lifted off by now. We have the luxury of *later*, of planning the next hour, the next day, the next year. Lauren does not—so why should I bother? Any of us could die at any moment. I could slip, fall, and crack my head open. A car could swerve into my lane. I could get caught in a cross fire, collateral damage.

"Maybe you should sit down," Nathan says, his hand on my elbow.

"I don't want to sit," I say, gripping the edge of the counter for support. "Did you notice Keith and Hedra acting like everything is normal? Keith, anyway. All he can think about is getting back into surgery."

Nathan lets go of my elbow, towel dries the wineglass, and holds up the goblet to the light, checking for water spots. "His patients need him. It's not like they can live without their hearts." He puts the wineglass away in the cabinet.

"But he can live without his." I reach into the dishwasher, bring out a mug that reads, *Live life on purpose*. But I don't know my purpose anymore, except as the keeper of memories—of those who have gone. My father, and before him, my grandparents. And now Lauren.

"You're right." Nathan laughs dryly. "I'm not sure Keith is capable of grief. But he's a damn good surgeon."

"And that's all that matters, right?"

"For someone with a damaged heart, yeah."

I turn to Nathan, leaning back against the counter. "He alluded to something when you were taking a shower . . . He almost suggested Lauren had it coming. That she deserved to die."

"You know how Keith is. I'm sure he didn't mean it."

"Didn't he?" I reach into the dishwasher, pull out spoons, throw them into the cutlery drawer. "How do you know he performs surgery to help others? What if it's just for his own sense of accomplishment? Or what if he enjoys cutting people open?" I shiver, pushing away the image of blood seeping out beneath Keith's scalpel.

"Maybe he does. He's got a dark side. You want to know what else he did when we were kids? He came in while I was taking a bubble bath and held me under the water. I was maybe five."

"What?" I drop dinner knives into the drawer. "Why would he be so cruel?"

"He thought I stole something. I can't remember what. I tried to hold my breath, but I thought for sure I was going to drown. He let me up at the last second, right before I lost consciousness. It was frightening." He looks out the window.

"Oh my God," I say, staring at the jumble of silverware in the drawer. "Why didn't you tell me?" I look up at Nathan. His eyes are glassy, his expression almost feral.

"Because I want to forget. Because he's my brother."

"In DNA only. Remember?"

"But it's in my DNA, too. That's what scares me."

"You're different. You're not like him."

Nathan looks at me, a dark worry in his eyes. "I'd like to think you're right. But sometimes I . . ."

"What?"

"I think about hurting people, like the person who killed Lauren, if she was pushed."

"Everyone gets those emotions. But you don't act on them."

His shoulders relax. "I don't. And neither does Keith. He's mellowed out over the years. He even apologized for the way he treated me—"

"Do you think he's cruel to Hedra? Does he cheat on her? I mean, the way he looked at Lauren . . . the way the two of them looked at each other. I wouldn't have put it past her to go after him. Or anyone else." The *anyone else* hovers between us, but Nathan doesn't take the bait.

He rubs his hands down his face, as if to erase his thoughts. "Come on. I wouldn't go that far. I know what she did in college. But now? You think she was still like that?"

"She could have been," I say, pressing the palm of my hand to my forehead. In truth, I don't know what kind of person she had become. Recently, she kept me at arm's length, rarely sharing her emotions. She talked about Brynn, difficulties at work. But we didn't go deeper. We didn't discuss our shared past.

The dishwasher is empty now. Nathan starts to load it again with leftover dirty dishes, the ones that didn't fit last night. "Look, I get it. You're trying to figure out what happened to her. But the detective is right. It seems she drank too much, wandered to the edge, and slipped. It happened, and there's nothing we can do to change that now."

"But she had bruises, and the blood . . . all over her. Her head was bashed in." I try to keep my voice from sinking into the deep end.

"That happens when people fall," Nathan says. He finishes loading the dishwasher, adds the soap, turns on the wash cycle.

"How can you talk about it in such a detached way?"

"I'm just stating facts. Ever see the simulation videos? They push a dummy off the edge of a cliff? The dummy falls over headfirst. Heads are heavy. You might try to stay upright but you won't."

I look at him, my throat dry as the dishwasher churns into action. "You watched videos of dummies falling off cliffs."

He looks at me with disbelief. "For my job, Marissa. I wasn't . . . researching how to throw someone off a cliff."

"Right," I say faintly, but my stomach twists. "Let's not talk about it anymore."

"Of course," he says gently.

I pick up another wineglass, the last one from dinner, a faint lipstick stain on the rim. Lauren's glass. She was the only one wearing this bright shade of red. I see her lips the way they looked on the beach— blue, dead. The memory of her clouded eyes punches me in the stomach. I put the wineglass on the counter, turn and dash to the bedroom.

I hear Nathan's footsteps behind me. "Are you okay? What happened?"

I sit on the edge of the bed. "I can't do this. I can't wash her away."

He sits next to me. "You don't have to."

"I just . . . don't want to act like life goes on the same as before . . ."

He pulls me into his arms. "We'll leave everything for now."

I lean into him, grateful for his warmth. I'm dimly aware of his cell phone buzzing on the nightstand. A text pops up, and I glimpse a few incoming words, . . . about you . . . can't stand this, before he reaches over and swipes it away.

CHAPTER TEN

Before I can ask Nathan about the text, Anna calls out to us from the backyard, her voice distant and muffled. We get up and go to the window. She crouches in front of a huckleberry bush, her breath smoking up in the cold. She holds up a giant pinecone and grins at us. "Look what I found!"

Nathan smiles and waves at her through the glass. "Come on back inside!" he shouts, but she doesn't seem to hear. She turns away, videotaping some small creature in the underbrush.

My gaze slides to his cell phone screen, now black and silent. "Who sent you a text?"

"Rianne, worrying about Anna. She doesn't want me to let her play outside. She could run away again. But she's nine, not three. I can't lock her inside. She loves being outside."

"She's certainly focused," I say.

"She gets that from Rianne, like I said. But her love of nature comes from her grandma. My mom. I wish the two could have met. My mom used to take long walks in the woods, maybe to get away from us. Or to think. I don't know." He heads back down the hall to the living room. I follow him, stand next to him at the bay window overlooking the backyard and the forest beyond.

"She was a stay-at-home mom," I say. "She never worked outside the home?"

"It was a full-time job for her, raising two boys. But she got restless. Took a night class. But Dad didn't want her to . . . They argued, to put it mildly." Nathan goes to the kitchen, pours himself black coffee. He never adds milk. The dishwasher softly churns.

"That must've been hard for you," I say, thinking back, trying to pinpoint a time when I heard my parents fighting. Never, not once. They lived inside a muted marriage. We played games and laughed. But it was all an illusion. If it wasn't, why would my mother have left?

"It was normal for us," Nathan says. "Everything that happens when you're a kid is your normal."

"But you have a new normal now," I say.

"For Anna," he says, gulping his coffee. "Everything was going to be different for her." His voice cracks. "It was supposed to be."

I go to him, rub his back. "She knows you love her."

"Yeah, right. Look at her. She ran away from me."

"She wasn't running away from you," I say, but for a moment I think, *Maybe she was.*

He sighs, wraps an arm around my waist. "She still can't find her cell phone. Rianne said she tried calling all morning. But I haven't heard any of the beeping and buzzing when texts come through. Where the hell could it be?"

"Probably in one of her pockets. In her coat?"

"We'll check again."

"Do you think she saw something out there?" I say. "When she was out in her pajamas? Could she have lost her phone?"

"It could be out there, yeah. We'll check the yard."

"I didn't see it in the tree house."

Anna rushes in, slams the door, and whips off her boots, her cheeks rosy from the cold. She waves her disposable camera, a temporary replacement for the camera on her lost cell phone. "I got video of a gray squirrel burying pinecones for winter. I love it when animals bury things, like they know to plan ahead." She seems to have forgotten her wish to run away forever.

"Great!" Nathan says. "Should we look for your phone again?"

"I'll look for it by myself." She waltzes into the kitchen, ducks her head into the fridge. "We don't have any food."

"Let's go shopping then," Nathan says, and he and Anna grin at each other, sharing a sudden sense of purpose. He turns to me. "Come with us?"

"I'll stay here and clean up," I say quickly. "I need a little quiet time." I'm not ready to face the world. I could burst into tears at the slightest provocation.

"We'll be back soon." He kisses the top of my head. "Enjoy your time alone."

After he and Anna leave, the silence oppresses me. I try to clean up, but I'm distracted, my thoughts drifting to the text on Nathan's phone. He didn't respond, didn't try to pacify Rianne. He simply swiped away her words. He has taken the phone with him.

Through the window above the sink, I watch an old, silver Buick creep up the Eklunds' driveway. Lauren's father emerges from the car. A tall man, he looks diminished, defeated. He hunches in his raincoat against the wind. Her mother gets out, moving stiffly, as if her joints are fused. I remember her hair, long and dyed blond, often plastered to her head when she returned from a twelve-hour shift at The Oyster Bar, a mediocre seafood restaurant in Silverwood. Now her hair is curly white, tinted greenish. They must have driven all the way from Spokane, where they've been living for the past several years. Can it really be only six hours since I found Lauren?

I'm glad they're here for Brynn. She needs family around her. I can't imagine what she's feeling, knowing her mother won't see her graduate from high school, won't come to her wedding, won't pick her up from a party or give her maternal advice ever again. My heart breaks for the shattered family next door. I wish I could take away their pain—and Anna's fear. What did she hear or see last night in those bird-print pajamas? Did she see what Arthur Nguyen saw? A malevolent shadow flitting beneath the motion sensor light?

Lauren's mother and father disappear behind the hedge, heading to the front door. I swallow a lump in my throat, escape from the kitchen, and go to the guest room to strip the bed. The large bay window faces the buffer of forest between the house and the road. We're almost at the end of the lane, where civilization runs away into wilderness.

It feels mundane changing the sheets, fluffing the pillows. Lauren did the same when she was sixteen, working as a candy striper at Silverwood Hospital. Already on her way to becoming a nurse. When I asked her why she didn't want to be a doctor, she said, *Bedside, that's where I belong. Out on the floor, caring for patients.* She tended to her frail grandmother when she moved in with the family, in the last stages of a progressive lung disease.

Despite Lauren's behavior at dinner, and the dark turn our friendship took, I feel the loss of her, the world's loss of a woman who was, beneath her seemingly selfish exterior, a caretaker. Unlike Keith, full of himself, and Hedra, fragile and uncertain, and even me, although I thrive on helping others in my own way, Lauren soothed the terminally ill, embracing challenges from which the rest of us would flee.

Keith and Hedra ran away from the guest room in a hurry, leaving the blankets in disarray and a black umbrella on the dresser. In the coat closet in the foyer, I spot a credit card on the floor. It must have fallen from someone's pocket. When I pick it up, I see it's not a credit card but a key entry card, with a black stripe on the back, a card used to enter a hotel or motel room or a private club. The logo shows an oak tree sitting on an oak leaf, but no other identifying words. The image looks vaguely familiar, but I can't place it.

I send a text to Hedra, asking if she or Keith left the card here. A few minutes later, she responds, It's not ours. Must belong to Jensen or . . . maybe it was Lauren's?

Maybe, I type back, a lump in my throat. Thank you.

I bundle up, tuck the key card into my coat pocket, and trudge over to the Eklunds' place to pay my respects. I can't bear to stay indoors. Lauren follows me everywhere—into the dining room, reaching over to refill Nathan's wineglass. Staring down at her phone. Hurrying out the door. But perhaps nothing she did last night was relevant. She lived an ordinary life, until that life was snatched away by a freakish, unexplained accident.

Out in the crisp, cold day, juncos chirp in the underbrush, as if life is the same. As I walk up the street, I expect Lauren to emerge from her house to pick up the newspaper, pull a weed along the path to the curb. Her hands were always moving, fingers combing her hair, plucking dead leaves off her plants. When we were little, she loved to braid my ponytails.

On the stoop, I knock tentatively. The door slowly opens, and I draw in a breath. Jensen stands before me in a rumpled sweater, jeans, and white wool socks, his handsome face as creased as the jeans. He's big, broad shouldered, solid. Our shared history comes rushing back. The three of us cavorting in the college apartments. Jensen laughing so hard, snorting beer out of his nose.

"Marissa," he says, looking past me.

"Jensen, I don't know what to say . . ."

In one motion, he hugs me so tightly I can hardly breathe. His body is tense, holding off a breakdown. "I can't believe she's gone."

"I know," I say, hugging him back. She barges in between us, the memory of her. She adjusts his collar, and her cloying perfume lingers in the air. I look over his shoulder, up the stairs. Brynn stands on the landing, gripping the railing, her eyes puffy. She's Lauren at sixteen. Almost. Same pout, same upturned nose and wide-set eyes. Only Brynn did not inherit Lauren's curvy build. Jensen gave her his solid frame. She shakes her head at me, as if I am to blame for her mother's death. Maybe I am. If Lauren had drifted out to sea, Brynn could still hope for her safe return. She could still be out there, treading water, waiting for a coast guard rescue. Lauren was always a strong swimmer. *Race you to the pool,* she says in my mind, running ahead to the community center near Old Town Lane, the street on which we grew up, her towel flapping behind her. *Last one in is a rotten egg.*

Brynn charges down the stairs, spins a hairpin turn, and rushes through the house. The back door slams.

Jensen releases me, wiping his eyes. "Don't mind her. She's not herself."

"None of us are," I say.

"Where the hell are my manners? Come in."

I step into the foyer. He's standing close to me now, closer than he has stood in many years. Since he married Lauren, we no longer touch, except briefly to say hello or goodbye. In a formal way. At times, I've caught him looking at me in private contemplation.

I glance toward the open coat closet. My throat goes dry. Everything of Lauren's is still there, of course—her bright-red snow jacket, her knee-high boots. On the foyer wall, framed photographs show the family on a ski trip. Why did I think that with Lauren gone, the evidence of her life would disappear, too? I tear my gaze away from the photographs, produce the key card from my pocket. "Is this yours? Did you or Lauren leave it behind? I found it in the coat closet, on the floor."

He looks at the card, and his lips turn down. "No idea. Never saw it before."

"Could it have been Lauren's?"

"Not that I know of."

I tuck the card back into my pocket, perplexed. "How are her parents?"

"Not good." His voice is low, husky. "They think . . . they're not happy with me."

"They think you should have prevented her fall?"

"Something like that."

"Give them some time."

"It might be a while."

I ought to order flowers, a card—something. "If there's anything I can do."

He nods, takes a deep breath. "When you found her . . . was she . . . ? I mean . . ."

"You saw what I saw," I say. He had raced down to the beach, shouting her name.

"Yeah," he says, drawing a shaky breath.

"Did Arthur Nguyen tell you he saw something in the backyard?"

Jensen nods, glancing in the direction of the house on the corner. "Who knows what Arthur saw? We get deer, bears coming down from the reserve all the time. Anything can set off the motion sensor light."

"Did the detective say anything? Does he think someone else could've been out there?"

"All he said was they found her cell phone broken on the rocks. She took it out with her. Was she trying to make a call in the middle of the night? What was she doing?"

"I'm sure the police will determine—"

"She was pissed off at me . . ." His eyes fill with tears. I want to reach up and throw my arms around his neck to comfort him.

"You don't have to say."

"I don't know what the hell I'm going to do without her."

I touch his arm, which seems okay, but he doesn't seem to notice. "I'm here if you need me. Us. We. Nathan and I are here."

"Thank you, Marissa." But he's looking past me, as if I'm not even here, a haunted expression in his eyes.

CHAPTER ELEVEN

I could go straight back to Nathan's place, but once outside I feel drawn toward the gazebo. Brynn's silhouette forms a lonely figure beneath the cupola. I step up beside her, rest my elbows on the wood railing. "How are you holding up?" I say.

"I told her I hated her. Last thing I said." She looks at me morosely.

"I said that to my mother, too, when she left my dad. I was old enough to know better."

"Did she ever go back to him?"

"I hoped she would, but it never happened." She returned to visit only twice after she left—once for a conference, and once for my father's funeral.

Brynn's mouth trembles, and I regret making the comparison. Unlike my mother, Lauren wanted to be here for her daughter. Her eyes lit up whenever she mentioned Brynn.

"My dad wouldn't let me go to the beach to see her," Brynn says. "Was she . . . ? Was it terrible? He wouldn't tell me."

"No," I lie. "She looked peaceful."

"Like she fell and that was it. She was gone."

"That was it." But I wonder, How long did Lauren live after she fell? How long did she suffer?

"That's good then," Brynn whispers.

"Look, I won't say she's watching you from heaven. I don't know what comes after death. But I'm almost a hundred percent certain she knew you loved her. And she loved you, too. She talked about you a lot."

"You guys were good friends, right?" Brynn kicks the floor slats at her feet. Leans over the railing again.

I let the air out of my lungs, a heaviness inside me. "Yeah, we were great friends," I lie. "Best buddies."

Brynn glances back toward the house. "They're all bawling. I don't want to go in there."

"You don't have to. I'm here if you need me. You could come over."

"I keep thinking she's going to come out of her room or something."

"I know," I say. There is nothing else. No answers, no comfort.

"How can she be gone?" Brynn's face contorts in pain. Her fingers grip the railing. Her face looks drawn, the skin pulled tight, as if the shock of Lauren's death has siphoned the life out of her.

"I know," I say, touching her back tentatively.

She shrugs away. "I can't even cry. I feel emptied out. Like I don't even believe this. Like it didn't even happen."

"I know what you mean." I look up at the sunlight breaking through a thin cloud, indifferent to the suffering below. Lauren's voice plays back. *Everything is the end of the world when you're sixteen.* How can I explain to Brynn that her life will go on, when I'm not sure I even believe this myself? "Just focus on being with your dad," I manage to say, but it sounds like a cliché. "You two need each other right now."

"He's in his own world. He doesn't know anything about me. He didn't even know my mom was going to send me away."

"She wouldn't do that. Send you where?" Images of straitjackets and mental hospitals flash through my mind.

"Wasatch Academy, a boarding school in Utah."

"You applied there?"

"Hell no. She just wanted to get rid of me."

"I very much doubt that was true. Were you having trouble in school?"

"I guess you could say that." Brynn grimaces. "It's my fault. Mom took me to counseling. And she told me all about how she was wild when she was young, and how she wished she had buckled down. How she wanted the best for me. I hated those talks. But now . . ."

"I get it," I say. *Now you would do anything to have her back again.* I thought the same thing when I graduated from the University of Washington with a Master of Science in Speech Language Pathology. My father watched me from his seat in the stands, and I imagined my mother beside him, applauding. I would've done anything to have her there.

"I wouldn't have gone anyway," Brynn says. "My mom and I . . . We butted heads about it."

"You fought about the boarding school thing."

"Yeah, it sucked. No way was I going to go. She would've tried to drag me there. I would've run away. But now I guess I don't have to worry about that." Her jaw hardens, and she looks at me with sudden coldness in her eyes.

CHAPTER TWELVE

The rain catches me on my trek across the yard. In the house, Brynn's cold gaze haunts me as I take off my wet clothes and stuff them into the dryer. I know so little about her, aside from what Lauren told me. Evidently, Brynn was a willful toddler, loud, fond of saying no to everything. Then she said yes to everything, excelling in sports, her classes, reading, and writing. Smarter than most kids. Prone to brooding silences. Fond of Anna, whom she babysits on occasion. She even volunteers to read to the dogs at the local Humane Society. But when she looked at me just now, her eyes were empty. Is she only pretending to grieve? Ridiculous. What am I thinking? She loved her mother.

The washing machine is broken, laundry piled in a basket on top. I pull out Anna's bird-print pajama bottoms from beneath a wet towel. How did she get those mud stains on the cuffs and knees? Did she kneel in the dirt? What was she doing out there in her nightclothes?

I hastily throw on jeans, a sweater, and shoes, and rush outside again, slip around to the back of the house. Anna's shoeprints disturb the ground beneath her window. But why was she out here? The wind shudders in across the sea. An alder stump rises from the soil, close to the window. She could hoist herself up this way. I look over toward the Eklunds' house. If I crouch outside Anna's window, I have a partial, angled view of the gazebo. And beyond the gazebo, Arthur Nguyen's rows of vegetable gardens, next to his oversized fishing pond. He's out there with Bert on a leash, waiting while the dog does his business.

Inside the house again, I take a hot shower, change back into the same clean jeans and sweater. My body feels tenuous, as if I might melt away. As the dryer tumbles, I tidy up some more, straightening the jumble of shoes by the front door. I tuck the key card into my purse, the one I found with the oak tree logo. To whom could it belong? I sent Nathan a text, but he said he knew nothing about it. That leaves Lauren. The key card must have been hers, even if Jensen didn't know. Husbands don't know everything about their wives, do they? And vice versa?

I stand at the kitchen window, soothe my nerves with a cup of chamomile tea. Lauren's parents come out to their car, Jensen and Brynn in tow, watching as Lauren's father backs down the driveway. In the passenger seat, Lauren's mother blows her nose with a crumpled tissue. I hope they're not leaving already. Maybe they're only going into town. Brynn is looking at me, watching me watching her. I can't read her expression, but I sense the coldness in her eyes.

I step back into shadows. The blood rushes in my head as she breaks from her father's grip and strides through the yard toward the path leading down to the beach. She's holding her cell phone to her ear.

Cell phone. I drop the cup in the sink, head back to Anna's room. I know I'm trespassing on her private space, but I can't help being nosy. I check her desk drawers for her phone. The photograph of Anna, Nathan, and Rianne taunts me from the desk, the quaint forest in the background. Rianne appears to be the queen of calm. But she wasn't calm today when she stormed through the woods. The first time I met her, when she had come to pick up Anna from school, she wasn't calm, either. Her eyes were filled with worry. *Anna's devastated by the separation,* she said. *She blames me.*

Maybe she blames herself, I said. *Children often do when their parents split up.* Rianne was so distraught when she arrived today, she didn't even acknowledge my presence.

I check under Anna's bed, find a stray balled-up sock. In the closet—shoes, a backpack, shirts and dresses on hangers. Board games piled on the top shelf. A pink tutu hangs in the back, the one she wore in ballet class a year ago. Her pink ballet slippers gather dust on the floor. This year, she wouldn't be caught dead wearing pink.

In her desk, I find a jumble of multicolored rubber bands, paper clips, and construction paper, and in the next drawer, beaded bracelets and a do-it-yourself jewelry set. She keeps art pencils in the bottom drawer, on top of a photo album. No cell phone and no jewelry box.

I pull out the photo album, sit on the edge of the bed and flip through the pages. The pictures begin in a sunny place—flowers and bright skies. She notices what other people might overlook—the subtle range of colors in the autumn leaves, the reflection of tree branches in puddles. A pileated woodpecker, a barred owl. Her family. Dad, Anna, Rianne. Dad and Anna. Anna and Rianne.

I'm turning the last page when I spot a photograph peeking from the pocket in the back cover. I remember now. Nathan handed his iPhone to a stranger, who snapped the shot of the three of us—Nathan, Anna, and me—grinning into the camera, each of us holding a large stick of swirling cotton candy at the county fair last summer. Nathan's on the left, Anna in the middle. I'm on the right. Or at least, I'm supposed to be. The entire right side of the picture has been snipped away, leaving only Anna and her dad.

CHAPTER THIRTEEN

When Nathan and Anna return, I wait until she has gone back outside with the camera, and in the living room, I show the vandalized photograph to Nathan. "She cut me out."

"I'm sure she didn't mean it," he says, frowning. "She loves you."

"Love? She told me to go home."

"She didn't know what she was saying."

"Remember when I first stayed over here?" I say, sitting heavily on the couch. Could it have been nearly eighteen months ago already? We hadn't been dating long.

"What about it? She was fine with it."

"You thought she was fine, but she came to me while you were in the shower, and she told me I can't move in and we can't get married. She said it would be weird." I remember feeling my stomach drop.

"Why didn't you tell me this?"

"At the time, I wasn't planning to move in or get married. And I thought she would get over it."

"She did," he insists. "But if you had told me, I would've talked to her."

"Maybe we are rushing things, especially now."

He takes my hands in his. "No, don't say that. She needs you. We need you."

"Last week, she got on my case for not recycling an empty carton of milk. She took it out of the trash and accused me of killing the environment."

"What the hell?"

"To be fair, Anna's not always this way," I say. "Plenty of times we've had fun together. But there was something else."

"What?" He looks out the window at her.

"A couple of weeks ago. She said her mom always leaves the blinds down. She doesn't like that I pull them up. It gets too bright."

His shoulders tense, and I feel a wall go up between us. "She's a kid. Cut her some slack. She has to get used to the idea of someone new moving into the house."

"I'm not someone new. And I haven't moved in yet."

"But in Anna's eyes, maybe you have. It's hard for her. When I was almost sixteen, a nurse practically moved into our house. She pulled up the blinds, too. Drove me crazy. My mom was dying, and here was this nurse acting all cheery, yanking up the blinds and letting in way too much light."

I touch his arm. "You lost your mom so young—"

"She had a weak heart. Ironic, isn't it? She married a cardiac surgeon, but in the end he couldn't save her. Every time the nurse raised those damned blinds, the light gave me a headache. All I wanted to do was sleep forever."

"Who could blame you?" I feel that way now sometimes—like I could lie down and let the earth take me. Anna has the right idea, crouching out in the grass close to the ground.

"The nurse eventually left, but you're not—"

"I'm not going to leave Anna," I say. "But maybe we should step back, give this some time."

"I told Anna she would still have her mom," Nathan says. "She would have all of us. This is all new for her, but you're good for us. For her."

"I doubt that's easy for her to understand at her age. She must come first for you—and now with this tragedy. What if she runs away again? But farther this time. I should go home for a while."

"Don't you run away from this now," he says.

"I can't see the merit in staying. My presence agitates her."

"Your presence calms us," Nathan says.

"I need some calming myself. My mind is going a mile a minute. Everyone I see, I wonder if they killed Lauren." I run my hand along the rough, thick fabric of the couch cushion, trying to calm my nerves.

"That's because she just died, and your brain is trying to make sense of it."

"Something is off. She didn't jump. Someone wanted her gone. I can't let go of that thought." I focus on the fireplace, on its pattern of masonry bricks which appear a uniform, pale pink at first, but the more I look, the more complicated the colors become—black and white and yellow all mixed in.

"She didn't have any enemies," he says, following my gaze.

I turn to look at him, the sun falling in the sky behind him, his shadow elongating across the area rug. "Why was she so adamant about talking to me about something important? About you? Don't you think it's strange that the next morning she was gone?"

"Coincidence," he says, but his voice falters. "If there was any meaning in what she said, the police will find it."

"What if they don't? The police aren't omnipotent. They don't know everything. So many cases remain unsolved."

He steps closer, blocking my light. The angular coffee table plunges into shadow. "It's not your job to solve their cases."

"I don't care what you think my job is," I say, surprised at the edge in my voice. "Lauren was my friend, and I'm going to do what I can to help."

Nathan moves a little to the left, a pale shaft of sunlight escaping past him, onto the couch next to me. "It will kill you to play this guessing game," he says. "What if you never find an answer? Some things aren't explainable. We don't always know why people do things."

"You're assuming she killed herself. Still. But anyone around her could've been harboring a secret hatred for her." My voice rises, and I wonder, briefly, if I'm talking about myself. If our attempt to recapture our friendship had always been doomed.

"Who could possibly have hated her? She got drunk and flirted, but she was a nurse. She made a life of taking care of others."

I lean back against the cushion. "What about Brynn? Lauren was going to send her to boarding school . . . I don't know why. And she told me that everything is the end of the world when you're sixteen. When I went out to the gazebo to talk to Brynn, she seemed aloof. Her mom had just died but she couldn't cry."

"People grieve differently."

"But Brynn seemed cold, closed off. Like something was missing inside her."

"You're not suggesting that Brynn would resort to murder to avoid boarding school, are you? She wouldn't kill her own mother."

"It's been known to happen."

"I could see it happening if a kid is abused or disturbed—"

"Maybe Brynn is mentally ill. Do we really know her? Or maybe she got into an argument with Lauren and accidentally pushed her."

"You don't really believe that."

I grab a throw pillow and hug it to my chest. "Oh God, I don't know what I believe. I'm losing my perspective."

"Who wouldn't?"

"I need to go home . . . take some time," I say, although in truth, I don't know what I need or what to do. My shadow bleeds out next to me, diffuse, unformed. The more I look at it, the more I see Lauren's face, her opaque eyes. I'm shaking all over again, fighting off tears.

"Go if you need to. Just stop trying to figure out who killed her," he says. He picks up a pile of magazines from the coffee table, starts tossing them into the wicker recycling basket next to his armchair.

"I'm never going to stop, Nathan. You know that."

He looks up at me. "But you're driving yourself crazy. Take a step back and let the detective do his job."

CHAPTER FOURTEEN

On the winding drive along the bay, the trees lean in, forming a narrow tunnel over the road. And on the waterfront strip, the quaint shops seem to watch me, their window eyes lit by antique streetlamps. I pass through the old section of town, a patchwork of ramshackle apartments growing between stately Victorians and boxy cottages from the early days of the fishing and logging industries.

I'm relieved to turn onto quiet Juniper Lane, where my cottage sleeps in pale blue and white, the curtains drawn. The porch light casts a faint glow across the front steps. The newspaper is propped against the fence. There is no headline yet about Lauren—maybe there will never be one. Maybe she's not a front-page story, even in a small town. I don't yet know. But maybe she made the internet. Internet news, real or fake, pops up at lightning speed. On the front porch, a bouquet of autumn flowers waits for me in a vase on the welcome mat. Flowers. At a time like this. They can't be condolence flowers. I'm not family. These . . . What are they?

A card is tucked in between two of the sprigs of fern, written in an unpracticed hand by someone at Vase of Flowers.

Welcome home, is all the words say.

Welcome home?

I send a text to Nathan. Thank you for the beautiful bouquet. When I said I needed to come home today, he must've ordered them for rush delivery.

Flowers? He texts back.

The bouquet, I text.

Secret admirer?

You.

Nothing, then Thoughtful of someone.

You.

Again, nothing, and then Keith and Hedra?

I frown. *Welcome home?* Why would they welcome me home after he'd proposed, and I'd agreed to move in with him?

I snap a photograph of the bouquet and send it to him. The phone makes a whooshing sound.

Wow, stunning, he texts.

A mystery, I type.

You okay?

No, I text back. My eyes well with tears. I text him a heart, and he texts one back.

I unlock the door and carry the bouquet inside. I love the creak of the hardwood floor, my cozy rooms lined with bookshelves, my comfy living room couch in a deep shade of indigo. Most of all, I love my Baldwin spinet piano, inherited from my dad when he passed away. I keep his photo on top, his hazel eyes twinkling, gray hair perpetually falling over his forehead. He resembled an exuberant sheepdog.

As I arrange the bouquet of flowers on the table in the foyer, a faint perfume wafts toward me—an alteration in the air. The flowers? No. Maybe I left a window open, and a smell seeped inside from a neighbor's house. Or has someone been in here?

The living room appears untouched, but there's a patch of dry dirt on the floor, almost like a footprint. Heart pattering, I tiptoe down the hall to the kitchen. A half-eaten apple sits on the countertop—did I leave it there? I race into my small home office. Nothing appears to be out of place, but the window is open—air wafting in. I shut it, my heart racing. I must have left it open. I've been scattered lately.

But in the bedroom, a hurricane has struck. My clothes spill from the closet. Shards of glass litter the floor, liquid splashed across the wall. A bottle of perfume. Someone threw the bottle at the wall. Who would do such a thing? The other bottles line up on my dresser, untouched. I check through the drawers, the piles of clothing. Nothing seems to be missing. Except one thing. My vintage blue silk dress, the one Lauren gave me all those years ago, the one I was planning to wear at the wedding—it's gone.

CHAPTER FIFTEEN

"You say your door was locked when you got home," the young officer says. She's sitting next to me on my couch. Her fresh, round face looks familiar. Her broad shoulders rival Nathan's. He hasn't called me back. I left him a frantic message half an hour ago. Her partner, a young, wiry man who springs on the balls of his feet, disappears into the bedroom, maybe to look for evidence or dust for fingerprints.

"Whoever it was came in through the window in my office," I say.

"We did see footprints outside, and we'll try to pull prints off the sill," she says. "Anything missing that you know of? Other than the dress?"

"Nothing else. Everything's still in my jewelry box. My filing cabinet is still locked."

She reaches out with a reassuring touch on my arm. "Are you doing okay?"

I'm shaky, light-headed. "Not really."

"Is there someone I can call for you?"

"I left a message for my fiancé. He'll call me back soon, I'm sure."

She nods, looks around. "Do you keep any other valuables in the house, cash under the mattress, anything like that?"

"I keep my money in a bank."

"Never know—I've seen it all. Any idea why someone would break in here to steal one dress and throw your clothes around?"

"I have no idea. It must be someone who knows me, someone who's angry at me." Lauren and I found the dress together, so long ago. We both tried it on in the store, but she bought it before I could. She wore it a couple of times, then she gave it to me. *It looks way better on you. It's yours.* In retrospect, I wonder if she gave me the dress out of guilt. As atonement for a sin I had not yet discovered.

The officer narrows her gaze. "Anyone you can think of who might be angry with you?"

"Maybe, but she's dead."

She sits back, looks at me. "You're the one who found Lauren Eklund."

"You recognize me, great."

"I was on the forensics team. Small town. You know."

"Oh," I say, the word *forensics* punching me in the gut. I picture the police swarming her body, dusting her fingers, clipping off strands of her hair.

The officer gets up. "Listen, I'll write up a report. You should install an alarm system. We've had a string of burglaries lately. But this one—"

"It feels personal."

She tucks a pen into her pocket. "Could very well be. Do you have somewhere else to stay?" she says as she walks to the door.

"I might go back to my fiancé's place, or maybe to the neighbor's house." Part of me wants to rush out of here right now, to keep running until I'm miles away. But I look around at the cottage I so lovingly painted, at my potted plants and matching furniture and all my books and my piano. This is my home, where I have always felt safe, and I'm damned if some trespasser is going to scare me off.

"Don't hesitate to call 911 if anything at all happens, okay? When you're here, lock your doors and windows."

"I certainly will," I say.

She steps out onto the front porch, and I close the door after her. In the living room, I pull aside the curtain, and as I watch her drive away, the streetlight flickers across the road. The neighborhood feels too quiet. I need a sound, music, anything. I sit at the piano and play a slow version of Beethoven's "Für Elise" to banish my fear. To fill the void. To tell any burglar who might be lurking outside that I am not scared. My dad smiles soothingly from his photo, but I wish I could talk to him for real; he would know what to say, but he's nearly ten years gone, his ashes scattered across the sea.

CHAPTER SIXTEEN

"I'm coming over," Nathan says on the phone.

"But what about Anna?" I peer out at the empty street. "She needs you there."

"Then stay here. What if the burglar comes back?"

"It could happen. But whoever did this made a point of making sure nobody was home. I hope they're too cowardly to return."

"I'm on my way."

"Wait a bit. I left a message for Julie. She should be home from her conference by now."

"If she doesn't stay with you, I think I should. I'll see if Rianne will take Anna."

"Nathan, I—"

"I'll get back to you."

"No. Don't. I'll call you if I need you."

"You're stubborn."

"Stubborn is my middle name," I say.

"There's something I wanted to tell you—I know someone in the medical examiner's office. He said so far Lauren's injuries are consistent with a fall from a height. That's all I know. But they're treating her death as suspicious."

"You mean—I was right," I whisper.

"I wouldn't jump to conclusions."

"Are they going to check her body for DNA?"

"Your guess is as good as mine. But they don't usually perform a complete autopsy when someone falls off a cliff. It's not like on TV. They don't comb through every hair and bag every molecule as evidence. They have finite resources."

"Suddenly you know a lot about this."

"Hey, I'm in the field. And I ask questions. In a case like this, something must clearly appear to be unusual. Like, if a woman falls half-clothed, they might investigate whether a sexual assault was in progress when she fell—or was pushed."

"So, they think something was unusual—"

"They must. Otherwise they would assume it was an accident, especially since she had been drinking. But for some reason they're paying extra attention. Maybe because of what Arthur said. Or maybe because of something else. If they've found evidence of foul play, they're keeping it close to the vest."

Foul play. "You mean evidence of a struggle," I say. "I bet it was something under her fingernails."

"Maybe. Did you notice?"

"I was in shock," I say. "It was hard to tell."

"Right. Yeah. You okay?"

"I will be one day, I hope."

"I'm not feeling so hot either."

"Oh, Nathan—"

"I keep thinking about her down there on the beach. I dunno, maybe I could've . . ."

"You can't save everyone," I say.

"I know, but I can try."

I hang up, feeling spooked about everything. The break-in. Seeing Lauren on the beach. Brynn's cold eyes. Jensen so sad. Anna crouched in the corner of the broken-down tree house, telling me to go away.

Hang in there, Mari, my dad whispers. *I'm always with you.* I miss his wild laughter. I inherited his laugh and his thick brows, but my brown eyes and my oval face come from my mother, who was born and raised in India. As undergraduate students, my parents met by literally bumping into each other in the library at Washington State University. They both became accountants, crunching numbers for a living until my mother took off, abandoning my father after I left for college. I should have recognized her wanderlust much earlier, but in my child's mind, our home life was perfect. We laughed together, played endless rounds of Pictionary and Scrabble. For a while, Lauren practically lived at our house, since her father worked as a fisherman in Alaska, her mother long hours as a restaurant manager. My mother sometimes traveled on her own, but she always came back, until one day she didn't. I can't even call her to tell her about Lauren. I don't have my mother's number.

"What's going on, Dad?" I ask aloud. "Who would break into my house? Who would want the dress? And who would want Lauren dead?" He doesn't reply, but I know what he would say. He would tell me to trust my instincts, and not to become cynical. *You must always look for the good in this world.*

In my office, I page through old photo albums and extract the picture of Lauren in the blue dress. She and Jensen and I sit in a dimly lit restaurant, laughing. The Mediterranean. Wooden tables, a mirrored bar in the background. Deep-red walls. I'm struck by how young we all looked. In another life, and yet. Only yesterday. Lauren's face was rounder, her lips full, her skin flawless. The look in her eyes—carefree. I wore heavy mascara, my expression tentative. She said I looked better in the blue dress, but when she tried on the dress in the shop, I watched her admiring herself in the mirror, mouthing *Wow,* like a hand-stitched garment held the key to everything good in her life.

Is it coincidence that the burglar chose the same dress, the one I planned to wear at my wedding? I never liked the idea of the bride in white—generic, bland, the color everyone chooses. But the blue silk reminds me of the vast blue sky, of endless possibilities.

I look up to see the curtain fall over the window of the house next door. Bee Mornay. The quintessential nosy neighbor. I pull on my sweats and head over to talk to her. I can hardly believe I found Lauren only this morning, and now night is falling, and my house has been ransacked. A lifetime has passed in this one endless hell of a day. As I approach, Bee peeks out her front door and waves. Like she only just now saw me coming. She's retired from the social security office, where she determined who would receive benefits and who would leave empty-handed, all from her desk behind bulletproof glass. Now she spends her days knitting, pruning her garden into alarming submission, selling antiques on eBay, and spying on her neighbors.

"Evening!" she calls out, stepping out onto the porch.

I force a smile. "Evening!" I weave past her espaliered hedges, chopped into unnatural shapes.

She opens the door to let me in. "I saw the police out there. What was going on?"

"Someone broke into my house," I say, inhaling the smell of chocolate chip cookies. One good thing about Bee Mornay, she likes to bake. She's perfectly made-up, as usual, although she rarely ventures out. She's too busy keeping an eye on the neighborhood. She ushers me into a cluttered living room, furnished in quirky antiques. She collects ceramic cookie jars—they're lined up on every available shelf and table.

"A break-in," she says. "How terrible. We are in a low-crime area, but criminals look for nice neighborhoods like ours. You must be so upset."

"I'm all right."

"Sit, sit." She moves a pile of laundry from the couch to a chair.

On the couch, the cushion barely yields beneath me. "I'm wondering if—"

"I heard the awful news about Lauren Eklund."

85

A. J. Banner

"Yes," I say, my throat tightening. On the mantelpiece, she has lined up photographs of her family—her late husband, her daughter, who lives in Hawaii, her toddler grandson. In one picture, surprisingly, Bee is decked out in scuba gear.

"A terribly sad business," she says. "You heard then?"

"I heard," I say. *She doesn't know I found the body. She doesn't know.*

"Sordid things happen in this town. You wouldn't think. I do watch out for you, not in a nosy, critical kind of way. I'm glad we don't have a cliff anywhere near here."

"Yes," I say. "I'm wondering if—"

"I can't believe someone broke in. I make sure nobody steals from your mailbox, if I'm watching. What did they take?"

"A beautiful old dress. I'm wondering if you might have seen anything."

"No, but I'll watch out for you. Very scary. You call me if you need anything."

"Thank you," I say, my heart falling. I was hoping she could help. I get up and go to the door.

"Of course, there was the car."

I turn around. "What car?" My heartbeat thrums.

"Across from your house earlier. You know how the dog barks over on the next block sometimes? I've got very sensitive ears."

"We're all grateful for that."

"The dog went on and on, so I came to the window to see what the fuss was all about. There was a car parked right across the street from your house."

I look over in the direction she's pointing, toward a stretch of dark forest, an undeveloped greenbelt. I swallow a dry lump of fear. "Could you tell what kind of car it was?"

"Honda, silver, SUV. I think . . . Newish model."

Lauren's car? But Lauren is gone.

"Did you see anyone inside?"

"A shadow in the driver's seat, that's all. Then whoever it was drove away. I didn't get a license plate, but next time I will."

"Let's hope there's not a next time," I say.

"You need to get an alarm system, young lady. I have one."

"Thank you." I step out onto the porch. "One other thing."

"Yes?"

"Did you see anyone deliver flowers to my house today?"

She frowns, then nods slowly and points at me. "I saw the white van from the Vase of Flowers! But I didn't see it stop at your place. I'm not looking out the window all the time, you know. I've got other things to do."

"You're so helpful to look outside at all."

She looks smug. "I do my civic duty."

"You didn't see a flower delivery."

"The van turned around at the dead end and left. Why, did someone send you flowers?"

"It appears that way," I say.

"Special occasion?" She looks at me as if expecting some interesting tidbit of gossip.

I smile sadly. "Yes," I say, sighing. "It's an occasion of mourning."

CHAPTER SEVENTEEN

Back home, I make sure the doors are locked. Windows, too. But I can't lock out this malaise, the specter of Lauren following me around. The mystery of the disappearing wedding dress. The feeling that Bee Mornay is watching me again.

Of course, there was the car.

Lauren's car.

Brynn. She might have been driving. Why? Who else could it have been? Jensen? Unlikely. I retrieve the detective's business card from my purse and call him. His deep, lazy voice tells me to leave a message. "This is Marissa Parlette. Someone broke into my cottage tonight— your officers came out. I'm not sure, but I have a feeling I know who it was. It could have something to do with Lauren Eklund. Could I come down and talk to you?" I hang up, and as I tidy the bedroom, I grit my teeth. Someone threw my clothes all over the room. Broke a perfume bottle against the wall.

How would Brynn know about the dress? Lauren must have mentioned it to her. Why the violence? What did I ever do to her?

Brynn's only sixteen—maybe Lauren told her about my engagement, about the dress, about how it once belonged to her. Maybe Brynn concocted some twisted explanation for her mother's death. A reason to blame me. I consider calling Jensen—but Lauren's family is drowning in grief. And then someone complains about a missing dress?

My cell phone rings, and Julie's soothing but worried voice fills my ears. "You got broken into? Are you okay?"

"I'm a bit freaked out." I brief her on everything. Lauren, Anna running away, the detective questioning us. The shocking events of the day roll out of me in a rush.

"I can't believe this," Julie says. "I'll be right there."

I hang up, feeling Lauren close, although she never set foot in this house. I was planning to invite her over. *Well, I'm here now. The ghost of me.* She leans back on the couch, crosses her legs, and swings her foot. *You need a little color on these walls. Be bold. Like me.*

She took her boldness to a whole new level that rainy spring afternoon, in our college apartment. How long had it been going on? Afterward, she moved out, and I refused to speak to her. Ignored her calls. Walked away when she approached me on campus. All the while, my heart fluttered off in tiny pieces of confetti.

After college, I did not return to Silverwood, the town of our childhood. I didn't want to run into her, in case she went home. I worked in Seattle for a while, immersed in private practice for a few years, but the setting didn't sit well with me. The noise, traffic, congestion. I yearned for the forest, the rustling trees and chirping birds and stars crowding the sky, so when the job cropped up in Tranquil Cove four years ago, I hopped aboard. I scoured the real estate listings for a quaint, affordable bungalow. My own space, away from memories.

But the past wouldn't leave me alone. When Lauren moved here, she looked me up, called me. I drove to the hospital to meet her in the cafeteria. *Remember when we popped over on the foot ferry, and we talked about moving here?* she said, sliding into a booth across from me. *Well, I did. After they built the hospital. I got a job in the ER.* She didn't move here to follow me. But she might as well have. She did persist in her quest to renew our friendship, inviting me for coffee, showing up at school to say hello. She had a built-in reason for dropping by. Brynn's high school is right across the street from the elementary school.

I stand on a step stool to reach the top shelf in my bedroom closet. The box is still there. Not stolen. I haven't brought the memories down in ages—some good, some bittersweet. I drop the box on the bed, and as I flip off the lid, the doorbell rings.

"You look like hell, and not even warmed over," Julie says as I let her in. She plunks her bag on the couch and squashes me with a breath-stealing hug, pulls back, and rests her hands on my shoulders.

"Thanks," I say. "You look amazing as always."

"Don't I know it." She stands half a head shorter than me and I'm only five feet, six inches. But she's larger than life, clad in an oversized purple sweater, leggings, and boots. Flashy, jangling jewelry. Heavy-lidded eyes, one a little smaller than the other, as if she is always squinting a little. The first time I met her at school, a boy was yelling at me in the hall outside my office. Julie rushed over and performed magic—calming him with what she called "positive reinforcement," "ignoring and distracting" from his "challenging outburst." She taught art, but she'd learned the psychology of calming her students. "I go to a conference, and all hell breaks loose."

"One good thing happened." I hold up my hand to show her my engagement ring, but my excitement feels muted, as if I'm sitting at the bottom of a swimming pool, trying to smile up through ten feet of water.

She takes my hand and gasps. "I knew it. He's perfect. He has impeccable taste in jewelry. Congratulations, my friend." But when she sees my expression, the smile drops off her face. "You look like you could use a drink."

"Or two," I say, twisting the ring on my finger. "Or three."

She yanks off her boots and shoos me into the bedroom. "I'll pour you a glass of whiskey, or whatever you've got. Vodka?"

"Maybe chamomile tea instead. But it's my house. I'll make the tea."

"No—you've been through too much today. Relax. I'll take care of you. I'm staying."

"I might snore. I don't know. I don't hear myself."

"You don't snore. Trust me."

I unpack my suitcase, flinging dirty clothes into the laundry basket, while I listen to Julie humming in the kitchen, opening the fridge and cabinets. Comforting sounds. She returns to the bedroom, surveys the mess, the box on my bed. "There's nothing in your refrigerator. You do realize that, don't you? One blackened banana and moldy cheese."

"I was planning to stay longer at Nathan's."

"That's no excuse." The kettle whistles in the kitchen. "Be right back."

I sit on the bed and pull a postcard out of the box, a missive from my mother, splashed with the words *Le Palais du Louvre,* showing images of the museum and the *Mona Lisa.*

Julie brings in the tea in a mug, places it on a coaster on the nightstand. She takes the postcard from me, reads the back. "'Dear Marissa, Happy twenty-first birthday. We're so enjoying Paris. Love, Mom.' Oh, hell, you're not going to wallow in this drama tonight, are you? You've got enough grief."

I throw the postcard back in the box, sip my tea. "You know, I didn't even have her address. She had moved to France. She wasn't on vacation. She was never planning to come back."

"Have you seen your mom since then?"

"Twice," I say, staring at the stain the broken perfume bottle left on the wall. "The first time, she had a client in Seattle. She became a financial advisor. Still a CPA under a different name. I met her for lunch. Stupid idea." I take a deep breath against the pressure on my chest.

"Why stupid?"

"She wanted to talk about herself. Not, 'How has my daughter been doing? What is your life like? I've missed you.' No, she went on about how Europe had called to her. She left and never looked back.

Her life was exciting now. She did travel when I was little, but she also found time to throw me amazing birthday parties, and help me with homework. Maybe she was going through the motions of being a mother the whole time. Or did she enjoy taking care of me and later changed her mind?"

Julie's brows pull together in the shape of an A-frame house. "You'll make yourself crazy speculating. It's her loss, not staying in touch, not getting to know her kid again."

I look at the pile of photos and papers in the box. "Or maybe I'm not that interesting."

"Don't talk that way. Call my mom if you need a mom, anytime, you know. You can even go stay with her."

"You're the best," I say, smiling at her. "I wish I still had my dad. He would've offered some sage advice in a situation like this." The memory of his singsong voice brings an ache to my chest. After my mother left, he put on a brave face, but he dried up like an autumn leaf. Every year, he grew smaller, more diminished by her absence, until finally he disintegrated. I can't even visit his gravesite—but he's in the waves every time I look out across the ocean. And in his photographs. And in my heart. What did my mother think would happen to him? He was devoted to her.

"You need some serious downtime." Julie sits on the bed next to me, stretches her legs out in front of her, propping herself on pillows.

I look at a tiny rip in her black leggings. "I didn't even ask you about the conference. How was it?"

She runs her hand across the bedcover. "It was freaking awesome. I learned new ways to tap into kids' creativity, you know? Art comes in many forms. I took a fun session on how to use toothpaste and hand lotion to make faux batik."

"Whoa. You're always trying the quirky classes."

"Quirky is my MO. But enough about me. Why the hell would someone steal your wedding dress?"

"I have no idea. I know it sounds crazy. But I'm wondering if it might be Brynn."

"What, her mom died so you should suffer, too?"

"It's possible. I don't know."

She taps her fingers on the bed. "She just lost her mother. Why would she care about a dress?"

"What if she was the one who killed Lauren? I know that sounds ridiculous."

"Why, what makes you suspect that? Kids have been known to kill their parents. But wait, you think she was killed?"

"Nathan says her death is being treated as suspicious, and I'm almost certain she wouldn't jump," I say. "The question is, who pushed her?"

"Could Brynn have been having deeper problems? Maybe she thought her parents were going to split up, and she fought with them. Maybe she got into an argument with her mom?"

"I would only be speculating, but maybe Brynn perceives a threat to her family. She responded with hostility. Kids do that, don't they?"

"What do you mean, exactly?"

"Well, Anna cut me out of a photograph," I say, a churning in my gut. "I want to believe she's just acting out, but—"

"Divorce is hard on kids." Julie crosses her arms over her chest. "But chopping you out of a picture. Now we're getting into twisted territory. Did she replace you with her mother?"

"Not yet."

"The key word being 'yet.'"

"It's not going to happen. She's a good kid."

"And adept with a pair of sharp scissors. I know this firsthand. She's in my art class."

"She wouldn't do anything like that—"

"Probably not. I've seen her get upset, but you're right, she's never mean to anyone. But then, we don't always know children as well as we think we do."

"Anna does run hot and cold. She's complicated . . ."

"And kids with antisocial tendencies can act as if they have compassion. Fly under the radar. We wouldn't be able to identify them."

"What, you're a psychologist now?"

"Just saying. I've read about this stuff. We never know about people."

"Anna's not a sociopath," I say. "Stop freaking me out. We know about her."

"Okay, we know about her."

"I mean it."

"We do. We know about Anna. But Nathan. Now he's a different story."

"Stop," I say.

She laughs. "Okay. He's a good guy. A catch."

"He is a catch," I say. When I met him, sunlight reached in through the window and lit our hearts. In the weeks that followed, on our giddy dates, our late-night walks, the long talks, maybe we didn't think enough about Anna, about how all of this might affect her. When I showed him the photograph with the edge clipped off, he couldn't explain. Or maybe he didn't want to. Maybe he couldn't admit to himself that his daughter could feel such anger toward me.

Even I can't quite believe it when I remember her smiles during speech therapy when she articulated a sentence without stuttering. When we made lemon cupcakes together, when I took her shopping for school supplies and indulged her. *Marissa,* she whispered to me once. *You're the best.*

But then, the next week, I wasn't the best. When I stayed overnight, sat too close to her father. When it seemed to her that I might move in.

I pull out a clothbound journal, sit back on the bed next to Julie. "This one is old," I say. "From our freshman year at UW. When Lauren and I were still friends."

"You sure you want to look at it now?"

"I wrote about her." Even after all this time, I feel a twinge beneath my ribs when I read my own immature handwriting. The melodrama of youth. "I wrote good things about her at first. But afterward, I hated her. I wanted her dead. Makes me cringe now."

"You had good reason," she says, taking the journal from my hands. She throws it back in the box. "This is the time for self-care, not self-pity. Think about the future, not the past."

"But Lauren is dead. She's fucking gone. I found her. You should have seen her. She was covered in bruises. Her head . . ." I double over, my chest imploding, as if I've forgotten how to breathe.

"It sounds horrible—beyond horrible. Oh, Marissa."

I hold back tears and slowly exhale. "I should burn these old journals. All of them."

"No." She touches my arm. "Don't do anything hasty. The past is the past. Your emotions were real. But you're not responsible for her death."

"Maybe I am. I think she wanted me to forgive her. For us to be friends again. The pain dulled over the years. I've matured. I have a life. I met Nathan. But I don't know. A part of me never let go. Maybe I never completely forgave her. And now . . ."

"I get it. Your relationship with her will always be what it was."

"Unfinished," I whisper. "Broken. I wish she was still here so we could hash it all out. Mend things. Start again. But life doesn't work that way, does it? Nothing is ever resolved. Nothing is fair."

"Yeah, sometimes it's not. But I'll say it again. This was not your fault."

"Easier said than believed." A text from Nathan pops up on my phone. Is Julie there? Should I come over?

She's here. I'm fine, I say.

I'm thinking about you.

An image of his phone pops into my head, the text from Rianne. . . . about you . . . can't stand this. My mind fills in the blanks. What if the text was from someone else? *I'm thinking about you. I can't stand this . . .* No, the text could have been about anything. *What about you . . . I can't stand this weather.*

"I should catch up on a little work," I say. "I've got hundreds of emails to read."

"I'll go and watch the tube," Julie says, getting up. "There's a new episode of *Poldark.* I'll sleep on the couch. I know where to find the linens."

Grateful for her presence in the living room, and the comforting drone of the television, I catch up on correspondence for work, search the internet for news of Lauren's death. Nothing.

Despite my fatigue, I can't sleep at first, my eyes propped open by invisible toothpicks. But after a while, I slip into amorphous dreams. Lauren laughs, pouring Nathan's wine, his goblet overflowing. The merlot becomes blood soaking into the tablecloth. Lauren smiles. *I need to talk to you.* Then we're on the beach, and she hands me her pail. Her dark hair blows around her face. She pushes her tongue through a hole where she lost a front tooth. How old are we? Seven? We add sticks of driftwood around our sandcastle, forming a moat. We've created a work of art, but when I turn around, Lauren is gone. Panic rises inside me. The waves reach up across the beach, clawing at my feet. I see her, several yards away, sprawled out, limbs askew. *You let me fall.*

I jolt awake in a sweat, the dream evaporating. Morning sunlight leaks into the room. I pull on my robe and stagger to the kitchen. Julie has already made coffee. She's seated in the breakfast nook, perusing the newspaper, her hair a tousled mess. Even her nightgown is larger than life, splashed with pictures of the countries of the world. "Hey, stranger," she says, looking up at me.

"Thank you for staying over. I feel like crap."

"A good dose of caffeine will help. Look." She hands me the newspaper, points to a short article about Lauren's death, impersonal and objective.

> A 36-year-old woman who apparently fell off a West Beach bluff onto the beach below has been identified as Lauren Eklund of Tranquil Cove, WA, the deputy police chief said. . . . The body was sent to the King County Medical Examiner's office, where an autopsy will be performed. Toxicology results are expected within a few weeks . . .

"Toxicology results," I say. "What could've been in her system besides alcohol?"

"Antidepressants, maybe? There's nothing about an investigation."

"They wouldn't tell the public," I say.

I pour a mug of coffee, look out the open window, the cool air wafting in, every sound sharp and magnified—the wind in the trees, the chirping of towhees mingling now with the melodic ringtone on my iPhone. It's the detective, his voice casual and friendly. "Miss Parlette, I just got your message. Next time, call my cell."

"I thought this was your cell," I say. "I think I might know who broke into my cottage."

Julie looks at me, raising her right eyebrow.

The detective, I mouth at her. She nods, eyes wide.

"Would you be willing to come down to the station?" he says.

"Right now? But it's Sunday. Don't you go to church or something?"

He sidesteps the question. "We could meet. I'd like to know what you're thinking, and I would like to ask you a few more questions."

I look around at my kitchen, stippled with light and shadows from the surrounding forest. There's a chink in the wood of the breakfast table—I don't know how it got there.

"I'll come to the station," I say. I hang up, gulp the rest of my coffee.

"What is it?" Julie says, turning the mug around in her hands. "You look pale."

I see the detective in Nathan's living room, his gaze shifting to my hands, stained with dirt or blood. His pencil scratching on his notepad. The forensics team on the beach below, gathering evidence. What more could he possibly want to ask me? "It's nothing—just, I think the detective knows more than he's letting on." I give her a brief hug. "I need to get dressed and go down to talk to him."

CHAPTER EIGHTEEN

On the drive into town, I'm jumpy, my breathing shallow. A mist blows in from the sea, shrouding the old brick buildings in an ominous blanket of gray. As I pass Rianne's boutique, Afterlife Consignment, a historic storefront dating back to 1929, I see the ghosts of Lauren and myself walking past the window. *I got married in a dress like that one,* she said, pointing to a vintage white wedding gown adorning a shapely, headless mannequin. Unwittingly, she opened a door to my pain, but I smiled, and she showed me her diamond-studded wedding ring. She told me all about how the best man had shown up drunk, how her mother had broken down crying, how the dress had to be altered to hide the baby bump. But in the end, the ceremony had gone beautifully, without a drop of rain although the weather forecast portended a storm on that early March day. As she chattered on, I was shocked to feel a little happy for her. The buffer of years had made a difference. Thoughts of Nathan brought a smile to my face. Intimate thoughts I kept all to myself.

Now I turn onto Overlook Road, where the Tranquil Cove Police Department looms two stories above the hillside. The paint looks new, mauve and gold, rectangular picture windows reflecting rare autumn sunlight. Steam escapes from the gabled metal roof, burning off the recent rain.

I park in the lot, my fingers gripping the wheel. I take a deep breath and get out of the car. Detective Harding opens the door as I approach the glass entryway. He looks freshly shaven. He leads me into an open lobby, the floor gleaming in large, gray tiles that stretch away down a wide hallway lined with glass-doored offices. Nobody else appears to be here.

"Coffee?" he says, smiling.

"I had two cups this morning. I'll bounce off the ceiling if I have any more."

"We wouldn't want another head injury."

I smile, although his morbid humor gives me little comfort. I follow him down the hall into a conference room marked "Interview." Fluorescent overhead bulbs cast a grayish light on two high-backed office chairs flanking a rectangular table.

"Have a seat," he says, gesturing to a chair.

I sit and try to find a focal point, but the walls are bare. I look out the window at the alder trees swaying in the breeze. "I feel strange coming here," I say. "I've never been in a police station. I've never had reason to be in one."

"Now you do." He pulls a notepad and his signature pencil from his pocket, lays the notepad on the table.

"Do you need to record this?" I say, looking around for a device.

"Do you want me to?" he says, giving me an unblinking gaze.

"Not really, no."

"You say you know who might have broken into your cottage?"

"Possibly Lauren's daughter, Brynn. But she's grieving. I wouldn't want to press any charges."

"You think it was her because . . . ?"

"My neighbor saw a silver Honda SUV across the street. Lauren drove a silver Honda SUV. Coincidence? Maybe. And the dress is gone, a special one Lauren gave me years ago. She's wearing the dress in a photo. It's hard to explain."

"So, you think Brynn wanted the dress. Why?"

"At dinner, I mentioned I wanted to wear the dress at our wedding. Lauren remembered giving it to me. But that was a long time ago, and soon afterward, we had a falling-out."

"You fought about the dress?" His gaze doesn't waver. I wonder if he ever blinks.

A sharp ache presses in beneath my ribs, a physical memory of betrayal. "Not the dress, no. Silly college stuff."

He sits back, taps his pencil on the table. "Fair enough."

"Recently, we started talking again, going for coffee, like I said before." *Indulge me,* she told me last fall. *I'll buy you banana-nut cake at the Tranquil Cove Bakery. Let's start again. I've missed you.* Her eyes brightened with hope. She held her breath, as if her entire future depended on my answer. I agreed to meet her. I wanted to build a new bridge between us, and when I got home that day, I dug through old photographs—of Lauren smiling as I blew out the candles on my birthday cake, the two of us splashing in the kiddie pool, smearing her mother's lipstick on our faces, coloring outside the lines.

"So, you were friends again?" the detective says, urging me to continue.

"We were working on it," I say, taking a deep breath. "At the dinner, when Nathan announced our engagement and I showed everyone a picture of the dress, Lauren had this look on her face. Of longing. She remembered everything about the dress. She left early to pick up Brynn from a party. What if she mentioned the dress? And Brynn came over to get it?" Even as I say the words, I know my musings sound far-fetched.

"Without proof of Brynn's presence at your house—"

"I wouldn't want you to accuse her of anything."

"Could the dress fit her?"

"I don't know, maybe."

"Does she have any history of stealing? Shoplifting?"

"I don't know," I say.

"Does she dislike you for some reason?"

"I'm not sure I know her very well."

"Seems like quite an act of aggression, to break in and steal the dress from you. All because her mother once wore it?" A fleeting look of skepticism crosses his face.

"Lauren said everything seemed like the end of the world to Brynn."

"I have a teenager myself. Lives with her mom," he says. "I can relate."

So, he was married once. "Do you ever see your daughter?"

A brief sadness flickers in his eyes. "Now and then. Summers and Christmas vacation. I'd like to see her more often, but it's not in the cards."

"Does she live near you?" I ask, surprised that he has shared something so personal with me. But this is what detectives do, isn't it? They reveal bits of their private lives, get chummy with their interviewees to tease out information.

"Not far," he says. "She prefers her mother's place. They get along, most of the time. They have their disagreements, but it doesn't lead to murder."

I prickle at his words. "I'm not saying Brynn did anything to her mother . . . but someone did kill Lauren, didn't they? I want to know who did it, because the thing is, Lauren loved life."

"What makes you think someone killed her?"

I tell him about my chat with Arthur, about what he saw. About Anna's wet pajamas, her escape to the tree house. "I can't say for sure that she saw something, but maybe she did. Someone else must have been out there. But you know this. Did you talk to Anna when you were at the house?"

"I did talk to her briefly," he says. "But she gave no indication that she knew anything. Do you have any idea who might want to hurt Lauren?" The detective lays the pencil on the notebook and leans back in his chair, assessing me.

"You're investigating, aren't you?"

"Lauren and her husband, how did they seem to get along?"

"They seemed fine. She flirted, but . . ." I see Lauren leaning over Nathan at dinner, filling his wineglass. "Jensen would not have hurt her."

"She didn't mention any problems with her marriage?"

"No, not that I know of. Did Jensen tell you there were problems?" I see Nathan's face in the night, lit by his cell phone screen. My insides flip over.

"I'd like your impressions."

"Jensen seemed devoted to her. Is he a suspect in her death? He's so sad. I can't imagine it."

"He's a pilot, leaves for days at a time, right?"

A clawing pain digs into my forehead. "She mentioned his schedule . . . He sleeps at a crash pad in San Francisco. He's based there, even though they live—lived up here."

"He flies down and stays there?"

"In bunks with other pilots, and then he flies out of San Francisco for a few days at a time."

He picks up the pencil, taps the eraser end on his notebook. "How were the others at dinner acquainted with Lauren Eklund? Your fiancé, Nathan—his brother, Keith? Hedra?"

I see Keith's gaze disappearing down Lauren's dress. He reaches out to hold Hedra's hand—she pulls away. Outside, Lauren casts a furtive glance toward the dining room window, from which laughter emanates. *I need to talk to you,* she says. Nathan pulls on his clothes, sneaks out just after 2:00 a.m. No, at 2:05.

"Keith and Hedra knew Lauren as a casual acquaintance," I say.

"Nathan?"

"Neighbors. That's all."

The detective puts the pencil on the notebook. He sits back, elbows on the arms of his chair, and steeples his fingers. "So, she and her husband bought the house next door to Nathan Black, just like that."

"She pushed Jensen for it—the market was tight. She loved the house." I shift in my seat. My left leg begins to tingle, going to sleep. "We talked about it when we were kids—Lauren and I always wanted a log house. She thought if she and Jensen bought the place, we might see each other more often."

"You were once involved with Jensen, isn't that right?"

The question shoves me backward, like a sudden gust of wind. My hands break out in a sweat. I hide them on my lap beneath the table. "That was a long time ago." How does the detective know? Jensen must have told him. But how did my name come up in conversation?

The detective leans forward again, picks up the pencil, and jots something on his notepad. Then he looks up at me. "Were you interested in getting back together with him?"

I clasp my hands in my lap, the overhead light glaringly bright. "Why would I be? Don't you have ex-girlfriends? Don't we all have relationships we've left behind?"

He taps the pencil on his notebook, leans back again, a hint of amusement in his eyes. "Answering a question with more questions."

"The answer is, I was once intimate with Jensen Eklund, but I have no desire to be with him again. Nathan and I are getting married." My words come out shaky. I have a sudden urge to dash out of here.

"But you still like Jensen enough to invite him and Lauren to an important dinner. Big event—your engagement."

"I thought—we could get along again. I was hopeful."

"I see," he says, drumming his fingers on the table. He exhales through his mouth, blowing upward, disturbing his mustache.

"Is that it?" I say, getting up. My legs feel wobbly.

"For now. Unless you have more questions for me."

I look around at the stark room, its vacant walls giving up no secrets. The detective's eyes are just as blank. "You're not going to tell me what you're thinking, are you?"

He gets up and shows me to the door. "I can't comment on an ongoing investigation."

"Lauren and I . . . we were best friends, a long time ago. Even with our differences, she meant a lot to me. It's important to me to know what happened to her."

"As soon as I have anything I can share, I'll let you know."

I rush out to the parking lot and sit in my car, practice deep breathing. I tell myself he was only doing his job, delving into my past with Jensen. It's not relevant, what happened in college. What matters is what Lauren was doing outside in the night, wandering so close to a treacherous cliff. I try to banish the image of her on the beach—her hair blowing in the wind, her head turned at a strange angle. I conjure a soothing picture of my piano, my plants, the view of the swaying forest from my kitchen window. I close my eyes and take steady, deep breaths, and I count in my head, *One, two, three.*

CHAPTER NINETEEN

As I drive away from the police station, I peer through the rain at the road ahead, trying to stay focused on the white lines. But the years unravel, and I remember running back to the apartment I shared with Lauren on the north side of campus. A bald eagle sailed through the sky above me, and I felt lightweight, too, like a feather. I was thinking of Jensen, of the way we'd curled up together, mapping out the size of our future family. If he returned to me now, asked me to travel back in time by seventeen years to marry him, I would refuse. And yet. I can't let go.

I pull over to the curb and call Nathan.

"I just needed to hear you talk," I say when he answers.

"You sound like a bus ran over you. Are you okay?"

"I'm fine. Just keep talking. Like you used to."

"When we first met?"

"Yeah, like that." I close my eyes and absorb the rich tenor of his voice. I feel ephemeral, as if a part of me has been slipping too far into the past.

"Pack your stuff and come back to my place. You're not safe at home."

"Are you there right now?" I open my eyes. I'm gripping my phone too tightly.

"No, but I will be. My home is your home. You know that. You have a key."

"It's not the same there without you."

He laughs. "What about when we live together?"

"You'll be home all the time, right?"

"That's my plan, eventually."

A truck roars past, and my car vibrates a little. This metal cage feels insubstantial, too easily crushed. "I met with the detective—it brought up . . . stuff."

"What stuff? You don't need to answer his questions." I hear voices, an engine running in the background.

"It was my idea to talk to him. I'm okay. It's just—"

"What? What is it?" A sharpness creeps into his tone.

"Remember the first night we spent in Seattle, when we caught the ferry on a whim and walked the downtown streets and stayed over in that seedy hotel?"

"How could I forget?" His tone softens. "What was that nightclub called?"

"I don't remember. All I remember is how strong my vodka tasted. Like pure alcohol. I can't believe I got so drunk."

"You were only tipsy. But I liked it. That was the most fun I've had in a long time."

"We've made some good memories," I say.

"And we're going to make more . . . Maybe we could go back to that hotel, for old times' sake."

"The mattress sagged. The pillows were flat."

"I didn't notice. As long as I'm with you, a bed is a bed."

I smile. This. This is what I needed. "Would you sleep with me on a bed of nails?"

"Sure, but you need a soft bed. You're like the princess and the pea."

"You got me there."

"What's this all about, Marissa?"

"I just needed to hear your voice."

"I'm sorry your house was burglarized. I'm sorry about Lauren. I'm sorry about the dress."

"If I never get it back . . ."

"You'll wear something else, and we'll still get married."

"I know," I say.

"I love you like crazy," he says.

"I love you crazier."

I hang up and pull the photograph out of my pocket, the one of Lauren and me and Jensen at the restaurant so long ago. Lauren in the blue dress. I took it to the police station but didn't show it to the detective. I almost wore the dress last June, the night of Anna's ballet recital, when Nathan and I had just started dating. But in the end, I chose a more conservative pantsuit. I dreamed of many more recitals, spelling bees, and outings with Nathan and Anna. But after the performance, when she rushed toward me with arms outstretched, she veered off at the last moment and ran to hug her mother. Rianne had been watching from a back row, keeping a polite distance from us. She'd arrived with a nondescript man, perhaps a boyfriend—I hardly remember anything about him, only the relaxed relief on her face when Anna hugged her.

I put the picture back into my pocket and pull out onto the road. But instead of returning to my cottage, I head out of town, along the winding, forested drive to Nathan's house on Cedarwood Lane. I park in the driveway and hurry over to the Eklunds' front door, ring the bell. The melodic tones echo through the rooms. No answer. The silver Honda sits innocently in the driveway. I ring again. Still no response, so I head over to Arthur Nguyen's place. When I ring the bell, he comes out on the porch, Bert in his arms, tail wagging. The scent of pipe tobacco wafts out. Arthur's wearing the hat, thick reading glasses perched on his nose. I pet Bert's head. "Marissa," Arthur says. "Want to go fishing? Pond is stocked."

"Um, thank you, no. I wanted to ask you about what you said before. I didn't get a chance to talk to you. We were worried about Anna."

"She was in the tree house, wasn't she?" he says, looking toward Nathan's place.

"You were right. Thank you."

"My kids loved it up there, especially my oldest daughter. She's going to Berkeley this year. On scholarship."

"You must be so proud of her."

"Oh, she was always the studious one. Stayed up till all hours to get those As."

"Speaking of staying up till all hours. You said you saw someone outside Friday night, with Lauren?"

"What I saw was a shadow. I thought I heard voices, but I didn't pay much attention. I realized in the morning, when the detective came over, that maybe I saw a murderer and didn't even know it. Or maybe it was nothing. Who's to say?"

"I heard Bert barking. Was he barking at the shadows?"

"I don't know, but he got pretty riled up."

Bert wriggles from his arms and jumps down, tail wagging. He trots over to lick my hand. "Good dog, Bert," I say. "Alerting the neighborhood to danger."

"That's my boy," Arthur says.

"Bert doesn't usually bark at people he knows. Does he?"

"He'll bark if he senses trouble," Arthur says thoughtfully. "He also barks at squirrels and rabbits. He's a dog. But you're right. When it comes to people, he alerts me to trespassers or strangers."

"So, either a stranger was wandering around, or he got overexcited about the wildlife. Other than his barking, did you hear anything else? Maybe an argument?"

"I couldn't tell. I wasn't paying a whole lot of attention. Bert needed a potty break and I needed to go back to sleep. I wish I could be of more help."

"You've been a great help. Thank you."

"No problem, anything I can do."

On my way to my car, I head up the Eklunds' driveway and into their backyard. I know I'm trespassing yet again, but nobody seems to be home. I'm drawn past the gazebo to the crime scene tape, which extends like a twenty-foot party streamer between two tall fir trees. I hunch against the wind, following the boundary line, scanning the ground. Dirt, grass, a flat area leading to a tangle of bushes clinging to the cliff edge. A thicket of rose hips. There, scuffed bootprints in the soil. Lauren's? Or someone else's? On either side of the scuffed prints, spindly rhododendrons grow to a height of eight or nine feet. If not for the sheltering branches of a fir tree, the rain would have washed away the prints by now.

Something looks wrong. I peer closely at the rhododendrons. A few branches are broken, snapped off at chest height. The police must have seen this. It's as if someone grabbed the branches to keep from falling.

I step back, my breathing fast. Lauren struggled, grasped those branches. I rush across the yard, hurtle down the stairs to the beach. Retrace my steps to the place where I found her. Or close. I can't be sure of the exact spot. There's no tape here, no markers, no sign. The tide rose and scoured the beach, then receded, leaving behind new shells and pebbles. Here, just past this promontory. This is where I saw her. I look up toward the bluff. Impossible to tell what happened at the top. Madrone and tree roots protrude where the soft ground is steadily eroding from the cliff face. Boulders have tumbled down, rubble piled at the bottom.

What happened to you, Lauren? I kneel and run my fingers through the sand. No sign that she was ever here. I walk the waterline, scanning the shore. On this deserted stretch of beach, wild things wash up— cockleshells, the occasional seabird, an overturned crab. Silvery-purple oyster shells in clumps. I glimpse a feathery reddish creature fluttering in the shallows, at the edge of a barnacled rock. Occasionally, a clear jellyfish flops onto the sand, but never one so colorful. As I approach the flash of red, a glint of something shiny catches my eye. Something man-made. Glass or metal. I crouch for a closer look. The red material is a swath of delicate, waterlogged fabric—a neck scarf, perhaps. A metal button shines at one end, imprinted with an intricate leaf pattern.

I look around, but all along the beach only kelp, broken seashells, and driftwood are scattered across the sand. How did the scarf get here? Could it be Lauren's? Could she have lost it on the way down? But she never wore scarves. She didn't like the feel of fabric around her neck. Could she have pulled the scarf off someone else? Or has someone been here on the beach since yesterday morning? I pull out my cell phone and call the detective.

"Have you touched the scarf?" he says.

"No, but it's in the water. Snagged on a rock," I say.

"I'll be right there. Any chance it could float away?"

"The tide is coming in."

"Keep an eye on it." He hangs up.

Keep an eye on it? Until the water laps up past my legs and I'm swimming? Until the waves crash into the cliff? The tide does rise that far now and then. The scarf whips back and forth in the water as if it's alive.

Ten minutes later, when the detective hurries down the steps in his long black coat, I feel I've been waiting for days. He retrieves the scarf with gloved hands, drops the soggy fabric into an evidence bag. "Did you find anything else?"

I squint up at the bluff. "I walked over to the yellow tape. I didn't cross the line, but I saw the broken branches at chest level, near the bootprints. I'm guessing you logged all that as evidence."

"We don't miss much," he says, heading back to the steps. "Neither do you. Want to come work for us?"

I hurry after him, bracing against the wind. "She was holding on, wasn't she? Trying to. Before she fell over the edge."

"We're trying to figure out what happened," he says, turning his head to look back at me. He ascends the stairs two at a time.

I race to keep up with him. "That's your standard line," I say. "You know the scarf is evidence, or you wouldn't have come all the way down here."

"Did I say that?" He strides on a diagonal path across the lawn, like he can't wait to shake me off.

"I saw the look on your face." I follow him to his black sedan, parked at the curb.

"What look was that?"

"Grim concentration. Like this is important."

"Everything's important," he says.

"She didn't wear scarves, you know."

"Who didn't?" He clicks a button on his key chain. The headlights flash on the sedan, the doors clicking.

"Lauren. She never wore scarves or necklaces or turtlenecks. She said it felt like she was being strangled. The scarf can't be hers."

"Good to know."

"Then where did it come from? Could she have pulled it off someone? Whoever pushed her?"

"Anything is possible," he says, getting into the car.

"If the scarf washed in from far away, it would be frayed or faded. What are the odds?"

He looks at me, a quizzical expression in his eyes. "You tell me. You seem to have it all figured out."

"Can you test the scarf for DNA?"

"Difficult to extract DNA if the evidence is submerged in salt water for very long. If that scarf passed through a few owners—"

"There would be lots of different DNA on the fabric."

His brows rise, and he shrugs. "Maybe."

"You won't tell me what you're thinking, so what can I do except speculate? She was my friend. She falls off a cliff, grabbing at branches, and now here is a scarf. I think it was here the whole time, but you missed it."

"That's entirely possible," he says. "Have a good day, Miss Parlette. Try to get some rest." As I watch him drive away, I want to run after him and pound on the window, demand answers.

"Marissa?" a small voice says behind me. I turn to see Brynn emerging from the wooded path to the gazebo. "Who was that?"

CHAPTER TWENTY

I tell Brynn about the scarf. "Was it yours? Your mom's?" I take a deep breath, try to dispel the image of Lauren losing her balance, branches snapping as she falls . . .

"We don't wear scarves." Brynn shivers, glances toward her house. A leaf drifts from her tousled hair. "Is it evidence?"

"They don't know yet. I need to ask you something. Do you know anything about someone breaking into my house?"

"What? Are you kidding me? What are you talking about?"

"Someone broke in." I keep my voice modulated.

"Are you accusing me?" Her eyes go cold again.

"I'm not accusing anyone. I'm just asking."

"I sneak out sometimes, but I'm not a burglar."

"Only one thing is missing, a special blue dress. My neighbor saw a car parked across the street similar to your mom's car."

"Lots of people have cars like that," she says, kicking at the ground. "No way would I ever break into anyone's house."

"So, it must've been someone else."

"I did drive by yesterday—"

"You were there?"

"But I didn't break in. I can't believe you would say that."

"Why did you drive by?"

"I wanted to talk to you."

"But you didn't stop in?"

"You weren't home yet." She looks at her feet.

"You parked across the street and sat there in your car?"

"Yeah, so? I didn't know what to do. I wanted to just drive around."

"You don't have to explain," I say. The air sinks into my lungs like ice water. "I shouldn't have brought it up now. It just shocked me, with everything going on, to go home and find my house ransacked."

She shivers again and tucks her hands up into her sleeves. "I don't get why people do that, breaking and entering. I didn't see anyone when I was over there. Must've happened after I left."

I shove my hands into my pockets. My fingers are going numb. "Maybe the police will come up with something, fingerprints."

"They won't be mine," she says.

"It would be okay if they were," I say. "I would understand."

She glares at me, her nose red in the cold. "But it wasn't me."

"I get it. We don't need to say any more about it." But the stain on my bedroom wall, the glass smashed on the floor—the violence haunts me, the image of a stranger's fingers sifting through my clothes, opening my dresser drawers, invading my private space. Brynn says it wasn't her, and even if it was, I could chalk it up to the temporary insanity of grief. I take the photograph from my pocket, hand it to her. "That's the dress your mom gave me. The one I'm talking about."

She holds the photograph close to her face, as if its secrets will come into focus when pushed against her nose. "Where did you find this picture?" She turns it over, looks at the back, then holds the picture away from her face, toward the light.

"I've had it for years. It was taken a long time ago."

"That's an awesome dress. Looks like one of a kind. It would be hard for someone to hide it, you know, wear it around and not get caught."

"I agree with you there," I say.

"My mom and dad and you . . . you were all friends back then."

"You didn't know that?" I say, trying not to sound floored.

"You guys look, like, way young."

"We were."

Branches crackle in the woods, and someone emerges from the shadows. I freeze, but it's a slight figure, a girl with a mop of orange and black hair shot through with blond highlights. A distinctly feminine face, delicate features. As she approaches us, multiple earrings and nose rings shine in the light. She stops next to Brynn, shoves her hands into the pockets of her skinny jeans.

"Who is this?" I say. "A friend?"

Brynn squares her shoulders, juts out her chin. "This is Karina, my girlfriend. My *girlfriend* girlfriend."

"Okay," I say. I'm not shocked—although I did not expect a girl wearing quite so many decorations. Her dark eyes shine with boldness. "Hey," she says.

"Hey." I extend my hand, and she shakes it clumsily, her fingers warm. I look at Brynn. She glares at me, as if defying me to ask more questions.

"Is this why your mom was sending you to a boarding school?" I say. "Because of Karina?"

Brynn looks past me, blinking fast. She draws a deep breath. "My mom wasn't, like, totally happy. She caught us in my room. But she didn't care that I was into girls."

Karina takes her hands from her pockets, pretends to examine her fingernails.

"Does your dad care?" I say.

Brynn reaches out to grip Karina's hand, as if the two of them are on a life raft on a roiling ocean.

"He doesn't know, does he?" I say.

"I'll tell him when the time is right." Brynn looks at the picture again. "My dad was really into you . . . He's staring at you like he's totally in love with you."

He's in profile, turned to face me on his right, while Lauren looks on from his left. It's difficult to read his expression. Jensen, stuck in the middle. Who took the photograph that night? The waitress? It was Jensen's birthday. Cake crumbs litter our plates.

"It's an old photograph, like I said," I say. "I don't remember."

"Why are you carrying this around then?"

"I took it to show the detective the dress."

"My mom looks good in it."

"She does," I say, my gut twisting.

"But you and my dad were in love. Don't deny it. I'm not stupid. So why do you look sad?"

"Do I look sad? Really?" I peer closely at the photograph. Perhaps I already knew what was to come. "I think a sad song was playing."

"How long were you going out with my dad?"

Months. "I can't recall exactly."

"He never talks about it. I asked him once how he met Mom, and he said, 'Through a friend.' But my mom told me all these stories about how they were together so much, and their relationship was so strong, and they could, like, survive anything. But this is like, whoa."

"Totally a surprise," Karina says.

I swallow, the sky tilting. "Brynn, your dad and I . . . were involved. Maybe your parents didn't want you to know. I'm not sure why. It was so long ago."

"He left you for my mom. Didn't he? Is that how he met her? Through you?"

I inhale, let out my breath slowly, *one, two, three. I'm in the apartment, opening the bedroom door. There's a steady drip from the faucet in the bathroom. My answer for Jensen. I can't wait to tell him.*

"Marissa?" Brynn says. "Am I asking personal questions? It's just . . . this is about my mom and dad."

"I know, it's okay. The way things happened. It's a bit confusing now."

She blows upward, her bangs lifting from her forehead. "She never told me. And now I can't even ask her. Maybe I would've seen her going out if I'd even been home." Her voice breaks.

"But—I thought she picked you up from the party."

She wipes her nose with the back of her hand. "She did, but I sneaked out again. She probably thought I was in my room asleep."

"You were out with Karina," I say.

Karina plays with one of her many earrings.

"We went up in the tree house," Brynn whispers. "The moon was full, and . . . we saw Anna."

My heart stops—the air stops. My breathing stops. "What? When? Doing what?"

"She was out taking pictures. She sometimes does that. I don't know what time."

"Did you tell the police?"

"I couldn't. They would want to know what I was doing outside. Karina's parents are, like, really . . ."

"They would send me away for reprogramming or even worse," Karina says.

"You saw Anna. Are you sure?" My voice comes from far away, down a long tunnel.

"Like, a thousand percent sure," Brynn says. "I recognized her bird pajamas. She was crouching behind the hedge, near her room. I was going to go down and talk to her, but she climbed back in her window."

"You didn't tell anyone. Nobody at all."

"I knew she would get in trouble. I would've gotten in trouble, too."

"Did you see anything else? Your mom? Anyone? The motion sensor light?"

"No, I wish I did," Brynn says. "I wish more than anything. Maybe I could have saved her."

CHAPTER TWENTY-ONE

"Brynn lies about everything," Nathan says on the phone as I'm driving back to my cottage. "Jensen told me he's having problems with her. Think about it. She denied breaking into your house. How can you believe anything she says?" His tinny voice echoes on speakerphone, as if he's on an orbiting space station instead of at work.

"If Anna was out there and she saw something—"

"I don't want the police interrogating my kid. This will traumatize her even more. Give her some time at her mother's house."

"You don't think this is important?"

"She didn't see anything. She doesn't know what happened."

I pull over to the shoulder, the windshield wipers beating a relentless rhythm. "How can you be so sure? I understand you want to protect Anna, but Lauren was murdered."

"Whoa, we don't know that," he says.

"Maybe you don't, but I do." I hang up, irritated, and against my better judgment I call Rianne, my breath catching when she answers. She's reluctant to meet with me at first, says she must soon leave for work, but she finally agrees when I tell her it's about Anna. I make a detour to the southwest side of town, where Anna stays with Rianne in a rented yellow Victorian, one of the original homes built in Tranquil

Cove in the early 1900s, up a gentle slope from the waterfront. This is a risk, approaching the ex-wife, who thinks I'm a bad influence.

Yet here I am at her place. Delicate curtains obscure the windows; the manicured garden turns immaculate corners. Anna is riding her bike on the sidewalk. When she sees me pull up, she pedals toward me and stops next to the car, resting her feet on the ground.

"I'm here to see your mom," I say.

"You c-c-can't talk to her. I'll get in trouble." Oh no, the stuttering again. My heart sinks, but all is not lost. She's distressed by recent events. This isn't a permanent condition.

"Why will you get in trouble?" I say, smiling to hide my concern. "This is between me and your mom."

"You're not sup—posed to come here." She's holding the bicycle handlebars so tight, her knuckles are white.

"I won't be here for long," I say, looking up at the house. I squint in a blade of sunlight. "Do you like your room here? Did your jewelry box go on a shelf?"

Her lips quiver, and the bike wobbles a little. The helmet slips down over her forehead. "Wh-wh-what do you want to talk to her about?"

"Hello there!" Rianne peeks out the front door, waving. Her vintage gold jacket shines in the sun. "Come on up. Anna, you have ten more minutes outside."

Anna frowns at me, hesitates, then pushes off and pedals down the road at top speed. I resist the urge to chase after her, to reassure her.

Rianne invites me inside the foyer, where leafy plants flourish on side tables beneath vaulted ceilings.

"Anna seems upset," I say. "Her speech fluency—"

"I noticed the stuttering, too," Rianne says, her voice threaded with worry. "Is that why you're here?"

"No, I didn't notice it before I got here. Look, I apologize for what happened, with the tree house. We . . . should have been watching her."

"I should apologize for my rudeness when I was there. I'm concerned about our daughter's well-being, that's all. After what happened Friday—"

"Actually, I came here to ask you about that night."

"Yes?" She looks at me with an unblinking gaze.

"Anna might have gone outside. Maybe she was taking video and she saw something."

"She's not allowed out at night."

"Nathan knows that. We know that. But Anna is willful."

"It's Nathan's job to—"

"I'm to blame, too. But if she saw something, it could be what scared her." I tell Rianne about the pajamas in Anna's backpack.

She ushers me into the living room, furnished in shades of muted beige. She sits in a cushioned chair, gripping the padded arm as if on a turbulent flight. "Do you think my daughter is hiding something? Something she knows? Could it be why her stuttering returned?"

I sit on a couch across from her. "I have no idea."

"I see," Rianne says.

"Nathan doesn't want to tell the authorities. He thinks it will further upset her. I'm wondering if . . ."

"You want me to talk to the detective. I'm not sure. What is Nathan even thinking?"

"He doesn't know I'm here. Would you be open to sending Anna to talk to someone else, if not the police?"

"A therapist. That's what you're suggesting." Her voice is distant, distracted.

"Whatever you think is best," I say.

"I'll talk to Anna. What you're saying . . . It does explain her panic. Her urge to run away. The stuttering. And what happened to Lauren . . . on top of what happened the night before, has only compounded Anna's trauma."

"What happened the night before—you mean our engagement."

"Anna has trouble with too many changes all at once. Sometimes she doesn't even recognize them. Here's an example." She picks up a glazed, red clay bowl from the coffee table. Lopsided, imperfect, but imbued with charm and originality. "She made this in class a few weeks ago. Look at the inscription." She flips the bowl over, showing me the engraving on the bottom, in tiny letters. *4 Mom+Dad.* ♥ *Anna*

"How sweet," I say, although the words jab at my heart. But what child wouldn't want her parents together again?

"She still sees the three of us as a family unit." Rianne frowns as she places the bowl back on the table. "Things like this . . . I let them go. I don't need to remind her that her father and I are no longer living in the same house. That she can't give the bowl to both of us. She's anxious enough as it is. And, she's finally realizing the truth. Friday night, she sent me numerous texts. She seemed frantic."

"She did rush off to bed early. I was worried."

Rianne looks up at me, the brooding light reflected in her blue eyes. "She was wound up about the engagement. I wouldn't be surprised if she went outside, as you say. Do you think she saw Nathan? He told me he was stepping out when I sent him a text."

"So, he wasn't lying. You did text him."

"It was late, I know. Could she have seen him out there, I wonder?"

"You mean, maybe she thought he had something to do with Lauren's—?"

"Oh, he wouldn't hurt anyone," Rianne says, but her words sound frail, unsure of themselves. "She knows that. I know that. But still."

I look at the photographs lined up on the mantel. Anna in a school play, dancing, in a formal school picture. "Maybe I can convince him to talk to her, find out if she saw him, and he can clear up any strange ideas in her head."

"I'll talk to Nathan, too," Rianne says. "She so desperately needs stability. She acts out these days."

"Acts out?" I think of the photograph with my face cut away. But I won't mention it to Rianne.

"She gets into moods. Always did, but more so now. She needs a predictable schedule, a calm life."

"I agree with you. I care about Anna."

"I know you do."

"We didn't want to bring drama into her life."

"Oh, I know that," she says. "I didn't mean to imply. I only mean, she deserves happiness. I never wanted her to grow up the way I did, in a broken family."

"She's resilient. We'll work this out."

Rianne smiles at me. "Sounds as though you already have— Nathan's schedule isn't too difficult for you? He gets called in at all hours. Does he still go out on long calls at night?"

"Not too often," I say. I get up, on edge. She walks me to the front door.

"Maybe he's settling down. His schedule was always crazy."

"I suppose it's the nature of his job." I can't shake the image of Nathan slipping out of the bedroom, his face lit by his cell phone screen.

"He was always eager to run into work if someone called in sick or needed a replacement. He was dedicated to that job. It goes way back."

"You mean because of his mother."

"He told you." She opens the door, gestures to Anna to come back. She's pedaling up the road, her hair billowing from beneath her helmet.

"He said his mom suffered from an irregular heartbeat once when his dad was in surgery. A first responder saved her life, and Nathan never forgot. The paramedic became his hero."

"There you go," Rianne says. "You know him pretty well now, after such a short time."

I smile tightly, resisting the urge to defend myself. It's none of her business, but in a way, she's right. Nathan and I have been together a short time in the large scheme of things.

I step out onto the porch, squint in the sun. Anna's pedaling up the driveway. She parks her bike against the detached garage, unstraps her helmet.

"Thanks for taking time to talk to me," I say to Rianne.

"You're still worried. I understand that feeling. You're so much in love with him, and yet . . ."

I look at her, my heart fluttering against my rib cage. Anna puts her helmet on the handlebars. "I'm not worried," I say, a lie.

"But you're questioning things." Rianne smiles wistfully. "I know. I've been there. When he takes off at night, sometimes it's hard to believe he's going to work, to help people—sometimes, well, you know, the imagination can wander off in all directions."

CHAPTER TWENTY-TWO

"Why the hell did you talk to Rianne?" Nathan says. We're out for a late dinner at Tranquil by the Bay, our table overlooking the water, candle flames flickering between us. At nearly eight thirty, a few couples linger in quiet corners; moonlight ripples across the sea. Nathan beguiles me in that pale-green flannel shirt, the top buttons open as usual, those faded jeans, and that haphazard smile.

"Rianne was willing to talk to me about Anna," I say. "She's not in denial."

"You went to her house. She's unhinged."

"That's a harsh statement." I look at him and realize, I don't know what's true. His damning of Rianne seems so extreme.

"Is this why you suggested dinner, to push me about Anna again?"

"Not only about Anna." He doesn't know that I tried on five different pairs of earrings before settling on a pair in filigreed gold to match the engagement ring, or that I fretted before choosing a black satin skirt and a soft, chestnut sweater. That I am uncertain. That Lauren's apparition materialized from the shadows, her face bloody and caked in sand. *What are you doing, going out for dinner, when I'm dead? How dare you?*

"Drinks for you two?" the waitress says, laying the menus on the table.

"Water, please," I say. No alcohol for me tonight. I need a clear head.

"A glass of white," Nathan says, still looking at me.

"Coming right up." She bounces away, and I unfold the cloth napkin on my lap, open the menu. Mango kale salad, risotto primavera . . .

Nathan sets the menu on his plate, leans forward, and reaches for my hand. I hold on to him, instant relief. I didn't realize how much I needed his touch, the warmth and firmness of his grip. "What's this all about?" he says.

"It's about us," I say. "Everything feels out of balance. Like somehow, through all this, a happy future might be out of reach."

"What makes you say that? Nothing has changed between us. We can weather this. Families fall apart and come back together in different ways. People are born. People die. We laugh and cry and mourn those we've lost. Grief is part of life."

"I know all that. It's just . . . I feel like Lauren died, and everything changed. I'm looking at the world through a foggy window, and I can't clear the glass."

"Lean on me," he says. "Wait, isn't that a song?"

I withdraw my hand from his and smile as the waitress returns with our drinks. Nathan orders the fish and chips; I choose the risotto. I glance at the couple two tables over, their gazes locked together.

"Why did you and Rianne split up?" I say after the waitress walks away. "You never really told me, and when I visited her, she implied . . ."

"Oh hell no. Let's not talk about her." He presses his fingers to his forehead, flicks them away, as if to dispel any thought of her.

"She implied that she was afraid during your marriage. Maybe she suspected you of cheating on her. She talked about your night shifts."

"That . . . Jesus. I can't believe this." He closes his eyes, takes a deep breath. Opens them. "You shouldn't talk to her. Her ideas are way out there."

"Way out where?"

"She was overly suspicious."

"That's an extreme thing to say about your own ex-wife, the mother of your child."

"I'm shocked by that fact every day."

The waitress brings our appetizer salads, butter lettuce garnished with radishes and onion, a mustard dressing on the side.

"You're going to have to explain," I say. "Tell me why you think she's unhinged."

Nathan digs into his salad. He looks at me, the tightness returning to the muscles of his face. He takes a deep breath. "I didn't know what Rianne was like when I married her. She got pregnant, and when Anna was born, I fell in love with being a dad. But Rianne got possessive and demanding."

"That's vague. How exactly?"

"She's insecure. To put it mildly. Had to know where I was every minute, what I was doing. I stayed too long in a bad marriage, because of Anna."

"To keep the family together. Rianne suggested your night shifts were—"

"They were night shifts. Still are. I've stayed in my profession to take care of Anna, too, to make sure she has food, clothes, birthday presents. I could have quit. I've seen enough shit to traumatize a person for life. But having a kid, it changes things. I'd do anything for her."

"Like protect her from herself? You're not surprised that she was outside in the night."

"You told Rianne. Now she'll blame me . . . I can't live without Anna."

"You think Rianne will try to take her away. You think this is about Rianne's assessment of you."

He looks up at me. "No, it's about Anna! What if Rianne wants full custody? Thinks I'm an unfit parent? Anna doesn't want to live at her mom's house all the time."

A small stab in my heart. "Things didn't work out for you three as a family. But you can't keep trying to protect Anna—you have to address whatever is going on with her."

"She's confused. That's all. When I first saw you, when you were with her at school, she was smiling. She loved what you were doing for her. I hadn't seen her smile in so long."

"But that was then. This is now." The food on my plate is suddenly unappetizing.

"She'll get over this."

I look at him squarely. "Someone pushed Lauren off a cliff—"

"You still don't know that."

I lean forward, closer to him. "And you are as good as obstructing—"

"You can't believe that!" He glances over at the next table, then lowers his voice. "I want to know what happened to her as much as you do. You can't let this come between us. What Brynn saw, I don't know. She's seriously troubled. She fought with her parents. I could hear them sometimes. For all we know, she could have—"

"What? Thrown her own mother off a cliff? And lied about seeing Anna out there?" I look out the window, but I feel the possibility in his suggestion. I see Brynn's cold eyes, hear the anger in her voice. *Boarding school . . . She would've tried to drag me there.*

"Maybe." Nathan sits back. "Anna's coming to stay with me later this week. Let's just be with her. Be Dad and Marissa. Maybe she'll talk to us on her own."

I hesitate. "All right. You're her dad. If that's what you want to do."

"I do. Trust me on this."

"I always trust you," I say, but what if Anna saw Nathan outside that night? And if she saw her dad, was he doing something other than sending a text to Rianne? He said he needed air.

"Maybe a trip into the city this weekend?" he says. "It will be a distraction, at least."

I smile and nod, and as we order blackberry cheesecake for dessert, made from a local harvest, I push away my misgivings. I'm happy with Nathan. He loves me. He loves his daughter. I can't fault him for protecting her. Maybe I'm the one who is overly suspicious. Before I met him, I had only one serious relationship after Jensen. But I was never completely in love, so I broke it off after a year. I've always been okay alone, waiting for the perfect man to come along: someone exciting but also honest, caring, and seemingly incapable of betrayal. Nobody truly fit the bill—until Nathan. The first morning I woke in his bed, the soft rush of the ocean flowing in through the window, I was at peace. I knew I had to hold on to him. I still feel that way. But. The *but* crept into my mind Friday night and stayed there, the echo of what happened before, in the college apartment. The flutter of the curtain when I walked in early, the heaviness in the air, a hint of something I had yet to discover. But I can't look for signs of betrayal. I must believe in Nathan, or else what's the point?

We're the last to leave the restaurant, arms around each other in the cold. A black sky blots out the stars, clouds sweeping in for the night. On the way home in his truck, I sit close to him, my hand on his thigh. His warmth radiates through me, and I can feel his heartbeat, his slow, deep breathing. The smell of him, soap and wine, wraps around me. I allow my worries to wane, and I imagine waking next to him every morning, my clothes hanging permanently in the closet. My piano in his living room, my favorite blue armchair by the window. My pots and pans in the kitchen cabinets. I'll share breakfast with him every morning; he loves apricot marmalade, hard-boiled eggs.

Back in his house, we slip off our coats, and he kisses me, pulling me against him. His lips feel cool, urgent. He walks me down the hall, still kissing me, unbuttoning my blouse. We leave a trail of clothing on the floor, landmarks on the path to the bed. I drink him in, grateful for his gentle touch. In the darkness, we could be on another planet, in another universe where grief doesn't exist. He knows how to heighten

129

my pleasure with a simple caress, a whisper in my ear. He urges me to let go, to give myself over to him, and I do.

Afterward, as I lie in his arms, languid and half-asleep, the air seems to buzz with ambient energy. He strokes my arm absentmindedly. "I've been thinking about work," he says softly into my hair.

"How romantic," I whisper, although I don't need to be quiet. We're the only ones here.

"No, I mean I want to retire early. It's why I'm taking so many shifts. I want to get rid of this job, spend more time with you and Anna."

I sit up and turn to look down at him in the darkness, at the rough etching of his face. "Are you serious?"

"I've never been more serious in my life." He reaches up to touch my cheek. "You're so beautiful. Do you know that?"

"When you say it, I feel beautiful."

"You should always know it." He runs his thumb along my bottom lip. "When I'm at work, I miss you all the time. I need to get off this treadmill. Life is short, Marissa."

"But you're helping people. You're saving lives. Remember that woman who hit the telephone pole?" As we were driving home from the grocery store, she drifted to the shoulder right in front of us. Nathan pulled over and ran to her aid. She was sweating, shaking. I thought she was drunk, but he quickly determined she was diabetic, suffering from low blood sugar. He gave her half a cup of orange juice from the store, and we waited for the ambulance to arrive.

"I'm burned out," he says. "I can't do it anymore."

"But how could you possibly retire now?"

"I figure I need to work two more years, and I'm there. My inheritance from my dad and my savings should carry me until my retirement kicks in—"

"Are you sure? What will you do instead? You're an adrenaline junkie. You like the rush of going out to the scene of a crisis."

He pulls me back down into his arms. "There are other ways to get my fix. I could teach, write a book. Work on the house. I need to replace the windows, repair a few roof shingles . . ."

"You are good with your hands," I say, nestling into him.

"That's the idea," he says softly, kissing my forehead.

"It's an exciting idea. I know you can pull it off. When you set your mind on something—"

"I make it happen," he says.

My mind whirs with the possibilities. Could I go part-time at school, embark on a new adventure with Nathan? As I'm drifting off, the beep of a text on his cell phone jolts me back to awareness. He turns away from me to check his phone on the nightstand. The clock reads 12:11 a.m. "Who is it this late?" I whisper sleepily. "Is everything okay?"

"Fine," he says, turning back toward me. "Just work, but I'm not going in."

An alarm rings in my mind, but it's a distant bell. I'm too tired to think. *Just work,* his voice echoes as I fall into sleep. In the early-morning hours, Lauren visits my dreams, surrounded by sand, the blood pooling at her feet, a vast and black reflective pond. *I need to tell you about something,* she says, her features sculpted by the rising moon. *It's about you and me, and what happened before. It's about my family. Brynn and Jensen. It's about us, Nathan and me.*

CHAPTER TWENTY-THREE

In the morning, the dream fades. Nathan is on a day shift. He comes and goes like a phantom, but at least he left me a note.

I loved last night. I love you like crazy.

"I love you crazier," I say aloud.

I lose myself in the comfort of strong coffee, try to forget his text from last night. *Just work,* he said, not missing a beat. I choose to believe him. When he proposed to me in the shower, before we made the dinner announcement, I was immediately sure of my answer. I nodded beneath the soothing hot water, whispered *yes* into the steam, and he held me tight.

But I wasn't so sure of myself, all those years ago, when I skipped my last class that February afternoon. I'd bought a new perfume, Coco, to prepare for my dinner with Jensen at the Great Northwest Soup Company. I'd been holding off for a week, and now I would finally give him my answer. I pictured holding out my hand so he could slip the engagement ring onto my finger, and I imagined the smile that would spread across his face. I was giddy, full of anticipation.

Back in the apartment, I peeled off my wet rain gear, left my knapsack by the door. I saw Lauren's coat draped over the couch. A math textbook lay open on the coffee table. She'd left her dishes on the kitchen counter as usual. Carelessly scattered her belongings around the living room. Soon I would no longer have to deal with her annoying habits. I would move out, and Jensen and I would find a place together.

I'd just removed my wet socks when I noticed a man's black trench coat thrown over a chair. I tiptoed down the hall to her bedroom door, which stood ajar. The strange whimpers and grunts grew louder. *In the afternoon.* How rude. *Does she ever study?* I sometimes woke in the night to the rhythmic squeaks of her bedsprings. I took to wearing earplugs. In the months leading up to that afternoon, she'd brought three different men—boys, really—back to the apartment after hours, and they skulked away guiltily in the morning. I saw them, their rumpled hair and wrinkly T-shirts, but I never knew who they were. She never bothered to explain.

Our friendship wavered on shaky ground. Playing together as children, patrolling the shopping mall as teenagers. None of it compared to having to live together in college. Her worst habits rose to the surface like pond scum. Maybe mine did, too. She snapped at me for leaving the cap off the toothpaste, for drinking the last of the coffee without announcing my intention. At least I didn't sleep with strange men.

She wasn't even trying to be quiet. She must not have heard me come in. Or maybe she and her lover didn't care. I pushed the door open a little more. They didn't even see me. I stared at her naked, sweaty back as she pumped up and down. I saw only part of him, my Jensen, his hair on the pillow, his eyes half-closed, not even looking at her. He was too far gone, his hands on her hips. His hands.

The noises he made, sounds I'd never heard. Deep, guttural. The lamplight illuminating Lauren's curves. Her hair tangled, messy—a pillow on the floor. During the thousand years I stood there, Lauren and Jensen became one, a single writhing beast moaning and keening and ripping out my insides. I wanted them to see me, to notice me, to kill themselves from the guilt, but they didn't look in my direction.

I doubled over, nausea rising in my throat, and I backed off in shock. The rain banged on the roof. I knew, as I ran to hide in my room, that I had become the jilted, betrayed girlfriend repeated through the annals of time. More than I hated Lauren and Jensen, I hated that I had become a cliché.

I quietly left the apartment, stepping out to the concrete walkway beneath the overhang. Then I pretended to come home, making a lot of noise with my keys, slamming the door, singing. I stood in the living room and waited, listening to the scrambling, their efforts to cover up. Then Jensen sauntered out of the hall, fully clothed but flushed. Lauren stepped out of her room in sweats, her hair a mess.

"Oh, hey, Marissa!" she said. "Jensen got here early."

He grinned, straightening his shirt. "Thought we could go to dinner from here. I was just in the john."

I stood there, wondering how they could look me in the eye. If I hadn't seen them, I might have believed them. Even with all the scrambling and messiness. I would have preferred the lie.

"I saw you," I said.

"What?" Lauren said. Her face reddened.

"I saw you two in your room. I came home. Your door was open. I saw you."

She laughed. "What do you think you saw? You didn't."

I was shaking so much, I felt my bones were breaking. "I. Saw. You."

"It wasn't what it looked like—" she started.

"It was exactly what it looked like."

"Damn it, Marissa," Jensen said. "Shit." The guilt on his face could've ended civilization as we knew it. But it didn't matter. I despised him. I ran into my room and locked the door. He knocked, said he couldn't help it. He didn't know what had happened. At least he owned up to his behavior. Lauren never did.

Now, as I spread peanut butter on toast, I mull whether to tell Jensen about Brynn. Maybe I ought to leave well enough alone, keep my distance. But what was she really doing outside in the night? It seems the entire town slipped outside, restless, drawn by the full moon. And what was she doing at my house? Did she genuinely need to talk? Or did she make up the whole story?

While I'm trying to decide what to do, I spot Jensen jogging toward the beach stairs, in Spandex pants and a windbreaker. As if he read my mind. I leave my toast on the counter, and I'm out in a minute, yanking my hat over tangled hair, running down to the beach in sweats and running shoes. I race to catch up with him, my lungs bursting. He slows to a fast walk. "Marissa, hey," he says, tossing me a sad smile.

"Any news?" I say.

"The detective came back. They're bringing a forensics team to rappel down the cliff. They want to retrieve her shoes and test them."

"What evidence can you pull off a shoe?" The blood rushes in my ears.

"They can see where she walked. Based on plant material on the bottom of her shoe."

"Where would she have walked?"

"We have a unique form of ground cover at the back of the property. They can tell if she walked straight back or took a detour."

"That seems a stretch," I say.

"It's really not. Different areas of ground have distinctive characteristics. They use a microprobe technique to compare soil samples from the shoe and the garden."

"Wow, they're definitely treating this as a murder investigation then."

"Word must be getting around. A reporter knocked on my door yesterday. She thought she could sweet-talk me to get her story."

"I hope you sent her away," I say.

"I told her to get off my property. I wasn't polite. I don't want the news all over this."

"I don't blame you." I take a deep breath, then I tell him what happened in my cottage to the dress. About my talk with Brynn. The broken branches and the footprints at the edge of the cliff. About the scarf. I don't mention Brynn's girlfriend, Karina—or Nathan's outing in the middle of the night. "Nothing else was stolen," I say. "Just the dress."

He's so quiet that I can tell he's stunned. "I apologize for Brynn if she broke in. She's taking everything hard. I'll see if she has your dress."

"I don't want her to get into trouble. I showed her a picture from . . . your birthday at the Mediterranean. From seventeen years ago. She guessed. About us, and about you and Lauren ending up together."

He looks at me, his eyes bloodshot. "Did you tell her the rest of the story?"

"I thought that was your job. You're her dad." I look at him, at his blocky profile leaning into the wind, aging but still handsome. He can still give me a faint flip-flop in my stomach, a distant echo from long ago.

"I never told her. Neither did Lauren. We didn't have the guts."

"That's refreshingly honest." Coward. I feel needles under my skin again, after all this time.

"Lauren was hell to live with. She didn't admit to anything. She argued about everything, drank too much at parties, flirted with strangers. But I loved her. Love her. I always will."

"I know." We turn around, head back along the beach.

"You intimidated her," he says. He wipes his nose with the back of his gloved hand.

"I intimidated her?" I say.

"She told me about how you helped her study for tests, but you never seemed to have any trouble getting As. She had to work at it. Other things came more easily to her. She admired you. She had a lot of guilt. She wanted to make it up to you."

"That's good to know. At least she grew a conscience after all these years."

"She didn't know how to apologize. You were so upset. You didn't talk to either of us for a long time."

I follow him back toward the beach stairs. "She didn't know how to apologize? Really? I don't believe it. Do you know why I got back to the apartment early that day?"

"You never told me . . ." He stops, the wind in his hair, and I can feel the pull of the past. He waits for me to go on.

"I had decided to say yes to you. I figured I would throw caution to the wind. I was one hundred percent ready to marry you and live happily ever after."

His face goes blank with shock. "You never told me that."

"I was going to tell you, but I didn't have the chance. It felt so special. I was walking on air. I was also scared. About the future . . . about everything. We were so young. But then I thought, people get married young all the time. You know what changed my mind? My sociology professor. In class, he was illustrating the concept of monogamy . . . He told us about how he'd met the love of his life in high school and they'd been together for forty years. He was about to retire and travel the world with her. He inspired me."

Jensen's face blanches. "Seriously? You're not making this up?"

I turn my face into the wind, inhaling the cool sea air. "Why would I make up something like that?"

"Marissa—I had no idea. I loved you."

"I know you did."

"If you'd told me sooner . . ."

"What difference would it have made?" I take a deep breath. He and Lauren stopped seeing each other after I found them together. Jensen kept pursuing me, meeting me everywhere, telling me he wanted to try again. He professed his love for me on his knees outside the psychology building when I emerged from class. Finally, I relented. I would date him, no promises. We lasted another six weeks . . .

"You weren't the same," he says. "We went out, and you didn't talk to me, sometimes all the way through dinner. I tried to be with you again."

"You're making it sound like it was all my fault what happened, and all my fault that I couldn't forgive you!"

"I know . . . I'm not saying that. We would have worked it out. We could have . . ."

"Really?" I'm climbing the stairs. He follows. "Maybe Lauren wouldn't have come to you and told you she was pregnant. From that little tryst that afternoon? Maybe if you'd stayed with me, she would have had an abortion, and Brynn would never have been born."

He flinches. "Don't say that."

"Or who knows? Maybe Lauren would've become a single mom. Eventually you would've gone back to her."

"We can't speak in what-ifs. What happened . . . happened."

"No, you made a choice, and then you made another choice. And then, well, the rest is history." We're at the top of the stairs. I stop to catch my breath, then I keep walking.

He falls into step beside me. "Why didn't you tell me all this before?"

"It was a long time ago. I might never have told you if it weren't for what happened to Lauren . . ."

"I know," he says, taking a deep breath. "I need to tell you something, too. She got depressed a couple of months ago. She didn't want me to tell anyone. About what happened at the end of August . . ." He wipes his nose again with the back of his hand. I give him a crumpled tissue from my pocket, which he probably won't use. He was never fond of blowing his nose.

"Hedra mentioned that Lauren was sneaking a cigarette at the barbecue last time she saw her. And crying."

"Yeah, she was broken up. After we had Brynn, she wanted a boy. We tried forever, but she couldn't get pregnant. Finally, a few months ago, she did, and the ultrasound showed it was a boy."

"She didn't tell me," I breathe.

"She didn't even tell Brynn. Her doctor suggested we wait. He said the risk of miscarriage increases with age, and Lauren was thirty-six. She wanted to keep it quiet. And then she lost the baby."

"Oh, how terrible for both of you. I had no idea." I search through my memory—of Lauren downing more alcohol than she should, flirting with Nathan. Was all this to numb her sorrow?

"She kept things to herself," he says.

"What a devastating loss—it must have been so hard."

"It was, but she wouldn't go near that cliff. Not if she was sober. Not if she was her normal happy self. But she wasn't."

"Are you saying you believe she might have jumped? Even with all the indications—"

"I don't know what to believe," Jensen says, a pained expression in his eyes. "She wanted to be happy again. I know she did. She was trying her hardest. But when the baby died, I think a part of Lauren died, too."

CHAPTER TWENTY-FOUR

I return to my cottage, and the day tumbles around me like laundry on a fast spin cycle. Even though I'm taking a few days off, I respond to emails from parents, from teachers who want to send students to me for testing. I work on Individualized Education Programs, and I click through the wedding invitation templates, the mock-ups I created for Nathan and me. One has a border of leafy vines, another version with interlocked wedding rings, a third style with roses. But I'm only going through the motions. My mind strays back to Jensen, to the surprise in his eyes when I told him I had planned to marry him, his expression turning to grief when he told me about Lauren.

Her actions reveal themselves in a new, sadder light. I could have been more forgiving if I had known. I would not have put her off when she said she needed to talk. But I was still holding a grudge, imprisoned by the past.

To anchor myself in the present, I pull out the romantic birthday card from Nathan, the one he gave me last autumn, with a heart made of red yarn on the front.

I'm in love with you. That's all.

I read through my texts from him. I can't wait to see you . . . new pillows . . . when you get here, let's take a shower . . . Anna's at her mom's . . . can't stop thinking about last night . . . you were wild. And the gifts—a thin silver necklace with an orca pendant, commemorating our first whale watching trip to San Juan Island; a handmade journal with a linen cover. I see him propped on pillows in my bed, laughing. My long-ago loss became a gain. If Jensen and Lauren hadn't found each other, perhaps I never would have met Nathan. But for all I know, Lauren would still be alive. Or not.

Jensen is right. I can't play the What-If game. Perhaps everything would have turned out the same way no matter what. I must let go. I try to find solace in the details of my life, in folding laundry, putting it in drawers. I come across a lace bra like the one Lauren loaned me years ago when mine was stolen at the high school swimming pool. A girl from school grabbed my bra, threw it out in the hall. I stood in the cold, covering my chest. Lockers slammed, faucets squeaked in the showers—giggles, the slap of flip-flops on the tile floor. The smell of chlorine hung in the air.

Why did you do that? I yelled. The girl laughed at me. Lauren shoved her, ran out to look for my bra, but it was gone. Someone had picked it up. She gave me hers, and she went without one that day. She came to my defense not only against drunken frat boys, but also against the cruelty of other girls. And yet. Falling in love with Jensen was the unkindest thing she ever did to me. Not on purpose, but still.

I return to Nathan's house in the evening, tell him what Jensen told me. "This whole thing is tragic," Nathan says, resting his hand on mine at the dinner table. "How are you holding up? I know it's bringing back memories."

"Good ones as well as bad," I say. "I wish she had told me about her miscarriage. But sometimes the saddest things are the ones we keep most secret. We can't bear to talk about them. And she and I weren't close friends anymore."

"Did she have any close friends?" Nathan says.

"A couple of nurses at the hospital, I think. She worked long shifts."

Nathan nods, staring off into the distance. He's trying to be attentive, but I can tell he's distracted. He pushes his green beans around with his fork, checks his phone.

"Is something bothering you?" I say.

He looks at me, opens his mouth, closes it, looks at his plate. "It's been a tough day. Two fatalities. One was a kid. Traffic accident. He wasn't wearing his seat belt. I hate those calls. Deaths that could've been prevented. And . . ."

"And what?"

He squeezes my hand. "A friend is in a bind, I think."

"Do you want to talk about it?"

He lets go of my hand. "I don't want to trouble you."

"It's no trouble," I say.

"You've got enough on your plate. I can take care of it."

"You shouldn't have to take care of it alone."

"No, I do. It's a complicated situation."

"Okay," I say, pulling back. "If you want to talk, I'm here."

"I know you are. I appreciate you." After dinner, he's quiet as we clean the kitchen, and he pours himself a scotch, as if to calm his nerves. While I curl up on the couch and jot notes about what I'll say at Lauren's memorial service, I catch him looking at me now and then, his eyes troubled. I know he encounters horrific, tragic situations every day. I don't push him. I give him the space he needs.

~

I wake to a low rumbling sound—a truck—but while I slept, I felt Lauren close, haunting me in unformed dreams. For a moment, I forget where I am. Then I remember I'm in bed with Nathan. I reach over, squint in the darkness. The covers are in disarray. But he's not here. Did he get called in to work? There it is again. The motor noise, tires crackling over gravel. My breath catches. I slip out of bed, reach for my robe, tie it around my waist. I hear my breathing as I race barefoot down the hall into the kitchen.

Nathan stands in the driveway. His truck is running, the exhaust pluming up in the waning moonlight. He gets in, backs out onto the street. I reach for my car keys, pull on my boots, slip out the door and lock it. I'm surprised at how quickly I can move. No time to worry about getting dressed. His truck has already disappeared around the bend when I back out. He is turning right. I follow—he's far ahead.

I forgot my cell phone. No time to go back. I follow Nathan all the way into the sleeping town, past the grocery store, the bank, along Waterview Road, past the closed boutiques, the library. I stay far behind him. Why am I doing this? My dad once told me to keep my trust in the world, my sense of wonder. After the debacle of Lauren and Jensen, he advised me not to shut down, not to suspect everyone of deception. Yet I can't help myself.

Nathan's truck climbs the road out of town. I expect him to hang a right at the turnoff to the ambulance station, but he keeps going. "You missed it!" I slam the palm of my hand on the steering wheel. "You're going to turn around, aren't you?"

But he doesn't. We're on the narrow highway hugging the shoreline. He keeps on for another two miles, past a diner, and then an RV pulls out into the road in front of me, blocking my view. "Get out of the way!" I shout. I can't pass on this winding, two-lane road. The RV slows to a crawl and soon turns into a campsite. The road is dark ahead. I speed past a hotel, a dark forest, a gas station. No sign of Nathan's truck.

I pull over to the shoulder, rest my forehead on the steering wheel. Now what? A sheriff's patrol car cruises slowly past me. I duck my head, pretend to look at a phone in my lap, but I stupidly forgot my phone, and I stupidly forgot my driver's license, too . . . All for what? *Hey, Dad. My sense of wonder went down the toilet.*

That was a long time ago. We've all grown up. Nathan must have an important reason for driving all the way out here. I pull out into the road, turn around, and head back. As I pass the hotel, driving slowly this time, the sign jogs my memory. The Oak Terrace Hotel. The logo shows an oak tree sitting on an oak leaf. The logo on the key card I found. My heart jumps. I've driven past this hotel, but I've never stayed here. I slow down, peer into the parking lot as I pass. Silly, what am I looking for?

I take the turnoff to the ambulance station. Nathan parked his truck in his usual spot next to the building. Of course, he's at work. What was I thinking, tailing him in my nightgown and slippers, hunched behind the steering wheel like a suspicious wife?

CHAPTER TWENTY-FIVE

I lie awake in Nathan's bed, in this familiar room with skylights and a rustic chest of drawers, accompanied by the comforting lullaby of the sea. Morning light textures the ceiling in shadows. The longer I look, the more shimmering colors appear, bits of hidden red and gold woven into the gray.

I grab my cell phone off the nightstand, send Nathan a text.

Checking in, couldn't sleep.

I miss you, he texts back.

Is everything okay?

Yeah, why?

Any problems at work? I type.

Always. Why?

I mean, I thought you were leaving in the morning.

I got called in early.

I want to ask, *Why did you drive past the ambulance station?* He probably needed to stop at the store or to fill the gas tank.

I get up, get dressed, and go home to gather my thoughts. I wish I could share a cup of mint tea with my dad. Mint was his favorite. "I need you to remind me about the good in the world," I tell him. He keeps smiling at me from his photograph, his eyes soft and forgiving.

In the afternoon, the police call to tell me they don't have any leads on the burglary. Nathan sends me a text letting me know the medical examiner will soon release Lauren's body and that her family settled on a date for the memorial service. I'm still on leave from work, but paperwork keeps piling up, and my mind keeps straying to the Oak Terrace Hotel logo. Could Lauren have gone there? Nobody else claimed the key card.

I call Julie at work. She's between classes.

"The kids miss you," she says. "But it's crazy here. Glad you're taking some time off."

"Can we talk? I'm freaking out a bit."

"Meet me here after school?"

"I'll be there." When I pull into the Tranquil Cove Elementary School parking lot at three o'clock, students are spilling out, racing to catch their buses. Although I've missed the vibrant, frenetic activity, I don't want to talk to anyone right now. I slide down in the driver's seat, trying to remain incognito, but I've been made. Tommy Aaronson, a delightful ten-year-old boy I'm treating for speech issues related to Down syndrome, sprints across the parking lot toward me, backpack bouncing, and taps on my window. I sit up straight, smile at him, and roll down my window. Still no sign of Julie.

"Miss Parlette, Miss Parlette!" he says, shaking with joy. "I thought you died."

"I'm very much alive," I say, opening the door and getting out to give him a hug. His mother rushes after him, pushing her purse strap up over her shoulder. "I'm sorry," she says. "I was talking to—"

"No worries," I say.

"When are you coming back?" he asks.

"In a couple of days."

"Are you sick? I miss you. I'm forgetting how to talk."

"I miss you, too," I say and burst into laughter. "You'll never forget how to talk." His loving smile turns my heart to mush.

"Come on," his mom says, grabbing his hand. "You want to go to swim class?"

"With Jimmy and Shawna and Cass and—"

"With all of them." She grins at me. "You're probably trying to be on vacation?"

"On vacation, yes," I say, relieved to meet someone who does not seem to know about Lauren's death. I watch the two of them rush off, Tommy waving over his shoulder. Julie bursts out of the school and dashes toward me as if she's making a prison break. She yanks open the passenger door and slides inside.

"Hurry, let's get out of here."

I drive off, down to the trail near the waterfront park, and I could almost believe our lives are normal.

"What a day," Julie says, changing into her walking pants and purple running shoes in the back seat once we park. In a minute, we're striding down the trail. "I almost had to stay late for a meeting. You saved me. What's wrong? You look like all the blood has been drained out of you. Been hanging out with a vampire lately?"

"I didn't sleep well." I tell her about Nathan leaving in the night, me following him. I show her the key card with the oak tree logo. "He might have turned into this hotel."

"You think he met a lover there?" She laughs.

"No, I don't, but I lost him for a bit when I followed him."

"Seriously, think about what you're saying. You're about to marry this guy, and you're tailing him. Do you really believe he would have an affair?" She pumps her arms as she speedwalks. I race to keep up.

"You're right. I don't know what I'm doing. I trust him—"

"But you followed him. Why not just call him? Or ask him what he's doing?"

"That would give him a chance to lie to me, to make up a story."

"You think if you follow him on the sly, you can catch him in flagrante delicto. I just read that phrase in a novel. I love the sound of the words *in flagrante delicto*."

"Stop! I'm not going to catch him with another woman. I wasn't thinking . . . It was just . . . Lauren just died. He went outside that night, and then he went out again. He overshot the ambulance station."

"Jesus, Marissa. You're going to drive yourself insane."

"I know—my head is turned around."

"Do you think this is about what happened in the past? With Jensen and Lauren?"

"No, I don't know. I'm not suspicious. I'm . . . uneasy. Okay, I'm suspicious."

"Then talk to Nathan. Tell him you followed him in what . . . a lace teddy?"

"A regular nightgown."

"Oh, how boring. Or go to the hotel. Ask about the key card."

"They won't give me any personal information about a customer. They'll just take back the key, and that will be that."

"We could go there and try all the doors. Would that help?"

"We'll get arrested," I say, laughing. "The key card wouldn't work anyway."

"Look, your fiancé is not a philanderer. Maybe I shouldn't say that. Famous last words, right? I'm pretty sure he's not a cheater. Like, 99.99 percent sure."

"But maybe Lauren was," I say. "Nobody else claimed the key card. Jensen and Hedra said it wasn't theirs."

"What about Hedra's husband . . . what's his name?"

"Keith. I'm sure Hedra asked him when I texted her."

Julie jabs a finger in the air. "Ah, but see, if it was his, he would say it wasn't, wouldn't he?"

I stop cold. "You mean, if he'd been meeting Lauren at the hotel?" I shake the thought from my head. "I can't go there. That's a huge leap. Now we're way out there."

"Just saying. It could've been his."

"Or it could've been Lauren's," I say. "It wouldn't be out of the realm of possibility."

"Do the police have any leads? How is Jensen holding up?"

"He's devastated. He told me something about Lauren . . . I don't know if I should say."

"I'm your best friend!"

"Don't tell anyone. Okay? Lauren had a miscarriage not long ago. She was very upset about it."

Julie's mouth drops open. "Poor Lauren. Now you're thinking she might have jumped? That's more tragic than murder."

"She may have been depressed, but she wasn't suicidal. But for some reason it felt like Jensen wanted me to think she was."

"Now you think he killed her."

"I don't know," I say.

"The memorial service is tomorrow." Julie stops to look out at a raft of ducks on the water. "They say killers like to go to funerals. If someone offed her, they'll be there."

"I think you've been watching too many cop shows."

"It's true," she says. "There's always someone who isn't crying."

"That doesn't mean anything. Some people are stoic, especially if they're in shock."

"But you're so intuitive. I bet you can tell," she says. "Just keep your eye on the crowd."

CHAPTER TWENTY-SIX

The church next to Tranquil Cove Cemetery is a modern wood-and-brick building surrounded by a forest. A plaque on the wall reads, "St. Barnabas Episcopal Church, lovingly built by local residents." I've been here before—not in the church, but I've wandered through the cemetery, reading the inscriptions on the headstones.

A solemn procession files inside, some mourners clad in black, others in colorful attire. The wind picks up, rustling through the treetops. The scent of pine needles wafts into my nose.

A dapper young church officiant greets us at the entrance. "Welcome." He hands us the program for the memorial service. On the front of the brochure, Lauren smiles out from a color photograph, her dark hair spilling around her face. Full lips curved upward in a playful grin. Her eyes sparkle, alive. *In loving memory of Lauren Eklund . . .* With her birth and death dates below. *Oh, Lauren, what happened to you?* I imagine she will walk in the door any moment now, wave and smile and say this was all a joke. She was only on vacation.

We file into the church and I sign the guest book *Marissa Parlette.* I write in black pen, and I wonder if I'll change my name, start signing guest books *Marissa Black.* Where is Nathan? He is supposed to meet me here.

I sit in an empty wooden pew near the back, scanning the church. No sign of him. Bibles and small packets of tissues are tucked into the seatbacks. Rectangular stained-glass windows overlook the forest. At the front of the church, a much larger stained-glass window casts a warm rainbow of light on a small, golden box holding Lauren's remains.

In the pews, I see Lauren's colleagues, friends, Brynn's teachers from school, and other familiar faces. Rianne is clad in a black pantsuit, seated beside Anna in a middle row. Anna is in a deep-turquoise dress and a black sweater. The detective sits off by himself a few rows ahead of us, wearing all black.

Jensen comes in with Lauren's parents, Brynn, Karina, and relatives I can't identify. The family sits in the first row. A priest dressed in a white robe enters through the back door and glides down the center aisle to the front of the church. No sign of Keith and Hedra.

Julie slides in next to me. I nod slightly but keep my gaze straight ahead as the priest addresses us with no preamble. "I am the Resurrection and I am the Life . . . Whoever has faith in me shall have life . . . We remember before you this day Mrs. Lauren Eklund . . ."

Brynn is softly crying in the front row. My heart folds into itself. In a flash, I see the church in North Seattle, the funeral for my father. A group of his colleagues and clients gathered to honor him on that sunlit summer day—I knew very few of them. I'd moved away at eighteen. I'd been living far from him for nearly eight years. My mother flew back for the service, and at first, I wanted nothing to do with her, but when she sat next to me and took my hand, I felt temporary comfort and a deep longing—for what? For my mother to stay, for my father to come back to life? I yearned for the happy family I thought I'd once had, but it was only a fantasy. My mother left a few hours later, and that was the last time I saw her.

Lauren's family members go up to the podium one by one to recite poems and to reminisce. Tears, laughter, slide shows. I'd forgotten that picture of the two of us in bikinis blowing bubbles in her front yard.

Were we thirteen, fourteen? Lauren graduating from high school, her wedding to Jensen. I'm seeing the ceremony for the first time, the way she described it to me. Her baby bump is barely visible.

Tears prick at my eyes, and I reach for the tissues in the seatback in front of me. Detective Harding scans the crowd, working, watching. Nathan rushes in late, still in his uniform. My heart leaps when I see him. He rushes over to sit next to me. "Got held up," he whispers. I squeeze his hand.

Brynn's at the podium now, breaking down in sobs. "She was like the best mom ever . . ." Two girlfriends flank her, gripping her arms, as if holding her up. Their eyes are red and puffy. She talks about birthdays, about her friend's car breaking down on a trip and how Lauren left work and drove five hours to pick them up and didn't even get angry. About how she made the best three-layer birthday cakes, about how she told Brynn she could be anyone and do anything, about how she lived for others.

As a nurse, she did care for others, but what about in her personal life? Even before I caught her with Jensen, I once looked out the apartment window and saw her returning late, changing out of pumps into her running shoes beneath the porch light, as if she didn't want me to see. Was she already dating Jensen on the sly? Living for herself?

What about her relationship with Brynn? *My kid is so smart and focused,* Lauren told me last month over happy hour drinks at the Shoreline Pub. *Just like her dad.* After two gin and tonics, Lauren batted her lashes at the bartender. She seemed proud of Brynn, and yet she apparently planned to send her daughter to a boarding school. *She just wanted to get rid of me,* Brynn said. Is that even true? I remember Brynn's cold eyes, the way she seemed to boil when she learned that her mother had stolen Jensen from me all those years ago. But now, at the service, she seems genuinely distraught.

Rianne looks over at us. Anna waves solemnly. Her mother says something to her, and they look forward again. Brynn staggers down from the podium, apparently overcome by the immensity of her loss. If she's not grief-stricken, she's putting on a good show.

What I want to say is on a folded slip of paper in my lap, but when it's my turn to speak, I don't even refer to it. The moments with Lauren, her generosity, it all spills from me, and none of this is enough, standing up in front of people who may not have known the shadow side of her.

"Once, when I was little, my parents couldn't afford a Barbie doll with legs that bent, you know, at the knees," I say. "I got a knockoff with straight plastic arms and legs. Lauren saw how upset I was, and she gave me her Miss America Barbie doll. She gave me a lot of things. We lived on the same street. At sleepovers, we got the giggles under the covers. I don't even remember what started it, why we were laughing, but within ten minutes everything made us laugh. We would move a toe and laugh, burp and laugh." I glance at Jensen in the front row. He stares at me, absorbing every word.

Brynn leans against him, between him and Karina, her shoulders shaking. When I step down, Jensen reaches out to take my hand briefly as I walk by, tears streaming down his cheeks.

The priest gives the final invocation, and we all file out to the spot beneath the trees where Lauren's ashes will be interred. The priest and family members gather around the granite headstone, huddled in their private grief. I spot Rianne through the trees, leading Anna back to the car. I stay for the interment, and afterward we all hug Jensen and Brynn and the family, offer condolences, move inside for the reception. I have no appetite for the catered appetizers and cakes.

I've lost Nathan in the crowd, but Julie waves at me across the room. She's putting on a black fleece coat, which she had draped over her arm during the service. She weaves her way toward me through the throng. "I'm heading out," she says.

I freeze, staring at her collar. My plastic cup slips from my fingers and falls to the floor, spilling the last droplets of fruit punch. I retrieve the cup and wipe up the liquid with my napkin.

"Are you okay?" she asks, handing me a spare napkin.

"A bit clumsy today." I blot up the last of the punch, stand to face her. I point to her collar. "Where did you get that?"

"Get what?" she says.

"The coat." I can hardly choke out the words. "Tell me where you got it." I didn't notice the button before; she removed her coat before she sat next to me. Now the collar, rising to her chin, reveals the button, glinting beneath the fluorescent light. With its intricate leaf pattern and metallic sheen, it's identical to the button on the scarf I found floating in the water.

CHAPTER TWENTY-SEVEN

Julie gives me a perplexed frown. "What are you looking at? Is there a stain on my coat?"

"I recognize the button on your collar," I say, swiping through the photographs on my iPhone. The mourners flow around us in a river of murmuring voices.

"Which button?" She pulls out her collar, bends her head to look down at the button.

"Yeah, that metal one. It's distinctive."

"I know—I love the pattern." She peers at the pictures on my phone.

I scroll to the series of shots of the scarf, zoom in on the metal button. "You see?"

"It does look like that one," she says, touching her collar.

"Not like it," I say. "Identical. Here." I snap a photo of the button on her coat, swipe back and forth between images of the two buttons.

"Holy shit," she says, then covers her mouth. "I'm cursing in a church."

"You see? Did the coat have a matching scarf?"

"I don't think so, but it's possible—"

"I saw the scarf in the water near the spot where I found Lauren."

"Holy crap."

"There you go again," I whisper. "Cursing in a church."

"You think the scarf was hers?"

"She didn't wear scarves, but what if she—?"

"Pulled it off the killer? Jesus."

People turn to look. I steer her out the door into the autumn day. "Now you can curse to your heart's content."

She shoves her hands into the pockets of her coat. "Check at Rianne's boutique. That's where I bought the coat. Maybe the scarf came from there, too."

"You bought the coat at Afterlife Consignment?" A gust of wind lifts my hair. Guests are starting to leave, getting into their cars.

"Yeah, a few days ago. But I didn't see any scarf."

"Thanks." I fumble in my purse for my keys, determined to get back to my car.

"Wait," Julie says, hurrying after me. "You're going over there now?"

"I need to know about the scarf," I say, getting into the driver's seat.

"I can't go with you. I've got appointments. I could try to reschedule—"

"You don't need to go with me," I say.

"What about Nathan?"

"I'll catch up with him later. This is something I want to do alone."

∽

I step inside Rianne's boutique and hurtle back in time. A 1950s white vintage maxi dress hangs high on the wall next to a white camisole, a pink robe; mannequin heads display vintage hats; antique lamps send golden glows into the darkest corners. On every rack, satin, crepe, and cotton clothes mark the decades, from the 1920s through the 1980s. Not an inch of space goes unused. I browse through a wonderland of fabric—satin dresses, cotton shirts, wedding gowns, vintage coats, scarves, sweaters. A sign on the wall behind the checkout counter reads

"Afterlife Consignment." The scent of lavender combines with complicated, musty fabric smells. From two small speakers mounted on the wall, the reedy voice of Edith Piaf croons from the past. A couple of young women sift through the clothing carousels in the back of the store.

Rianne stands outside the dressing room, talking to a customer inside. She hangs a blue shirt on the door. "Here's a size four. Let me know if you need a different style."

She doesn't see me. I slip behind a carousel, my heart pounding. I thought I would come in here and thrust my iPhone in front of her face, demand to know about the scarf—to whom she sold it. Or whether the coat and scarf belonged to her. I should have gone straight to the detective, but he won't share his conclusions, and I need to investigate for myself.

I search the clothes for more metal buttons. Look through the coatrack, pretending to browse. No sign of any scarves or coats with similar buttons, but it would take forever to search through Rianne's entire inventory.

She goes to the checkout counter, leans over the glass countertop, arranging gloves and scarves across the top of the case. She's a walking display, clad in an eclectic style—boots, long sweater, retro jeans, beaded necklaces. She returned from the service and changed her clothes in record time.

Here goes. I walk up to her. "Rianne," I say.

"Oh, I didn't see you," she says cautiously as I rest my hands on the countertop. "You said nice things about Lauren. You did her justice." A woman glances over at us, then keeps browsing.

"Thank you," I say. "I want to ask you about a red scarf with a metal button."

She drops an embroidered handkerchief, which sails to the floor, billowing outward like a tiny parachute. She bends quickly to pick up the handkerchief and return it to the shelf. "What scarf?"

"It was in the water below the cliff, where Lauren fell."

Rianne's eyes widen, and she lowers her voice to a whisper. "The scarf is important to the case?"

"She might have pulled it from whoever pushed her off that cliff. The detective has it."

"I see. How can I help?"

"My friend Julie has a coat with an identical button. She said she bought it a few days ago from your shop. I took a picture."

"Let me see." Rianne leans across the counter. I show her the photograph.

"Ah yes, that's a very smart piece," Rianne says. "I sold the coat to Julie. Not my size. But I wished it was."

I swipe to the photos of the scarf in the water. "Identical button, the same pattern, see?"

Rianne taps her finger on her chin. "Wow. I do remember that scarf. I know it. Unusual button, hard to forget. The coat and button came from the same owner. I tried looking for similar buttons online but never found any. They're rare."

My heart is beating. My hands are clammy. "Do you remember who bought the scarf?"

She looks toward the dressing room, where the customer is throwing pants over the door. Then she looks at me. "I probably shouldn't look it up, but under the circumstances . . ."

"Please. Lauren was my best friend as a child . . . This scarf could be important. Whoever owned it, or lost it, might know something."

"Or might have killed her."

"Yes . . . that's true."

"It was the Saturday before last, before your engagement dinner. I remember because that scarf was so distinctive. My assistant sold it. When I came in on Sunday, it was gone." She taps the screen of her iPad, propped on a stand on the countertop. She scrolls, swipes, and taps, then motions me to her side of the counter. She points at the screen, to a transaction completed at 4:35 p.m. on the Saturday before the dinner party. A purchase of a few items made at various prices by debit card.

"Is the scarf listed there?" I say.

"The receipt doesn't show that level of detail. I used to enter every item with an image, but I've got so much stuff now, it all got away from me. There it is." She points to an item that sold for fifty-one dollars plus tax marked "Clothing—wool."

"How do you know it's the scarf?" I say.

"It was the only thing at that price, and it's the only wool item. I priced it high because it was so beautiful."

"Who bought it? Can you tell?"

"Only because she used a debit card," Rianne says, swiping through the screens. "Yes, here it is. We sold the scarf to Hedra Black."

CHAPTER TWENTY-EIGHT

Keith and Hedra are not answering calls. Back in my cottage, I try to remember what they were wearing when they arrived at Nathan's house. Hedra pulled off her coat, no scarf. She wore an emerald dress. In the morning, she had changed into slacks and a sweater. Did she pack a scarf or have one tucked into her coat?

"Do you think Hedra is a murderer?" I ask my dad as I play Chopin's nocturnes on my piano. The elegant, mournful melody flows from my fingers.

I think you miss your friend, my dad says in my head.

"But someone killed her, and I need to know who it was because . . ."

You feel guilty for not forgiving her before she died.

My fingers stiffen on the piano keys; my chest constricts. I get up and call Julie. I need to hear her soothing voice. She gives me perspective.

"You should tell the detective," she says on the phone. "He needs to know Hedra bought that scarf."

"I left him a message, but I feel terrible. Hedra's going to be my sister-in-law. I'm sure she can explain. I wish I could reach her."

"What did Nathan say?"

"I called him. He doesn't know what to think. Except he said it's probably a coincidence." I'm paraphrasing.

"He doesn't see that this is important? I mean, he's a good guy, but come on."

Yes, come on. "He's more inclined to see the best in people, to give them the benefit of the doubt. Like my dad. Maybe that's one reason I love him so much."

"Let's hope he's right."

For the rest of the day, while I catch up on reports and prepare to return to work, I think about Nathan's exact words to me when I told him about the scarf. *Coincidence . . . You're looking for connections where there may not be any.* But his tone was guarded.

I return to his house in time for dinner. He made a stir-fry, but he hardly eats. Shoulders slumped, he broods, spending more time looking at his food than at me.

"What's going on with you?" I say. "Talk to me."

He puts his fork on his plate, his vegetables untouched, rubs his hand across his forehead. "I'm sorry if I seem distracted."

"I'm not that fragile, Nathan. I can handle whatever it is."

He holds my hand between his, looks deep in my eyes. "I'm just tired. I'm okay, but you're not."

"I'm fine—"

"No, you're not. You try to hide it, but I see you crying."

"I'm okay, too, really I am," I say, but I feel the tears threatening again.

He kisses my cheek, pushes the hair away from my forehead. "It's hell to lose people we care about." He gets up from the table, goes to the liquor cabinet and pours us two glasses of dessert wine. I join him on the couch, his arm around my shoulders.

"I love sitting here with you," he says, "listening to the wind."

I settle into his arms. "Winter is coming. I can feel it."

He takes the glass from my hand, puts our drinks on the table, and kisses me, long and deep. He leads me into the bedroom, and when we make love, he's urgent, intense, as if he's trying to banish the ghosts that haunt him. Afterward, we lie quietly in the darkness, and I drift off. When I wake again, it's just after midnight. I sit bolt upright in bed, darkness curtaining the room. I'm alone. The house is unnaturally silent. Not again.

I get up, pull on my robe and slippers, go to the kitchen and peer out the window. His truck is gone. I should call him, send him a text. Ask him if he's been called in to work . . . yet again. Instead, I change into jeans, boots, and a sweater, and I head out to my car. This time, I bring my wallet and phone. I follow my instincts, taking the route out of town to the Oak Terrace Hotel in the clear, cold darkness. I could go home, sleep, pretend he merely left early for work again. Assume he had errands to run. After midnight? Or I could keep driving and hope I'm wrong.

I'm having a little trouble with my sense of wonder, I think to my dad. He smiles in my mind. I trusted him. He was always there for me, holding on to my seat when I learned to ride a bicycle, hugging me when I lost the spelling bee on the final round. Bandaging my skinned knees. *I trust Nathan, too. He's at work.*

But he's not. I drive past the ambulance station, and as I turn into the parking lot for the Oak Terrace Hotel, I spot his truck parked in front of a door marked "15," a two-story residence-inn-style unit far from the main building. Adrenaline pumps through me. My heartbeat kicks up; my eyes begin to water. I start to type a message to Julie. Nathan's at the hotel . . .

But I don't send the text. I park in a shadowed spot beneath a young cedar tree, its spindly branches swaying in the wind. He'll have a plausible explanation for being here. A confidential situation, a medical emergency. I imagine myself knocking. He'll answer the door, medical kit in hand, a bandaged patient beside him. They will invite me in, and I will feel ridiculous, like a jealous wife. Like Rianne. Or the way he describes her. Only she doesn't seem at all unhinged.

I get out of my car and slip around to the back of the unit. The two-story structure opens onto a small yard leading to a sandy beach. I duck down and sidle to the enclosed patio. A curtain obscures most of the room, but a sliver of light leaks in from the hall. I crouch and peek up over the sill, through filmy glass speckled with salty ocean spray. I make out the corner of a countertop, the shape of a fridge, Nathan standing with his arms crossed. I can't read his expression, but I recognize the general angles of his face. In a chair near the window, a woman sits in the darkness with her back to me. She gesticulates, perhaps arguing with him.

Nathan opens his arms, and she stands to wrap her arms around his neck. He pulls her close. The world turns in their embrace, the stars winking out, going nova, new stars born into the sky. I feel the passage of time, my body aging and turning to dust. He's burying his face in her hair, and I snap back to the cold, to the cramp in my legs as I crouch beneath the window. As he rubs her back, a disbelieving part of me withdraws, insisting this can't be real. But his bouts of brooding, his vague responses when I asked him what was bothering him. Their intimacy. The darkness. At a hotel. The ultimate cliché.

My engagement ring shines in the moonlight, winking at me, mocking me. Nathan looks up, pulls away. I think of all the names I'm going to call him when I move out. Not that I ever moved in. Was he having an affair with Lauren, too? All the questions crowd in my throat. Who is the woman? What is she saying to Nathan? Why did he even bother to propose to me? I want to run away, but I can't stop watching.

It could be worse, Julie might say. *You could have caught them in bed together like the last time.* No, that's my own brain trying to ease the pain. Trying to convince me that I haven't been royally screwed.

He rests his hands on her shoulders. Is she crying? Her head is bowed, her hair covering her face. I wish I could read his expression. I hope it's guilt, regret, shock at his own behavior.

He turns and strides away. Now the woman is a dark silhouette. As she turns toward me, I duck down, although my instinct is to smash a fist through the pane. I could stand up now, press my nose to the glass, scare the hell out of her. But I can't move. This isn't really happening. I'll wake up in Nathan's bed, and he will be there. Anna will bounce into the room, smile, and say, *I'm so happy you and Dad are getting married and living happily ever after.* Lauren will bring over a banana-nut cake. *I shouldn't have seduced Jensen. He always loved you best. And by the way, I'm alive.*

And this—this is a vivid nightmare. The woman pulls back the curtain. She doesn't notice me down here crouched in the darkness, but I see her face. The sculpted nose, long, blond hair. Everything distorted from my strange angle. I'm not surprised, not really. I already knew who she was. Her height, her elegant, willowy shape. But I wonder where Keith is in all this. I'm sure he'll be interested to know where Hedra has been.

CHAPTER TWENTY-NINE

I slide down against the wall, the concrete patio cold beneath me. The wind slaps me in the face. Voices murmur inside. Hedra has pulled the curtain closed. My memories of Nathan flood in, candlelight flickering on the dinner table between us, his hand reaching across to take mine. The late nights spent talking. *What are you most afraid of?* he asked me once. *Being left behind,* I said. *Not noticed. Unloved. What about you?*

I'm not afraid of anything. Okay, one thing. Not being able to save someone I love.

No sound now from inside. What does that mean? I should knock on that door, fling it open, but instead I dash back to the parking lot. I get into my car, take a deep breath. My heart collapses into itself. I wait five minutes, ten. Stare at my phone. My fingers grow numb. I could send a text to Julie, but I don't want to wake her. If I tell her what I've just seen, then it will be real.

In the rearview mirror, I see Nathan's truck sitting in the darkness. Finally, fingers trembling, I send him a text.

Woke up, you were gone.

I wait, my blood rushing. A few minutes pass before he replies.

Problem I need to solve. I love you.
We need to talk, I type.
Okay. Urgent?

The question mark mocks me. Is this urgent? As urgent as a patient suffering a massive heart attack? Accident victims? As urgent as his clandestine affair? Hands trembling, I throw my phone on the seat, flip the ignition, and floor it back through town to Nathan's place. I could have knocked loudly, demanded an explanation, but what good would it have done to make a scene?

In his house, the rooms feel dark, unwelcoming. Despite the heat wafting from the vents, I'm shivering. Mud sticks to my boots. I yank them off and leave them by the front door. I turn the house upside down, rummaging through drawers, cabinets, his desk. In his closet, I search his pockets while a part of me stands back, admonishing myself. *What are you doing? You're not even married to him.* This is crazy. But he has betrayed me. I convince myself that it's okay to furtively extract coins and rubber bands. In the pocket of his favorite windbreaker, I find the hotel receipt. He paid for a week. The receipt is dated three days ago. Heart pounding, I tuck the receipt back into his pocket. I've got the evidence I need.

I send him another text. I saw you and Hedra through the window.

A minute later, his reply balloons on my cell phone. You followed me?

I woke up, and you were gone. I knew where you'd gone.

It's not what you think.

I laugh, and yet I want to believe him. Looked clear to me, I type back.

Wait there, please. Don't go. I'll be home in the morning. I'll explain. I'm heading out on a long call.

Right, a long call. An emergency that requires him to stand by, maybe for hours. An apartment fire, a hostage situation, a water rescue. What do I care? But I don't run straight home. I wait for him. Perhaps I'm in denial. I need to talk to him face-to-face.

So, I stay at his house, resisting the urge to cut his clothes into pieces, smash his dishes on the floor. Spray paint the walls. I must remember: Anna lives here, too. She's innocent. I love her.

I can't bear to sleep in his bed, so I lie on the couch, dozing off now and then. I'm up early, aching and stiff. No word from Nathan. What am I even doing here? Maybe I should jump off the cliff, join Lauren in the afterworld. No, I'll wait, give Nathan a chance to explain. He'd better have a damned good story, an Oscar-worthy performance.

I follow the worn path through the yard to the Eklunds' garden. The wind blows stronger here, whipping in from the southwest. I start a text to Hedra numerous times, but I don't hit send. What the hell are you doing with my fiancé, you . . . How dare you? I don't trust myself to be civil, and why should I be? But still, I don't want to type words I might later regret.

From the gazebo, a spectacular view of the ocean rolls away to the horizon. I rest my elbows on the railing. The paint flakes off below my fingers, greenish moss growing on the wood. Flashes of Lauren return to me, her unseeing eyes, the bruises, the pallor of her skin. Unnatural.

I look back at the Eklunds' house, the dark windows revealing no secrets. I descend the gazebo steps, walk through the grass toward the cliff, north of the crime scene tape. My stomach tingles and my legs go weak. At this corner of the yard, the ground gives way and drops precipitously to the beach below. If I were to take one step, I could tumble all the way down without finding a foothold. Lauren fell from the cliff a few yards south of this spot.

Did Hedra push her? If so, why? What is the connection to Nathan? I dial Hedra's number. Her smooth voice tells me to leave a message. She must see my number popping up on her phone. But I get her voice mail. "I need to know what's going on between you and Nathan," I say.

I call her home number, no answer. I'm restless, impatient for answers. I look up Keith's number at the office. He must be there by now. He gets in early. A woman answers the phone. "Dr. Black's office. How may I help you?"

I can't think for the pounding in my head. "Could I speak to Keith? Dr. Black. I'm his . . . I'm engaged to his brother. It's a personal matter. He's probably busy or with a patient, so I could leave a message. It's urgent, sort of."

"I understand, of course," she says in a friendly, professional voice, although I surely sound like a lunatic. "But Dr. Black's away at a conference—"

"He's away," I say, stunned. I didn't expect this, but then it explains how Nathan and Hedra could meet at the hotel.

"He'll be back in three days. Would you like his voice mail?"

"I suppose you can't give me his cell phone number or tell me where he is."

I can feel her hesitation in the beat of silence. "I'm not allowed to give out any personal information or his personal contact—"

"That's fine. I'm guessing he checks in for his messages. Please tell him I called. And have him call me at his earliest convenience." I leave her my number and hang up, furious. This is it. I'm out of here. I gather my belongings, everything I own that I can stuff into my weathered suitcase. Toothbrush, toothpaste, lotion, clothes. I stop to peer into Anna's room, my heart plummeting. How will I explain this to her?

I tuck the key card into my jacket pocket, and just when I'm ready to head out, Nathan comes home. He stands in front of me in his living room, still in his uniform—dark-blue slacks and a light-blue, long-sleeved jacket with white stripes on the arms and patches on the shoulders. His jacket is speckled with blood. I wonder to whom it belongs. His face is pale, his eyes dark and angry. He could be a different person, someone I don't even know.

CHAPTER THIRTY

"We need to talk," he says. "It wasn't what it looked like."

"I looked in the window, and I know what I saw."

"No, you don't. You don't know what you're saying."

"This is not about me. This is about you. Lying. Sneaking around." I lift my left hand, point at the engagement ring. "It's about this. A promise."

His shoulders sag. "Whatever you thought you saw—"

"I saw you hugging Hedra. More than that."

"You shouldn't have followed me."

"How about, you shouldn't have been sneaking around with your brother's wife."

"I'm not, we're not . . . I'm helping her."

"Helping her. Helping her in bed, or what?"

"No, not that. I can't—she. I promised her I would maintain her privacy, but it's not an affair. I promise."

"I don't care what you promised her," I say, pacing. "Your promise to me is what matters. What the hell is going on? She won't answer my calls. I left a message for Keith."

"You what? Oh no. You shouldn't have done that!"

"Why the hell not? He doesn't deserve to know what his wife is doing?"

"You shouldn't have . . . You could get her into deep trouble."

"I certainly hope so."

"You could get yourself into trouble. You shouldn't be involved."

"Involved in what, Nathan? Your affair? Are you even serious?"

"It's not an affair!"

"You're right, it's not. You and I . . . We're not even married yet. I guess it doesn't qualify."

"I was going to tell you. I wasn't trying to lie to you or be dishonest."

"But you were! You were dishonest."

"Please, this has nothing to do with our relationship."

Rage darkens my vision. "It has everything to do with our relationship. You took off in the night—I don't know how many times—met Hedra at a hotel, and buried your face in her hair. There is no other way to see this except as deception."

"Not a deception aimed at you."

"Looked that way to me," I say.

"It's complicated. Keith, what does he know? It's very important that you tell me."

"What? I can't even."

"What does he know? Did he call you back? Did you talk to him?"

"I left a message."

"Don't tell him. I'm helping her leave him while he's away. But he didn't fly to another state. He's only in Seattle. He could come back."

"I hope he does." I head for the foyer, pull on my boots. Nathan rushes to block my path.

"I'm not helping her to be with me. I'm helping her to escape from him. To escape from an abusive situation."

"You're saying he hurt Hedra," I say, my mind spinning.

"Sit down. I'll explain." He takes my arm and leads me back into the living room, sits next to me on the couch.

"You're helping Hedra leave your own brother. You expect me to believe that?" But his childhood stories climb into my mind—Keith locking him in the shed, holding his head underwater.

"I wouldn't lie to you." He tries to take my hand, but I yank my arm away.

"Even if it's true, why wouldn't you tell me? We tell each other everything." I search his eyes for my answer. If he's a liar, how would I know?

"Keith is charming. Successful. But underneath all that . . ."

"He seems like an arrogant asshole to me," I say, shaking my head. "But I thought you said he outgrew his cruelty."

"I thought he had, but now I know he didn't. Hedra is in way over her head. I told her about our childhood when they got married so she would have the full story. I was sure he'd changed. Or maybe I . . . hoped." He pulls out his wallet, shows me a photograph, a staged family shot. Nathan is maybe four, rosy cheeked and cherubic, with his delicate mother holding him on her lap. Her radiant smile belies the vacancy in her eyes. Her tall, handsome husband stands behind her, one hand on her shoulder. Keith, seven or eight years old, stands off to the side.

"You all look happy," I say. "Except for your mother. She looks tired and a little sad."

"She is tired and sad. See my dad's hand on her shoulder? That was about control. He had a subtle way of bullying and belittling her."

"You're saying Keith took after him."

"I think Keith is worse."

"What am I supposed to believe, Nathan? If you were only *helping* Hedra, why did you bury your face in her hair? You're trying to make me doubt myself."

"No, that's not my intention at all. I know it seems like I crossed a line."

"Seems? I would be an idiot to interpret it any other way."

"That was the closest we ever got, Marissa. She was so down and out, talking about going back to him again. Worrying she'd made a mistake, even though he could kill her."

"Why doesn't she leave him? Why does she need your help? If what you're saying is true?"

"He's dangerous. He threatened to kill her, and I'm afraid he might be serious. But he would find a way to make it look like an accident."

"This is unbelievable. You should have told me."

"I didn't know until recently. I was about to tell you—"

"Oh, you were?" I whip out the key card and wave it in front of his face. "I found this the morning after the dinner party, so don't pretend you didn't know."

He looks stunned, as if he really has never seen the key card before. "That must be Hedra's. She told me she left Keith earlier for one night. She had already rented the hotel room. But then she changed her mind and went back to him."

"Right. What about the receipt I found in your pocket? You paid for a week."

His face hardens, but he does not accuse me of invading his privacy. He knows better. "I was extending her stay."

"Why couldn't she extend it herself?"

"She said she had paid cash, and she didn't want to withdraw any more, or Keith would become suspicious."

"So, you put the hotel room on your credit card instead." I can't help the animosity in my voice.

"Look, I wasn't going to keep this a secret forever. But I needed to protect you and protect her—it was a tough call. I was worried and conflicted. Last month, I went out on a domestic violence call. The husband beat the wife. I'll spare you the details. A neighbor called 911. The minute the bastard saw us coming, he killed his wife. Shot her in the head. Then he fired a few extra shots out the window at random. I felt I needed to keep Hedra's situation confidential for your safety, for hers."

Confidential. I step back, his words a blow to the gut. "That poor woman. But Hedra's situation is different, and I would have kept your secret—"

"How could I put you in that position? Of having to keep the secret?"

"So instead you kept her secret. You prioritized her instead of talking to me."

His eyes fill with pain. "I know. I see that I've hurt you."

"Hedra could have said something, too."

"She's not in her right mind."

"Clearly not."

"It didn't happen overnight," he says. "She told me it started with small things. She'd left a spot on a dish, hadn't folded the towels perfectly. I thought, shit, this is our dad, only worse. I overheard my dad yelling at my mom, telling her that she was ugly. He always monitored the amount of food on her plate. Keith is the same way."

"Why didn't Hedra walk away? How long have they been married?"

Nathan runs his fingers through his hair. "I was the best man at their wedding six years ago. It might seem like a long time to put up with his abuse, but he plays mind games. Don't you see? He piled on the charm, took her to Mexico, Hawaii, the Caribbean. She grew up with an addicted mom. They were often evicted. It was a big change, moving from poverty to luxury. The big house, the parties, the way Keith paid attention to her. She loves him. That's what worries me. She wants to leave, but she wants to go back. The asshole won't even let her make a phone call without his permission."

And this is your problem to solve because . . . ? I hate these thoughts, my desire to banish Hedra from the picture. She's in trouble. Maybe. Maybe not. The truth slips through my fingers. I sit back against the couch cushion, drawing a deep breath. The room feels heavy with secrets. "Something must have pushed her to finally leave. A little crush on his brother, maybe?"

"I had no idea what was going on until she asked me for help a few days ago. That bruised wrist—at dinner, when she said she fell off the stage during a photo shoot. Apparently, that was a lie."

"Keith did that? You could be making this up!"

"You have to trust me. Keith has connections. He's manipulative. A psychopath. He will try to come after her."

"Those are strong words. You're full of them. Rianne's unhinged. Keith is a psycho."

"A small dose of detachment helps a surgeon keep his cool," Nathan says, undeterred. "He's good at cutting people open without any emotion."

"He saves lives."

"So, he must care, right? He doesn't."

My stomach twists. I get up and go to the window. I need a view of trees, of the changing sky, the things I know are real. "I appreciate you telling me all of this, Nathan. But I need Hedra's side of this story, and it doesn't excuse your lies or what you were doing with her. I need to talk to her."

"Okay, but not right now . . . we need to see this thing through."

I spin around to face him. "Not right now? Are you fucking kidding me?"

He raises his hands, pushes down on the air. Trying to pacify me, which enrages me even more. "Let her get to a secure location," he says. "Away from the hotel. He might find her there."

"How would he find her, Nathan? You're the one who paid for a secret love nest." I can't help spitting bitter words. I can't stop myself.

"We didn't sleep together. She needed a place to go where he couldn't get to her. But now . . ."

"But now what? I didn't tip him off."

"He will know something is up."

"I'm going to talk to her."

"She could freak out and do something rash."

"You're afraid of what she might tell me. That the two of you—"

"After she's safe. Then talk to her. You don't understand. He could kill her."

"Maybe he could, but guess what else is dying, Nathan? Us."

He slams his fist into the palm of his other hand. "This isn't right. Damn it."

"Are you protecting her from something else?" I say, arms crossed over my chest. "Did you know about the scarf? Was she outside last Friday night? Did she push Lauren off that cliff?"

His face turns white. "Why would she push Lauren?"

"I don't know. Seems I'm being kept in the dark about a lot of things these days."

"I didn't know anything about the scarf."

"Uh-huh." I raise my brows, my mouth dropping open. I'm sure I look as incredulous as I feel.

"I swear. I don't know what it was doing in the water."

The connection hovers just out of reach, but it's there. I feel it in my bones, in my blood. Nathan, Hedra, Lauren, the scarf. Keith the monster chasing her. Or is he simply a buttoned-up, fastidious surgeon? Careful about his work? Loving in his own way? I don't know him at all, not really. I don't know Nathan, either. I thought I did.

I look around at the living room, in which I've enjoyed games, laughter, intimacy, a feeling of home. Now it's just a collection of furniture, the happiness leached away. I no longer belong here. "I have to go."

"Stay." Nathan steps toward me. I step back.

"Don't," I say.

"What will I tell Anna?"

Now he's using her to try to keep me here. A cheap shot. "Whatever you need to tell her. This is not on me."

"Don't go. There's nothing going on between Hedra and me."

"That is such bullshit." I tug off the engagement ring, put it in my pocket. As I walk out the door, I remember the first time I came over for dinner. I gave him the potted azalea now replanted in the garden, dormant in the autumn gloom. He admitted to googling "dinner recipes for first dates," picking one he wouldn't easily mess up—spaghetti carbonara. But he burned it, and that time I was the one who lied, because I was already falling for him. *This is the best meal I've ever had,* I said, and I kept insisting it was true.

CHAPTER THIRTY-ONE

The hours pass in a blur, like nondescript scenery from a train window. I draw the curtains, plunging my life into dimness. While I curl up in bed, feeling supremely sorry for myself, the months unravel. Was I too trusting? Too eager? Did I fall for Nathan too soon? I became infatuated with him when we first met, or was it two days later, at Career Day? I peeked into Julie's art class and saw him in uniform, answering questions about his life as a paramedic. He brought his gear for show-and-tell. Anna beamed as the students gathered around. He showed them his stethoscope, trauma shears, his automatic defibrillator. He told riveting stories related to each piece of equipment, holding the kids enthralled. I was enraptured, too, and when he looked in my direction, our gazes locked. I backed out of the room, feeling my cheeks flush. Half an hour later, Julie sidled in. "He asked about you," she said. "He's in the hall. Go and talk to him before he gets away."

I found him at the water fountain, bending to take a long drink. He straightened and grinned at me, shook my hand and introduced himself again. "In case you forgot, I'm Anna's dad."

"How could I forget?" I felt his firm fingers gripping mine. All eyes were on us, and then he let go.

"Could we talk outside?" he said. "About Anna's speech therapy."

"Sure, of course." I followed him out into the school yard. "She's making great progress."

"I wanted to thank you—she's so much more confident now."

"You're welcome," I said.

"Would you like to have dinner with me?" he asked point-blank. I expected him to beat around the bush, talk about the weather. But he looked right at me, asking a straight question.

I laughed. "Are you asking me on a date?"

"At my place? Is that too forward?"

"I should trust you, right? You're Anna's dad."

"Yeah, trust me, but I warn you, I'm the world's worst cook."

"I'm pretty sure my mother was," I said before I could stop myself.

"No, I am. See you Saturday night at seven? Anna won't be there. She's at her mother's house this weekend."

I nodded and went back inside, wondering if I had broken some school rule, flirting with a student's father on campus. But I didn't care. My heart was turning cartwheels.

Julie ran into my office, and I gave her the scoop. "Dinner at his place already?" she said. "No lunch or coffee first?"

"Your number is on speed dial in case I get into trouble."

"You'll be fine. He's a good guy, a good dad."

I could see she was right when I showed up at his house for dinner. I handed him the potted azalea, and he smiled. "Anna will love this," he said, putting the plant on the table in the foyer. "She's getting into learning flower names."

"Then I made a good choice." I took off my shoes and promptly stepped on a piece of green Lego.

"That's where that went," he said, picking up the piece.

"Did Anna make those?" I said, pointing to Lego birds on the coffee table—a blue jay, a robin, and a hummingbird.

"That's my girl," he said. "She was never much into dolls. Oops. Dinner." He dashed into the kitchen, attempting to salvage a pan of burning spaghetti. On the fridge, he displayed numerous photographs of Anna—proudly pointing to a missing front tooth, holding up a spelling test plastered with a big gold star, twirling in her pink tutu.

He removed a stack of her library books from the dining table before we sat down to eat. "She's a big reader, too," he said.

"She should come over and check out my books," I said. "I've got a huge collection. And, of course, you should come over, too." I blushed, and he smiled.

Over a candlelit, charred dinner, he related the best and worst aspects of his job, from the joys of delivering twins in the ambulance, to the pain of losing a child who'd fallen from a tenth-floor window.

I told him about my work at Anna's school. "I love my job. It's challenging. Sometimes we even work with a therapy dog. I have one student who refuses to read aloud unless he's reading to the dog. He's afraid the other kids will make fun of him."

"What kind of dog?"

"We've had a golden retriever, a yellow Lab. Recently we had a four-year-old Bouvier des Flandres named Penelope."

"A Bouvier des what?" He laughed, nearly snorting wine from his nose.

"You know, a big fluffy dog with pointy ears and a beard. Looks like a gigantic Jim Henson puppet."

"I loved Jim Henson movies! Anna and I just watched *The Muppets Take Manhattan*."

"My favorite is *The Dark Crystal*."

We discussed films, from horror to comedy to animation. The conversation inevitably circled back around to Anna, to her love of dance and nature. To her speech disfluency and my efforts to help her overcome stuttering. At the time, I'd been treating her for only a few weeks.

"Patience is important in my job," I told Nathan. "It's all about repetition, small steps, individualizing the treatment plan. I never say the word *stuttering* directly to the child."

"Rianne told me about that." He refilled his wineglass, and I held up my hand, indicating I'd had enough. The mention of his ex-wife put a slight damper on my enthusiasm, but I quickly recovered. Nathan and I talked late into the evening. It had been a long time since I'd become so absorbed in a conversation that I'd lost track of time.

At eleven o'clock, I leaped to my feet. "I should let you go to bed."

"Sleep is overrated," he said, but he graciously let me go. We could have easily fallen into bed together that first night, but he never tried to rush me. Always attentive, always excited to see me, he took me kayaking, hiking in the mountains, beachcombing, to dinner. He lured me in, so how was I to know what he would do?

I try calling Hedra again, still no answer, and no response from Keith. Nathan doesn't want me to talk to her now. I'll put her in danger. Right, in danger of having to explain herself to me. It takes all my energy, but I pull on a coat and head out to my car. Nathan extended Hedra's stay in the hotel, which means the key card in my pocket should still open the door.

CHAPTER THIRTY-TWO

I drive back to the Oak Terrace Hotel through a bright, cold afternoon. Nothing moves—not the sky, not the leaves. Autumn hangs suspended in time. The hotel units look benign in sunlight, even bland, lounging along a gentle hillside on the edge of a protected forest. No answer when I knock on the door to room fifteen. I look over my shoulder, nobody coming. A seagull soars overhead, squawking its way to the sea. I swipe the key card through the lock. The door opens easily. Part of me didn't want the key card to work. For all of this to be a mistake. But clearly Hedra has been renting this room for five or six days. My stomach clenches as I step inside and close the door.

"Hello!" I call out. "Hello! Anyone here? Hedra?" My voice echoes. No answer.

I look to my left, into a living room sparsely furnished in a generic style. A faint smell of onions drifts from the kitchen. I find the remnants of an omelet in a pan on the stove. Evidence of Hedra is littered all over the unit. A tube of lipstick has rolled to the edge of the countertop; a pair of women's shoes point toward me from beneath the coffee table. *Elle* magazine sits open to a celebrity page, next to an empty mug.

At the small dining table, someone recently sat, perhaps eating the omelet and toast from a plate still dusted with crumbs. I start up the stairs to the second floor. A knock on the door. My heart thumps. My hand slides down the banister.

"Housekeeping!" a woman calls out.

Housekeeping. Of course. I go down and open the door. A young woman stands there in a brown uniform. She's round all over. She gives me a broad smile. Her fingers curl around the handle of a rolling cart full of towels and toilet paper rolls. "You called about towels," she says.

"Ah, yes," I say, glancing up toward the second floor, then back at her. "I'm in the middle of something. Could you come back tomorrow?"

A shadow of irritation crosses her face. She pushes a strand of shiny hair behind her ear. "You still want pool towels?"

So, the hotel offers this luxurious amenity. "That's okay. We're good."

"What about your husband?"

My mind trips over the word *husband*. "Um, he's okay, too."

The maid nods and rolls her cart along the sidewalk toward the next unit.

I flip the "Privacy Please" sign face out, close and lock the door, and tiptoe upstairs. Straight ahead of me—a small bathroom. Toiletries laid out on the counter. Lotion, soap, toothbrush, toothpaste. Singles of each item. Hotel shampoo and soap in the shower. Only one bedroom up here.

"Hello?" I call out. I push on the open door. A curtain flaps in the window. Unmade queen-size bed. A pile of pillows. On the nightstand is an empty prescription bottle. I hear a moan. Someone is here, on the other side of the bed.

Adrenaline courses through my veins. I step around, and I see her slippers first, pale feet, the white lace of her nightgown. She's lying on her side, facing away from me. *Lauren, I see Lauren, lying on the beach.* There's a smear of blood on the corner of the nightstand, as if she stumbled and hit her head.

"Are you okay?" I say, rushing to kneel next to her.

Her hair covers part of her face, but I know it's Hedra.

"Are you all right? Hedra, talk to me." I gently shake her shoulders. She doesn't respond, but she's breathing. "Did you fall?"

No answer. "Hedra, wake up!" I fumble in my pocket for my cell phone. As I call 911, Hedra moans and shifts onto her back. The hair falls away from her face, revealing a thin cut on her forehead. I grab for a tissue from the nightstand, dab at the wound. The blood is clotting; she's not bleeding. My brain switches into high gear. "What happened, Hedra? Tell me!"

She mumbles, lashes fluttering. Her eyes open a little, those emerald eyes, sleepy, drugged.

The operator comes on the line. "Nine-one-one. Where is your emergency?"

"I'm at the Oak Terrace Hotel, room fifteen. Please send an ambulance."

"What is your emergency, ma'am?"

"A woman might have overdosed on medication." I try to keep my voice steady. "I think she fell and hit her head. I found her this way. I don't know what happened. She's breathing . . . and conscious, but she seems confused."

"Help is on the way. What is your name, please?"

"Marissa Parlette. I'm a friend."

"Are you in any danger there? Are you safe?"

"Yes, I'm okay. I don't think anyone else is here."

"Do you know what medication she took?"

"No, I'll ask her." I nudge her shoulder. "Hedra! What happened? What did you take?"

She mumbles an incoherent reply. I rush around to the nightstand. "It looks like . . . Sinequan pills," I say, reading the label on the bottle. "The prescribing physician's name has been removed. What's Sinequan?"

"It's a type of antidepressant," the operator says. "How many pills did she take?"

"I don't know. Hedra, did you take these pills? How many?"
Her lashes flutter. She moans again.

"She's not answering," I say.

"Any vomiting?"

"No, no vomiting. How long will the ambulance take?" My head swims; I sit on the carpet to keep from fainting.

"They're about three minutes out."

They must have had another call nearby—we're way out of town. Hedra groans, and I squeeze her hand. "Hang on, help is on the way," I tell her.

She reaches up and clings to my sleeve, clawing at me. Murmuring. "Nathan . . ."

"He's not here. I'm Marissa. I'm here. I'm staying with you." *Where are you, Nathan? What have you done?*

More mumbling, her fingernails digging into my arm.

On the telephone line, I hear beeping and indistinct voices in the background. The operator is asking more questions, but they pass right through me. A siren screams in the distance. I see lights flashing outside through the window facing the parking lot. "They're here," I tell the operator.

"Lauren . . . ," Hedra says.

"What about Lauren?" I say. "She's gone, Hedra. Remember?"
Her eyes roll back.

"Stay with me," I say. "The ambulance is here. I need to go downstairs and let them in. Okay?" She moans softly, fading. I extract myself from her feeble grip. As I stand up, she looks at me and says, "Lauren. Knew. Lauren. She knew." Then her eyelids flutter shut.

CHAPTER THIRTY-THREE

"I told you, she was like that when I found her," I say to Detective Harding as the ambulance speeds away, lights pulsing. Siren blaring. I didn't recognize the paramedics who raced up the stairs to tend to Hedra. Did I expect to see Nathan? I wanted to scream at him, accuse him, run into his arms, punch him.

"You came to this hotel because . . ." The detective points his pencil toward the overhead sign. Other hotel guests step out on their balconies, watching, the manager talking to a policeman in a nearby patrol car.

"I told you that, too. I followed Nathan here." My mouth tastes sour.

"Your fiancé." Dan Harding jots a note, an annoying scratch of the pencil.

"I found a key card in the closet after the dinner party. Hedra must have left it behind. But she denied it."

"You let yourself into the unit . . ."

"If what I did was against the law, arrest me."

"So you followed Nathan here last night and—"

"I saw them together, hugging, through the window. I came back to talk to her and found her." There, now I've told someone. The detective, of all people. What I saw, what Nathan and Hedra did. It's real. No going back.

"You came here to confront her."

"Maybe, if you want to put it that way."

"So, you would have good reason to argue with her? Get into a pushing match?"

"I didn't argue with her. I didn't do anything to her. I found her on the floor." I look up at the unit, the lights bright inside, the police combing through the rooms. "She took the pills, didn't she?"

"I don't know, you tell me."

"I saw the blood on the corner of the nightstand. I thought she must have fallen . . . Will she be okay?"

"We don't know yet." He looks toward the room, back at me. "Did you see anyone else in the immediate area?"

"Nobody. She was alone."

"You make a habit of following people, breaking into their hotel rooms?"

"I had a key, like I said. And I wasn't following *people*. I was following Nathan. Hedra said Lauren knew. I'm pretty sure that was what she said to me. Before she passed out. 'Lauren knew.'"

"What do you think she meant?"

"Maybe Lauren knew about her affair with Nathan?"

"Uh-huh." The detective runs his forefinger across his mustache. "Could your fiancé have a history of meeting women at hotels? Maybe he was involved with Lauren as well?"

The wind pricks my skin like a thousand needles of ice. "I have no idea."

"The night Lauren died, were you outside, checking up on Nathan? Like you were doing tonight?" He waves his pencil in a small circle in the air.

My face is going numb, the lights of the police cars blinding me. "No, I was in bed." My mind flies back to the morning I found Lauren, when I ventured out in my sneakers. They were damp, bits of grass clinging to them.

"Are you sure? Could Nathan have been meeting Hedra that night, too? Maybe a rendezvous on the sly?"

"What are you getting at?" I stare at him coldly. My breath steams up, clouding the air between us.

"Just curious," he says mildly. "Perhaps Nathan was here at the hotel with Hedra Black today, before you arrived."

"He couldn't have been here. He's working."

The detective nods. "Anything else you want to tell me?"

"Nathan said he was helping Hedra leave an abusive marriage."

"She was leaving Dr. Black. The cardiac surgeon."

"His profession is beside the point," I say. "But he's away at a conference."

"That's what I hear." I feel the detective looking at me, but I don't meet his gaze.

"I need to talk to her," I say. "I want to know what was going on, why she took those pills. Why she was here with Nathan. What did she mean, Lauren knew?"

The detective tucks the notepad back into his pocket. "All good questions, Marissa. I'd like to know the answers, too. We'll have to ask her when she wakes up."

CHAPTER THIRTY-FOUR

In the morning, as I park at the hospital, I look at my hands on the steering wheel, my ring finger bare. I drove here in a daze, the detective's questions still chipping away at my sanity. Does he think I make a habit of following people in the night? Could he seriously believe I would have hurt Lauren? What am I even doing here? What will I say to Hedra? She overdosed on an antidepressant, Nathan said when he called last night, but she would be okay. The blood came from a superficial cut, not life threatening. He wanted to keep talking, explaining, but I hung up on him, a tempest of rage rising inside me.

Now I sit here, feeling as heavy and inert as the vehicles parked around me. My body wants to sink into oblivion, but I get out of the car and stretch my legs, realizing how stiff I feel, my limbs heavy with exhaustion. I didn't sleep well.

I walk through the parking lot into the hospital, ride the elevator up to Hedra's room. Through the half-open door, I see the foot of her bed before I see her. A thin stream of sunlight spills in through a bay window, splashing across a tile floor, countertop, a bedside table, the linens. Mounted from the ceiling, a television silently plays out the news. I knock softly.

A soft, throaty voice says, "Come in."

I step inside, clutching my purse. Hedra sits propped on pillows, her head bandaged. An IV line snakes from the back of one hand. She looks toward me, and as I push the door fully open, Keith comes into view, hunched in the chair next to her bed. I've never seen him this way—sleepless, rumpled, his shirt and slacks like an unmade bed. He hardly looks like an abuser; he resembles a distraught husband.

"Marissa," he says. "Come on in." He reaches toward the bed, engulfs Hedra's hand in his.

"I came to see how you're doing," I say to Hedra. *I came to scream at you.* But she looks haggard. I try to tread softly, although my shoes squeak on the floor.

"Mild concussion," Keith says, conveniently leaving out the part about the overdose. "We're grateful to you for finding her." He doesn't mention what Hedra might have been doing at the hotel. What about the pills? Did she take the whole bottle?

"How long will you be in here?" I ask, trying to remain civil.

"I can leave tomorrow," she says, "maybe even today." The reason she was in the hotel remains unspoken, a wedge between us. She touches her forehead. "I don't know what I did. I must have passed out."

She knows perfectly well what she did. I want to yell at her to cut the act, but I can't bring myself to provoke her. I look around for another chair. Keith points to one against the wall, near a countertop with a sink. I pull the chair around to the other side of the bed. "I'm glad you weren't more seriously injured," I say. Or am I?

Keith squeezes her hand. "We're all glad," he says. He looks at me. "You're pale. When was the last time you ate?"

"I—can't remember." Maybe I had cereal this morning, or not.

He points to the bedside table next to me. "Bag of peanuts there. You should eat."

"I'm okay for now. I can't think about food."

"I don't blame you," he says. "It must be difficult, seeing this side of my brother."

"What side?" I say, my throat dry.

He glances at Hedra, then looks at me. "We can talk later. You'll understand."

"I'm not sure I understand anything." I want to shout, *I understand that he lied to me. That anyone or everyone might be lying.* "I don't understand what he was doing in your hotel room. What exactly was going on?"

Hedra blinks away tears, looks out the window. "I'm not sure it's anyone's business."

"What Nathan does is one hundred percent my business," I say.

"Then ask him."

"I already have. I need your story."

"My head hurts," she says.

"Nathan says you'll recover," I say.

Keith makes a sour face. "Nathan says, does he?"

"I'm not feeling well." Hedra touches the back of her hand to her forehead.

I want to say I'm not feeling so well, either, now that my engagement is shot, but I hold back. She's in a desperate condition, and I hate what she and Nathan have done, bringing out this bitter side of me.

"Marissa," Keith says gently. "Hedra should rest. She has a head injury."

I get up and pace, my body trembling. I stop and look at Hedra, assessing her. "Nathan told me you overdosed on a medication and your head injury is superficial."

Her hand rises reflexively to her forehead. "I have stitches."

"What, one or two? Never mind." I glare at Keith. "Don't you wonder what she was doing at the hotel with Nathan? Don't you want to know if your wife was sleeping with your brother? He said you were abusive to Hedra. He was helping her leave you." I'm aware of the way I must sound—disturbed, accusatory, maybe even delusional. But I feel as though I have no control over my life. First Lauren, then Nathan.

I'm on a roller coaster about to jump its tracks, and there's nothing I can do to stop it.

She gazes down at her left hand, fiddles with her wedding ring.

Keith looks at her, pain in his eyes. "Is that the story you both told?"

"No, it's not true," she whispers.

A nurse peers in the door. "Is everything all right here?"

"Fine," Keith says. "Everything is okay. I've got it under control." The nurse nods and leaves. He turns to me. "Look, this is not the time or place."

"Neither was the night before last," I say, "or any other night she spent in the hotel with Nathan. How long was it going on? Were you with Nathan even when he proposed to me?" I see her now, the way she excused herself from the dinner table, escaped to the bathroom. I see Nathan whispering to her in the hall.

"No," she says softly. "Nothing was going on." She picks up a plastic mug from the bedside tray and takes a sip, her hand shaking.

Keith holds the straw to her lips. "Slowly," he says. "You'll choke."

"How long then?" I say to Hedra.

She keeps sipping, staring blankly ahead of her.

Keith puts her cup on the table. "She's exhausted. She shouldn't talk too much right now. She and I have to discuss things first, and the detective is coming in to interview her."

So, I beat Dan Harding to the punch. I put my purse on my shoulder. "She needs to tell me. Hedra, I need to know. Why would Nathan propose to me if he was seeing you? If he . . ."

"That's Nathan," Keith says in a quiet voice. "It always has been his modus operandi. He's done this before."

"Stop," Hedra says, turning her head toward the window. The IV bag catches the light as it drips.

"He's had affairs before?" I say.

"Don't do this," Hedra says.

"Were you planning to be with Nathan long-term?" I say.

Keith stands abruptly. His shirt is untucked in the back. "She's not with him. She's coming home with me," he says in a broken voice. "Aren't you?"

"Yes, I'm going home," she says, not looking at me.

I rest my hands on my purse. "When I found you, you were mumbling. Do you remember?"

She glances at me sidelong, a furtive look. Then she looks out the window again. "I don't remember anything. Only . . . one minute I was standing by the bed, the next I was here."

My heart plummets. Could she have forgotten? "You said something about Lauren. It sounded like 'Lauren knew'?"

She shrugs, her lips turning down. "I don't remember anything like that."

Keith sits down again, the color falling from his cheeks. "I'm sure Hedra didn't know what she was saying."

"You're sure," I say.

"I don't remember," Hedra says, looking toward the window.

"But you know what I'm talking about. Do you know what happened to her? To Lauren?"

"She fell," Hedra says. "Everyone knows that."

"Did you lose a scarf that night, at our house?"

"What are you talking about?" she asks.

"I found a scarf in the water, where Lauren died. The detective took it . . . The scarf belonged to you."

Hedra looks up at me, her gaze sharp. "I have no idea what you're talking about."

There is something, a connection—the scarf, Lauren, Hedra, Nathan. But what? "Did you bring the scarf when you came over that night? How did it end up in the water?"

She pushes herself up against the pillows. "What scarf? I don't have any scarf."

"I saw the receipt in Rianne's boutique. From the Saturday before last."

She looks anxiously at Keith, then back at me, a veil falling over her eyes. "I bought stuff in her boutique, but—"

"You were in Tranquil Cove that day?" Keith is staring at her as if she is a strange creature who has just emerged from a cave. "You told me you were visiting a sick friend."

"I was," she says, but her voice wavers.

"What is Marissa talking about, Hedra? What is this about a scarf?"

"It's nothing. I don't know about any scarf in the water. What does that have to do with Lauren?"

"She struggled," I say, feeling myself shaking. "She didn't want to fall off that cliff. She was bruised. Branches were broken."

"I don't know what happened to her. I was asleep." Hedra's face is ashen now.

Keith stands again and steps right next to Hedra's bed, pushes the hair from her forehead in a tender gesture. She flinches, turning her head away from him. "If you know something, honey," he says, "we need to tell the detective."

She holds her breath, deflates on the exhale. "There's nothing to tell."

"Are you sure, honey? If you do know—"

"I don't. I don't know!"

"All right." Keith pats her arm. "But if you're trying to protect someone. Nathan?"

"I'm not. I told you. I don't know what she's talking about."

"All right," Keith says. "You're tired. Get some rest."

"That's all I've been doing!"

Keith ushers me out into the hall, and as he leans in toward me, I catch a whiff of his subtle aftershave. "We need to talk," he says. "You and I, about all this. We have the same grievance."

"Or a similar one," I say, sliding the palms of my hands down my jeans.

"What did Nathan tell you? About me?"

"I think you know. About the past, about the way you treated him—"

"I was a shithead. I admit it. But we were kids. You should watch out. Nathan's no saint. He can turn on the charm." He scratches his unshaven chin, runs his hand along his cheek.

"Funny, he said the same thing about you." Right now, neither brother succeeds with me in the honesty department.

"Whom are you to believe?" He straightens and steps away from me as a nurse strides by.

"Exactly my question. Maybe neither one of you."

"I can't blame you," Keith says, glancing back into the hospital room. He looks down at his black shoes, then at me. "But right now, Hedra's my primary concern. Do you know how many of those pills she took? At twenty-five milligrams, nine pills. Almost enough to kill her. Almost. Whatever problems we've had, they're not worth losing her. She's going to need therapy."

"Does she want to go into therapy?" I ask. Or was she trying to escape from him? From a life she couldn't bear?

"She'll agree. She'll see the wisdom in it. Whatever might have been going on between her and Nathan, it's over now. She assures me of that."

"You're assuming she even wants to go back to you."

He scratches his jaw again, looks down at me. "Why wouldn't she? We all get restless now and then, don't you think? Hedra wanders, but she always comes home eventually, one way or another."

CHAPTER THIRTY-FIVE

When I return to my house, my father tries to reassure me from his photo, his eyes always kind and forgiving. Too forgiving. He thought only the best of my mother, even after she left. *She needs a little vacation,* he said. *She'll be back.* But he was wrong.

She left in spirit long before she left in body. All those short trips on her own—to Arizona, New Mexico, California. She claimed to be attending conferences, visiting a cousin. Little did we know, she had been planning her final departure for years. Setting aside money, mapping a travel route. When I returned from my first year of college to spend Christmas with Dad, she had cleared out her belongings, including all the photographs of herself—anything that might remind us of her. But she'd left her Best Mom mug behind, the one I had given her for Mother's Day when I was twelve years old.

Her latest postcard catches a ray of filtered sunlight on the dining table.

Dear Marissa, Sven and I are in Milan for a gallery show. What a city. If I didn't love Paris so much, I could move here. Come for a visit. Thinking of you. Love, Mom.

The words lean to the right, trying to escape the paper, the way my mother longed to abscond from us. Well, why didn't she leave earlier? Nobody was stopping her.

I try to imagine an impossible scene: my mother calling to ask how I'm doing, what's been going on in my life. As if she genuinely cares. She boards the first plane home to support her daughter in her time of need—but she never will. If I contact her, she will react the way she did when she called on my nineteenth birthday, February 9, not long after I caught Lauren in bed with Jensen. *Love can be harsh. But you pick yourself up and keep going, don't you?* My mother's voice quickened, the words stumbling away from the telephone. *Mari, I've got to hang up. My taxi is here.*

Not that I expect anything from her anymore. Not that I've needed her in years. I write to her sister, my aunt in Mumbai, and other relatives scattered all over India, their support diluted in handwritten letters or brief Facebook messages. I ignored all the early signs of my mother's desire to leave, but they were all there. She stared off into space, rushed through meals before shutting herself in her study. I latched onto the times she laughed with me, brushed my hair, went shopping with me for school clothes. But she never used the mug I gave her, and she left it behind.

Did I ignore the signs with Nathan, too? How well do I really know him? How well can we know anyone? "Dad, help me," I say to his picture. But he offers me no comfort.

~

The day after I visited Hedra in the hospital, she went home with Keith. I haven't spoken to her in the nine days since, or to Nathan, although he has tried to call several times. Once, he showed up at my door, but

I didn't answer. As he returned to his truck, shoulders slumped, I saw Bee Mornay's curtain flutter in her living room window.

I'm grateful to be back at the school, immersing myself every day in the solace of work. This morning, a chickadee fluffs its wings in the birdbath outside my office window. With such ease, the feathers flutter, droplets of water flying in all directions. Buoyant, ethereal, the tiny creature takes flight above the planet's troubles. There is something timeless and otherworldly about birds, the surviving descendants of dinosaurs. Evidence of past eons. I could take comfort in knowing that millions of years from now, our lives will amount to nothing but a cosmic hiccup. Lauren's unseeing eyes will revert to stardust. Nathan and Hedra, locked in an intimate embrace, will disappear into ancient history. Of this I can be sure. Nobody will remember me missing Nathan and Anna and the life I thought we had.

I'm grateful for the routines of the school day—the kids running and yelling, the smells of books and markers. The view from my office, of alders and dogwood trees, has a calming effect on my students. If only I could relax, too.

"Earth to Marissa," Julie says from the doorway. She splashes in, a fashion statement in a cobalt dress and an oversized orange pullover, carrying a paper coffee cup from the Tranquil Café. She plunks the cup on my desk. "I thought you could use another pick-me-up this morning. Off the floor, by the looks of things."

"I've been a downer, haven't I?" I say, pushing back my hair. "You're my coffee angel." I gesture to a chair.

"Coffee angel, coffee angel," she sings in her melodic voice to the tune of "Earth Angel." She gives me an awkward shoulder hug. "But seriously, how are you holding up?"

"Work helps. I go crazy at home."

"Better to go crazy at school, right?" She slides into the chair, crosses her legs, and swings her foot.

"Work keeps me sane," I say, eyeing my paperwork, the seventy-three unread emails on my computer screen. "I've got Anna for a session this afternoon. I'm nervous."

Julie stares at me, her mouth dropping open. "Are you up for that?"

"Her stuttering is getting worse. Rianne called me yesterday, asked me to see her again."

"You can refuse. Someone else can do it."

"I thought about it, but I miss Anna. I know it's only been a couple of weeks, but she's . . . she's like my own daughter."

"Could a session with you bring up issues for her?"

"I worry about that, too, but Rianne said Anna wants to see me. I don't want her to think I've abandoned her."

"You didn't. Her dad abandoned you. Let's not forget who fucked whom. Oh, my bad. I forgot we're at school. But I'm angry at that man. On your behalf."

"Thank you, that helps," I say, sipping the strong coffee, grateful for a double shot of caffeine. "But I didn't actually catch him in bed."

"Only in a hotel room in an intimate embrace with his sister-in-law."

"Don't forget he had a perfectly plausible explanation."

"You're being facetious, aren't you?"

"I'm not sure, to be honest."

"Whoa, okay."

"I don't want to believe the worst about everyone," I say.

"You don't. You trusted him."

"You're right, I did. I just need time."

"Take plenty of it." She gets up and heads for the door. "Enjoy your morning. I have class in five minutes."

"Thanks for the coffee," I call after her as she leaves.

My first appointment is with an eight-year-old girl named Fria Walters, who was in speech therapy for six years before I diagnosed her with a cluttering disorder. I try to clear my mind before she tiptoes into my office. She sits across from me at the blue table in the corner, the binder of visuals between us. She keeps fidgeting, slouching in her seat.

"Good morning, Fria. How are you today?"

"I'm good," she says softly, turning to the right, then the left. Stretching her arms above her head.

"Let's practice our sentences. Remember what we learned? Take each card in order, left to right. Nice and clear. Take your time. I'll record you on my iPad." I open the app and click record.

"I want," she says, placing the first card in front of her. Second card: "to order a . . ." and then, the third card: "cheese pizza. I want to order a cheese pizza."

"Beautiful," I say. But the words of her next sentence—"For dinner, I want to eat some pasta"—pile together in a heap.

"How did that sound to you?" I say.

Fria shrugs.

"Let's listen to it. Then you can tell me if it was smooth or bumpy." I hit the play button in the app, and she listens.

"Bumpy," she says and sighs.

"I'll read the cards, and then you try again. You were a little rushed at the end there."

She keeps fidgeting, stretching her arms to the sides, sliding down, sitting up, kicking her legs. But she listens to me, and she tries again. And succeeds.

"Excellent," I say. "You're working so hard!"

After Fria, I breeze through my session with a boy who struggles with the /r/ phoneme. And a seven-year-old student named James, who spends ten minutes explaining his emotions, and how he talks just fine when he's around his friends.

"When you talk to a new person, what happens?" I say.

"I get stuck. My words get stuck," he says, gripping the arms of the chair. He leans to the right side, then the left, jumps to his feet, sits down again. "But only when I'm worried."

"It's good to know yourself. You're very observant." If only I knew myself, or the people I love, as well as James understands his own speech disfluency.

As the hours fly by, I find my rhythm. My sadness fades into the background. A busy day helps to dull the pain. But when Anna walks in gripping Rianne's hand, my emotions rise to the surface. Why is Rianne here? Normally, students come in on their own, directly from class. Maybe she has a bone to pick with me. Or worse, a bone to break into pieces. Julie was right; I should refuse to treat Anna. I hold my breath, then consciously exhale, forcing a smile.

"I'm so happy to see you," I say, hugging Anna. She hugs me back tentatively. Rianne gives me an anxious smile. I let go of Anna.

"We should talk," I say to Rianne. "I don't think I should—"

"Please," Rianne says. "Anna's been waiting to see you. I'll be out in the hall."

"All right," I say, trying not to sound alarmed. What's going on here?

Rianne leaves, closing the door gently behind her. Anna takes her usual chair at the table, an echo of the past. I remember Nathan peeking in the window, then striding in and stealing my breath away. Anna's radiant smile. But now, many months later, she's shuttered and silent.

"How do you feel about being back here again?" I ask her.

She says nothing, looks down at her lap. Unlike every other student I've seen today, she doesn't move. Doesn't fidget. She's a frozen child.

"Would you prefer to see someone else?"

She looks at me wide-eyed and mouths the word *no*.

"You're okay being here with me?"

She nods and nods, her eyes still wide.

"Anna, do you want to tell me about your speech, your fluency?"

She barely breathes. She looks out the window.

"Have you been having trouble speaking fluently?" I say.

She nods, still looking at her lap.

"What's on your mind? What are you feeling?"

She looks at the ceiling, kicks her heel against the chair leg.

"This is hard for you, being back here, but it's okay. We're going to work this out."

Her mouth opens, closes. Nothing comes out.

I point to a visual aid on the wall. "Remember what we learned? Take in enough air . . . easy onsets, light contacts, connect the words."

Anna shrugs, looks out the window. I try a few more questions, show her some pages, but she's disconnected, silent.

"Why don't you step out in the hall and let me talk to your mom for a minute?"

She gets up and slinks out the door. Rianne comes in, twisting her hands together, biting her lip. I close the door behind her. "What's going on with Anna?" I ask.

"She's been talking less and less, and apparently she hasn't been talking at school. You have to do something."

"My thought is, we should bring in some other—"

"Anna is perfectly capable of speaking," Rianne snaps. "It's just all of this—everything."

"I understand," I say, keeping my voice calm.

"Why can't you work with her again? Fix her stuttering?"

"I want to, but . . ."

"You did such a good job before." Rianne lowers her voice to a fierce whisper. "My daughter needs to talk again. You know how kids make fun of her. Now she's not even communicating. You know what you're doing."

"But I may remind her of what happened in recent days. And her dad and I—"

"You're not back together with Nathan, are you?"

"No," I say, "but—"

"Then what's the problem?"

"We're no longer dealing with stuttering. Anna is choosing silence here, with me. I'm not able to diagnose—"

"She needs to get back to normal." I can see the desperation in Rianne's eyes, her helplessness. I can't let on that I feel the same way.

"Why don't you talk to Nathan about taking her to see—"

"A psychologist? She wouldn't be happy about that, and neither would I." She paces back and forth across the tile floor.

"I can't force her to speak. I'm going to remove myself from Anna's treatment, under the circumstances. But I can refer you to someone else. I'll talk to my supervisor, and we'll work something out."

Rianne sighs and squares her shoulders. "Thank you. Well. This is probably the best course of action." She turns on her heel and stalks out.

I sit at my desk, collecting my thoughts, trying to calm my confusion. The day is over, students rushing down the hall in a stampede. What could have happened to push Anna into silence?

My office contracts around me, the air suddenly oppressive. I can't bear to stay in here. I get up and head for Julie's classroom, a rainbow of colors, paintings and drawings, ceramics and collages. The smells of crayons and glue mix with the lingering salty, tangy odors of the young children who've just left.

Julie is at her desk, on the phone. She waves to me. I look at the drawings on the walls, the imaginative musings of children giving me comfort. Until I see an illustration at the end of the row, with Anna's signature at the bottom, and my heart begins to thump. She has drawn a bizarre picture, moody and ominous. The question is, what does it mean?

CHAPTER THIRTY-SIX

Julie hangs up the phone. I motion her over to the picture.

"What is this?" I say. "It's beautiful—but so bizarre."

"I thought so, too. One of my exercises was to have the kids draw a picture of a family, a house, and a tree." She points. "That's Anna's interpretation."

"A dark sky and a two-story house with no windows," I say. "But Nathan's house has windows. Rianne's does, too. So, whose house is this?"

"I asked her. She said it was nobody's house and she accidentally forgot to draw the windows."

"Did you mention this to her parents?"

"Not yet. I didn't think of it . . ."

"Windows are symbolic. They give views, a way out . . . a way in. Curtains over windows, privacy. What house in the world doesn't have windows?"

She shrugs, staring at the drawing. "A house without windows offers no view. Possibly no escape. Or maybe it's not about escape, but it's about not being able to get *in*. I don't know. I'm not a shrink."

"But there's a door," I say, pointing.

"Yeah, but it could be locked."

I point to the shadowy figure of the man in the picture, standing next to the house. "He's tall. Almost as tall as the tree."

"She said that was the dad but not her dad."

"Then whose dad?"

"She wouldn't say."

"The woman. She's large as well. Very . . . tall. And dark. A silhouette. Who is it?"

"She said it was just a lady, apparently."

A tall woman. Could it be Hedra? I point at the third person in the picture.

"It's the kid," Julie says. "But she won't say it's her."

"Am I missing something? She doesn't appear to have any hands."

"She said she forgot to draw them. But she knows how to draw hands."

"This is disturbing. A child with no hands. A child who feels powerless?"

"I bet you're right. Didn't I say you're intuitive?" Julie removes the picture from the wall, puts it on her desk. "I'll mention it to her parents. And the other one. But the other one isn't as much of a worry, maybe. I don't know."

"What other one?" I say, my stomach flipping.

Julie leads me to the other side of the room, to a series of sketches on another wall. "I asked the kids to imagine the world in five hundred years. An archaeologist digs up history in their backyard. What would be found? These students are so creative. We used markers and oil pastels to draw objects that might be buried. When we finished, we painted over everything with a thin layer of watercolor, so it looks like the objects are all underground."

"These are fabulous," I say. "Toys, books, shoes, chocolate bars?"

"You know, nothing ever breaks down in a child's mind." She points to another stylized painting. "Anna's try at it. This is what would be in her yard. Butterflies and phones."

Butterflies and phones. I look at the picture, and the shapes leap out at me. I step in closer, hardly daring to breathe. "Oh my God." I touch the paper, the image underground, the box. "That looks like her jewelry box. It's missing from her room. I thought she took it to her mother's house."

"A jewelry box, huh?" Julie cocks her head to the side, squinting at the painting. "I thought it was her imagination running wild, creating an underground box from which butterflies are escaping."

"The butterfly pattern is on the jewelry box. They're monarchs. Her phone is underground, too."

"Yeah, a future archaeologist will find jewelry boxes and phones. Go figure!"

"You don't understand. Anna's iPhone is missing, too. Rianne got her a replacement phone."

"This is five hundred years in the future," Julie says.

"No, I think it's now. I'm pretty sure Anna buried her jewelry box. And her phone."

"What? But why?"

"I don't know. But I'm going to find out."

CHAPTER THIRTY-SEVEN

In the car, I search through my purse for my key ring, which holds my car keys, cottage keys, the key to my post office box, and the key to Nathan's house. I still have it. I call him. No answer. I leave a message, tell him to meet me at his place. As I drive to Cedarwood Lane, the afternoon grows blustery and bleak. Winter frets at the edge of autumn, waiting to barge in.

I park in the empty driveway, duck against the wind on my way to the kitchen door. I feel a jolt of sadness. This could have been my home, here with Nathan and Anna. If not for . . . I can't think about it now.

The house smells slightly of burned macaroni and cheese. In the kitchen, I find a crusty pot soaking in the sink. Otherwise the house is neat, just a jacket thrown over the couch, the usual shoes jumbled by the front door. Unread newspaper folded on the table in the foyer. The guest room is untouched, as clean and tidy as it was when I last left the house. Nathan's bedsheets are rumpled on one side, the other side smooth. In the bathroom, his toothpaste, shaving cream, and hairbrush are scattered across the countertop.

I peek into Anna's room. Her bed is made, her books and mementos lined up on the shelves. Her desktop looks neat, the photograph of the three of them still taunting me. I think of the dirt on the windowsill, her muddy pajamas. The missing jewelry box, her missing cell phone. Anna, hiding in the tree house, cutting me out of a photograph.

I grab a spade from the stuffy toolshed, slip around to the back of the house. Outside Anna's window, the ground is scuffed, her footprints still visible in the dirt beneath the eaves, where the rain can't reach. What if she climbed out the window and crouched behind the privet bush in her bird-print pajamas? And buried her jewelry box and her phone? If she did, why?

I start digging in the dirt below her window. It doesn't take me long to hit an unyielding object. On my knees, I brush dirt off the jewelry box and wrench it from the ground. It's in a sealed plastic bag. No, three plastic bags. My heart pounds through my skull; my gut twists. Rain spits down, a cold wind pummeling the trees. I fill the empty hole with dirt, smooth over the soil, clean the spade and put it away. I stamp the dirt off my shoes before going inside the house.

"What's in here, Anna?" I say aloud, removing the plastic bags, wiping off the jewelry box with a clean towel. I place the box on the coffee table. I try to open the lid, but it's stuck. No, locked. But it's a toy lock, maybe easy to pry open. My phone rings. Nathan.

"What are you saying about Anna burying the jewelry box?" I hear sirens in the background, yelling.

"She drew it in Julie's art class," I say.

"What?" The sirens grow louder.

"I'm at your house. Come back as soon as you can."

"I'll call you back."

"We should talk—"

But he has already hung up.

Damn it.

I go to the kitchen for a knife to pry open the jewelry box. On the countertop, I find a business card, a black-and-white image with a shiny pearl-themed background. The words on the left read "Divorce

Attorney"; the address and telephone number are on the right. On the bottom, in blue pen, someone wrote, *Hedra, Friday, 2 p.m.* An appointment? No doubt. Hedra plans to meet with a divorce attorney, Arthur Nguyen.

Of course. He thought he saw two shadows beneath the motion sensor light. A divorce attorney, hired by Nathan and Hedra. What could he know?

I throw on my coat and boots and jog up the road to his house. Evening is falling. The rain has stopped for now. Light shines in the dining room window; his red BMW sits in front of the garage. I take a deep breath, head up the walkway. The bell echoes through the house. Bert yaps in the distance. I look up the street; no sign of Arthur. The barking seems to be coming from the backyard.

I cup my hands to the window next to the door, peer into the dimly lit hallway. The light in the kitchen is on, too. I see the edge of a stainless-steel refrigerator, the corner of the dining table. I knock on the door. "Mr. Nguyen!" I call out. "Mr. N!"

No answer. I turn the knob. Not locked. A creak as the door swings open. I step into the foyer, trespassing. But people have been doing a lot of trespassing lately. A lot of crossing lines. "Mr. Nguyen! Hello! It's Marissa Parlette! You know, Nathan's fiancée?" As if I needed to announce this now-defunct fact. "Former fiancée," I mutter. Still, no answer.

I survey the gaudy interior furnishings, the dark colors, kitschy statues, mementos from his travels. Rows of photos line the bookshelves, showing his three daughters, his wife, who left for California. Maybe they got sick of Arthur representing philanderers. I know I'm bitter, but I can't help these thoughts.

If he's not here, why is his car in the driveway? Why is Bert barking somewhere in the backyard, the front door open, the lights on? Something doesn't sit right. I retrace my steps, hurry out the front door, race around behind the house, down the slope. A white shape hurtles toward me. It's Bert, dirty, tangled—a mop of a little dog.

I kneel to pet him. "Bert, it's okay. Where's your dad?" Usually, Arthur walks Bert on a leash, keeping him close. I turn toward the house—the back door is open, a triangle of light spilling out. Arthur never lets Bert run loose. Bald eagles often circle overhead. They've been known to pick up small dogs.

"Come on, let's get you inside," I say with growing unease. I pick up Bert and carry him back into the house. I head back out to the garden. "Mr. Nguyen!" I call out, my heart beating, beating. I follow the path past his vegetable patch.

"Mr. Nguyen," I call out again, heading for the pond. Something is there. Floating. I run, losing my breath. I recognize his red-and-white plaid shirt, billowing outward, his hat, a halo of dark hair. *A body.* Arthur Nguyen is floating facedown in the water. "Mr. Nguyen! Somebody help!" I call 911 on my phone. "This is Marissa Parlette," I say when the operator comes on the line. "Send an ambulance to the corner of Cedarwood and Waterview Roads in Tranquil Cove. Arthur Nguyen lives here. He's in the water, facedown."

The operator says help is on the way.

"Hurry!" I throw the phone onto the ground. I need both hands. I wade in, my heart racing, the icy water slamming into my legs. My muscles seize. The muddy bottom gives beneath my boots. I try to pull his arm. He's too heavy. I stumble, he starts to sink. I'm calling for help. I struggle to turn him over. His lips are blue, his skin ashen. "Mr. Nguyen! Arthur!" I shake him. Nothing, no response. I can hear my labored breathing. He's slipping from my grip, and then someone's running up behind me, fast footsteps.

"What's going on?" Jensen shouts, wading in.

"Help me get him out!" I yell.

"Shit, shit," Jensen says, hauling Arthur out. "What the hell happened?"

"I don't know—I just came over and saw him." I gasp for breath, shivering, waterlogged. "I called 911. They're coming."

"Is Nathan home?"

"No."

Jensen turns Arthur on his back on the ground, rips open his shirt, splays his fingers over his heart, interlocking them with the fingers of his other hand. He starts fast chest compressions. "One two three four five six . . . Come on, Arthur."

I call Nathan again; his phone sends me to voice mail. "Pick up! Arthur Nguyen's unconscious. He's not breathing. He fell into his pond. I called 911. Hurry!"

Jensen keeps performing chest compressions, a hundred a minute. "Damn it. He's still not breathing. Water in his lungs, maybe."

"Keep trying," I say, my voice breaking.

I think of the family photographs in the living room, his three daughters side by side, grinning at the camera. My teeth chatter, the sky darkens. In the house, Bert is going crazy, barking and throwing himself at the door.

"Did you see what happened?" Jensen says, still working. "Did he fall? Was someone else here? He's ice cold."

"I don't know. I came by to talk to him. The door was open. Bert was wandering around!"

"How long was he in the water?"

"I don't know."

"I hope it wasn't long. He's not bloated. I think that's a good sign."

In the distance, sirens rise on the wind.

"Is anything happening?" I say, frantic.

Jensen shakes his head, out of breath.

"Keep going," I say. Arthur's toothy smile comes back to me, the single dimple on his left cheek.

"He's on medication," Jensen says.

"What medication?" I say.

Jensen keeps up the compressions. "I don't know. Beta-blockers, aspirin. Blood thinners. He was complaining about all the meds the other day. Go and look. In the cabinets."

"Jensen," I say. He's in shock. So am I. "He can't ingest the medications if he's unconscious. If he's not breathing."

Jensen pants from the effort of pumping on Arthur's chest. But he keeps at it. "We need an automatic defibrillator. Maybe he has one. Check. It would be in an orange case. My dad has one."

I run into the house, the dog following at my heels as I check the bathrooms, the bedroom. Arthur is neat to a fault; no sign of a defibrillator.

The ambulance pulls into the driveway, lights flashing, siren blaring. I dash out to meet the medics in the driveway, leaving Bert inside, my lungs about to burst. "He's in the backyard!" I yell.

Two medics run down with their bags, in uniforms like Nathan's. But Nathan's not here.

We stand back as they check Arthur's vitals, his pulse. "Pupils equal and responsive but sluggish," one medic says. "No detectable pulse. Cyanotic." They attach a defibrillator to his chest, and a metallic voice says, "Analyze, stand clear, shock advised."

"I'm clear, are you clear?" says one paramedic.

The other responds, "I'm clear," and presses a button. The defibrillator shocks Arthur, and his body arches off the ground. As the defibrillator recharges, they fit an oxygen mask over his face. I stand back, Jensen holding my arm, my view blocked by the medics crouched over Arthur. They transfer him to a stretcher, rush him into the ambulance, continuing CPR as a black sedan pulls up next to them. Detective Harding is here.

CHAPTER THIRTY-EIGHT

"I told you, I saw him in the water, facedown," I say to the detective as the ambulance speeds away. No sign of Nathan. I pull the heavy blanket around my shoulders, handed to me by a medic. My clothes are soaked through. The cold night breathes on my face. The detective has already questioned Jensen, who has gone home.

Now the detective pulls me aside. "You rang the doorbell, knocked, heard the dog barking, went around back, and saw Mr. Nguyen in the water."

"Yes, will he be okay?"

"Too early to say. I'll let you know as soon as I know."

"I need to change into dry clothes," I say, drawing the blanket closer around me.

"Do you need a ride somewhere?"

"I'm fine. I have a key to Nathan's house."

"You seem to show up in these violent situations," he says. "You should put 911 on your speed dial."

"I don't know how it works out that way."

"Maybe you do know."

"What's that supposed to mean?" I'm prickling, moving away from him.

"Let me get this straight. You found a business card in Nathan's house. You think he and Hedra Black employed Arthur Nguyen as their attorney."

"I don't know why Hedra was planning to see Arthur," I say, shivering. "I came here to ask him."

"You didn't ask Nathan."

"I haven't spoken to him in a while."

"But you were in his house."

"I had to pick up something I left behind."

"Have you spoken to Hedra Black?"

"At the hospital after I found her at the hotel. But not since then."

"And when you arrived here, you—"

"I came around here and saw Arthur in the pond."

"Did you see anyone else in the house when you arrived?"

"Nobody until Jensen showed up."

"You came over to have a little chat with Mr. Nguyen. A little chat that turned into an argument?"

"What are you implying?" My throat constricts. I'm quaking all over, his accusation slamming into me. "We're done here." I throw off the blanket and head toward Nathan's house, but the detective grabs my arm.

"Wait." He pulls me back toward him. "Maybe you didn't argue with Mr. Nguyen; maybe you did. Maybe he saw you outside the night Lauren Eklund died."

I yank my arm away, shocked at the detective's direct accusation. I'm quivering with rage. "What? You can't be serious." The memory of my shoeprints flashes in my head.

"Like I said, you make a habit of showing up—"

"I told you, I don't know why. I've been trying to figure that out, too." My feet are ice, numbness traveling up through my body.

"Right." He looks at me, his nose pink in the cold. "Funny where your curiosity leads you. From one unconscious person to another. And the break-in at your house. Bit of a coincidence, wasn't it?"

I want to slap that mustache right off his face. "You think I made that up? You think I faked a burglary? Why would I do that?"

His breath condenses into vapor. "I don't know. Why would you?"

"You're on the wrong track. Don't look at me. I know what you're thinking. But I wasn't trying to deflect attention from myself. I would never do anything like that. You don't know me at all."

"All right. Maybe I don't." He steps back as Bert starts barking again.

I shift my gaze to Arthur Nguyen's house. "What's going to happen to the dog?"

"I'll keep him for now. I'm a big fan of dogs."

"Is that even allowed?"

He shrugs. "Probably not."

I nod, shivering. Bert goes quiet again. "May I go?"

"For now." He tucks the notepad back into his pocket. His phone buzzes. He answers. "Harding. Yeah." He listens, frowns, looks at his shoes. "Thanks for letting me know." He hangs up and rests a hand on my shoulder. "Looks like they were able to revive Arthur Nguyen. It will be a while before we know if he suffered any brain damage. He's unconscious, but he is alive."

~

Back in Nathan's house, I change into a pair of his jeans, which I roll up numerous times, a flannel shirt, and his thick cotton socks. I throw my clothes in the dryer, then I make a cup of hot tea and try to gather my wits. The neighborhood is quiet and dark with the police and the ambulance gone.

I'm still trembling with anger. The detective can't possibly believe I vandalized my own house, pretending my dress was stolen. He must be trying to push my buttons. But why? Does he really think I had anything to do with what happened to Lauren? To Hedra? To Arthur

Nguyen? Did someone try to kill him? If so, who would do such a thing? Did the same person kill Lauren? If Anna saw something that night, maybe her jewelry box holds an answer.

I pry open the lid with a knife, breaking the lock and the flimsy hinges. That's the thing about jewelry boxes. They give only the illusion of security.

A dazzling array of silver and stones winks out at me. A bracelet, a gold earring, a few smooth quartz specimens, rare coins. Found things. In the top drawer, an envelope bulging with small bills—from ones to fives. Anna's allowance? In the bottom drawer, her cell phone is carefully zipped into a plastic bag full of uncooked rice. She didn't lose the phone. It was here all the time. Did she bury the phone because it got wet? But why not say she got her phone wet? Why bury it? I press the buttons, but the battery is dead.

In Anna's room, I can't find a charger. Does she even have one? Did she take it with her for her replacement phone? Did she ever back up this phone?

From my own phone, I dial Rianne's cell phone.

"Marissa?" she says cautiously. She must have my name in her contacts list.

"I'm at Nathan's place, I—"

"At Nathan's! But I thought—"

"It's a long story. Could I talk to you about Anna?"

"You sound strange. Is everything okay?"

"It's a long story . . . This is going to sound weird, but . . . she buried her jewelry box in the backyard, under her window."

"What? That is odd. How do you know this?"

"In art class, she painted what an archaeologist might find five hundred years from now—"

"I didn't see that painting," she says, sounding slightly miffed.

"She didn't take it home. It's on the wall in the classroom. But she painted an identical jewelry box underground, and I noticed her jewelry box was missing from her room. I connected the dots."

"And Nathan dug up the box?" she says.

"No, I did," I say.

"Oh." A beat of silence. "Did you tell him? Is he there?"

"I told him, but he's working."

"Well. I'm on my way back with Anna. Did he forget that he has her this evening?"

"He and I aren't . . . I'm not—I mean, I don't know the details of his schedule these days."

"I'll try to get in touch with him to have him meet us there. Thank you for telling me about the box."

I hang up, feeling alone, my mind plagued by images of Lauren, her head caked in blood. And Hedra, incoherent, drugged. And Arthur Nguyen floating in his pond, his lips blue. The jewelry box stares at me from the coffee table, the monarch butterflies dusted in dirt. Outside, a soft rain begins to fall.

Only a few minutes later, Rianne's SUV pulls into the driveway. When she and Anna step inside, Anna stares at the jewelry box and races to snatch it off the table. She trails droplets of rain on the floor, leaving muddy bootprints.

"Not so fast, Anna," Rianne says, eyeing my baggy clothes, her brows rising.

"Long story," I say. "I waded into the pond after Arthur Nguyen. He almost drowned."

"What? Oh no!"

"He's still alive. But unconscious. I don't know if he's going to make it."

"The poor man. You were brave."

Anna's face turns white, the jewelry box clutched to her jacket.

"Give it to me," Rianne says gently. "Take off your coat and boots and get into some warm clothes. I'm going to talk about this with Marissa."

Anna opens her mouth, but nothing comes out. Her painful silence knocks the wind out of me. She won't let go of the box.

"Give it to me," Rianne repeats. "We'll keep it safe. Go and get changed. Now."

Anna doesn't move, as if in a trance. Rianne gently pries the box from her arms, and Anna turns and dashes down the hall, whipping off her raincoat on the way.

"She hasn't said anything?" I say, my voice cracking.

"She isn't mute all the time," Rianne says. "She talks a little to us. To Nathan and me. But in public, and at school . . . It's frustrating. I shouldn't have snapped at you. But I'm at the end of my rope." Rianne's face is pale. Her blond hair appears a dull gray in the dim living room light.

"I understand. Don't worry."

"I wish she would talk to us and tell us what's wrong."

"I hope I haven't traumatized her more by digging up the box."

"You think there might be evidence in here? Of what?"

I sit on the couch, run my hands down my face. A deep fatigue settles into my bones. "I'm not sure, to be honest. But she's hiding something."

"When you told me about the box, I thought—it makes sense. With everything she's done and said. And now, her silence. The way she's been acting. But I was still shocked when you told me about this." We're both looking at the jewelry box. "Do you mind?" she says.

"Go ahead."

She opens the box and takes out the jewelry, the money stashed in an envelope. Then she pulls out the cell phone, which I removed from the bag of rice. "I'm amazed that you dug this up. I don't understand why she would bury it."

"She takes videos out in the woods," I say. "My theory is the phone got wet, and it stopped working. She thought a bag of rice would dry it out."

"Which is a myth."

"But a lot of people swear by it."

She nods thoughtfully. "I feel as though I don't even know my own daughter. I didn't know about the drawings at school."

"Neither did I," I say.

She puts everything back in the jewelry box, and I try to gather myself as footsteps come down the hall. Anna appears in sweatpants and a T-shirt, face flushed, hair still damp. She stares at the jewelry box and mouths *No*, but no sound comes out.

"It's okay, honey," Rianne says, reaching for Anna's hand, but Anna rushes to the table, grabs the box again.

Rianne holds up the cell phone. "I've got this. I'm not sure why you hid the phone in your jewelry box."

Anna gasps, as if her lungs have been ripped right out of her chest.

"Anna," her mom says patiently. "Put the box down."

Anna puts the box on the table. Her arm darts out like a snake flicking out its tongue. She grabs her old cell phone from Rianne's hand, then rushes down the hall.

"Should I go after her?" I say. "Explain why I dug up the—?"

"Don't worry," Rianne says. "Give her some time."

"I shouldn't be here," I say, getting up. "With everything that's happened . . ."

Lights sweep across the wall, voices outside. "The Eklunds are home," Rianne says, leaping to her feet. "Brynn stopped into the shop yesterday. She said they were going away for a bit. I didn't get to offer my condolences at the memorial service. Would you excuse me a minute?" She peers out the kitchen window.

"Go ahead. I'll stay with Anna."

She throws me a grateful smile. "I'll be right back, promise." She pulls on her boots and rushes outside, pulling her sweater tightly around her. I watch from the kitchen window. The wind whips through her hair. Jensen approaches her, rubbing his gloved hands together. Brynn follows. I pour a glass of water and gulp down the cold liquid. What will happen once Nathan arrives to discuss the jewelry box with Rianne? What secrets will they unlock? I turn away from the window and nearly bump into Anna.

"You scared me," I say, pressing my hand to my heart.

In her sneakers, she stands on tiptoe to peek out the window, then presses her fingers to her lips. The whites of her eyes shine in the dimness.

"What is it?" I don't know why I'm whispering.

She places something in my hand—the damaged cell phone from her jewelry box, the screen lit by a photo of the ocean on the home screen.

"This is your phone," I whisper. "The one you buried. You had a charger?"

She nods, swallowing, makes an urgent motion with her hand. The indicator shows the battery is only a quarter charged. She clicks through on the screen, shoves the phone back at me, shows me a series of texts. As I read, my throat tightens and my heart races. The walls begin to pulse.

The texts are dated the evening of the dinner party when Nathan proposed to me. "Anna, these messages . . ."

She scrolls back through earlier messages from previous days, and I read them all, stunned. The missives from Keith are jokes. Let's shoot some squirrels. Oh, you mean with a camera. Anna's response: You're silly. I don't kill things.

The other texts, interspersed with the playful ones, make my blood run cold.

I look up for a moment. Rianne is walking down the driveway with Brynn and Jensen, out of sight behind the hedge.

"Oh, Anna," I say. "You were keeping all this a secret? The texts? Did you bury the phone because you wanted to hide them?"

Her face is pale. She clicks through the phone to her saved images. She scrolls through the pictures, stops at a video, and hits the play button. At first, I see a lone figure in the darkness, and then Lauren passes beneath the motion sensor light on her back porch, her features illuminated. She's in her long black raincoat, carrying my Laurel Burch umbrella. Seeing her alive this way wrenches out my heart. I want to reach into the phone and save her. She hurries out of the light, into the garden. She strides all the way past the gazebo, almost to the edge of the cliff. Hesitates. She's in shadow now. What was she doing there? She was afraid of heights.

She turns halfway, peering in Anna's direction. Maybe she saw a flash of light, a glint off the lens, or she heard a rustling in the trees. The rain has stopped. Was Arthur Nguyen already outside with Bert? The wind picks up, and the scene grows slightly lighter. Perhaps the moon is peeking through a break in the clouds.

Then from the left a shadow enters the picture. The shape of someone rushing toward Lauren. The umbrella points in the assailant's direction, the neon blue glowing in the night. The moon shines brightly now. *Watch out!* I want to scream. *Someone's coming. Look behind you. Run!* But she doesn't turn around. The shadow is right on her before she finally turns. A flurry of tussling follows, an altercation. A dog yaps in the background, a distant echo. Someone yells, *Hello?* Far away. A voice. Arthur's? More barking.

The umbrella falls, tumbling away into the darkness. *No, Lauren, hold on. Keep your balance.* Lauren stumbles backward, grabbing at branches, and the shadow seems to reach for her, but she is gone. Nothing but darkness. Not a sound. Her assailant turns and flies back toward the house. The motion sensor light floods the yard again, and in that fleeting moment every facial feature is visible, identifiable. There is no mistaking who it is.

CHAPTER THIRTY-NINE

Rianne shows her face to the camera, then she rushes out of the light, taking flight out of the camera frame. The video ends.

Anna's trembling.

"Your mom's face," I say. "It's clear. Did she see you?"

Anna shakes her head, and we both look out the window. Rianne is still talking to Brynn, but Jensen has started his truck.

"But why?" I say, my mind reeling.

Anna's eyes fill with tears.

I scroll through the texts:

Rianne: She'll never be your mother. I'm your mother.

Anna: I love you, Mom.

Rianne: I don't want you to call her Mom.

Anna: I won't. You're my mom. She's just Marissa.

Rianne: She needs to go away.

Go away . . .

And earlier:

Who is that woman your father is seeing? We need to be a family again . . . Don't you want us to be a family? As I read through the conversations, a picture of Rianne emerges—a woman full of hate and fear. She despised me, but why push Lauren off a cliff? My blue umbrella, flipped upside down in the sand. The umbrella I carried to work through the rainy season, until Lauren borrowed it.

"Anna," I whisper in growing horror. "You thought . . . Did you think your mom pushed me off that cliff? Did she think that Brynn's mom was me?"

Anna nods vigorously. No wonder she hid in the tree house, told me to leave. *Can a person be good and bad? Even me? Even you? Even—?* When I interrupted her in the tree house, was she about to ask, *Even my mom?* No wonder the stuttering returned. No wonder Anna won't talk.

"The picture in your photo album from the fair," I say. "Did your mom cut me out?"

Anna nods, tears spilling from her eyes.

"Don't delete this video, Anna."

She nods, shivering all over.

"I know it's your mom," I say, hugging her. "You're worried she'll get in trouble. That you'll get in trouble."

Anna nods again.

"Everything will be okay."

She cries softly. She loves her mother, wants to protect her, and yet.

I try to unwind everything Rianne said to me, try to separate the truth from the lies. But the texts to her daughter. The video. Rianne is coming back. The kitchen doorknob rattles. Anna slips the cell phone into her sweater pocket and backs up into the living room.

Rianne strides inside, the door slamming after her. She takes off her boots, looks at Anna. "You decided to come out of your room," she says, then turns to me. "Any word from Nathan?"

"He called back," I lie. "He wants me to bring Anna to him."

Rianne frowns, rubbing her shoulders and shivering. "Bring Anna to his work? Is he crazy?"

"He can be," I say, hoping my smile looks real, hoping she can't see the fast pulse in my neck. The words she sent to her daughter, the threats. The expression on her face in the video. Rage.

"We should hit the road." Will she let me take Anna? We need to escape. Rianne wouldn't physically harm her own daughter, would she? The emotional damage she has wrought upon Anna—maybe she doesn't even realize she's inflicting such pain. Or maybe she does, and she doesn't care.

"You're not taking my daughter anywhere," Rianne says. "I'll call Nathan."

"We're going," I say, pulling on my shoes.

"What did Anna show you on her phone? I see it sticking out." She points to Anna's pocket. Anna gasps, pushes the phone deeper into her pocket.

"I don't know what you're talking about," I say.

"She needs to tell us why she buried her phone."

"No, she doesn't," I say. "Not right now."

"She does. She's my daughter."

"She was showing me photographs," I say.

"I'd like to see them, too," Rianne says, holding out her hand.

I grab my purse, sling the strap over my shoulder. "Come on, Anna. Let's go."

Rianne stands in the way, hands on her hips. "Nathan didn't call you back."

"Yes, he did," I say.

"No, he didn't. Anna, honey, hand over your phone."

"Don't do it," I say. "Anna, keep your phone." I grip Anna's hand, sidle toward the front door.

"Who are you to give my daughter orders?" Rianne says, moving to stand in front of us again. There's a stillness about her, like the air before a storm. "I know there is more on that phone. I suspected something was up when you said you'd dug up the jewelry box."

Anna appears to be barely breathing.

"You're her mother," I say. "And you can't see how troubled she is."

"Oh, I see. I see how a broken family has done a number on her. Let go of her. I don't trust you with my daughter."

"You don't trust me? Seriously?" I tighten my hold on Anna's hand.

"You disrupted her life. Who knows what else you've done? Everyone knows you hated Lauren. You were jealous of her."

I see Lauren's face in the moonlight, my shoeprints in the dirt. *Who knows what else you've done?* I can't let Rianne get under my skin. "Anna and I are leaving," I say in a shaky voice.

"Give her to me. How do you think it affects her when you carry on with Nathan?"

"You don't think your behavior has any effect on her?" Only ten feet to the door, but I have to get past Rianne. She's bigger and stronger than me.

"Don't tell me how to raise my child." Her lips tighten, her eyes black beneath the ceiling bulb.

"You were never really concerned for her. This was all about you. You didn't want Nathan to marry me."

"How dare you? My concern is always for Anna, for our family."

"Did you send me those flowers? Welcoming me back to my cottage?" I'm playing for time. I can't make a call. My cell phone sits on the kitchen counter. If I backtrack, Rianne could grab Anna.

"You don't have much of an aesthetic sense," Rianne says. "When I spoke to Anna that day, she told me you'd gone home. I was so relieved and happy for everyone. I called Vase of Flowers to order the bouquet right away. I tried to be nice to you."

"Nice? You call that nice? I call it manipulative. You broke into my house, didn't you? Not Brynn."

"I wouldn't call it breaking in if you leave a window open. I call it an invitation."

"You admit it! You stole my dress."

"It's not a dress anymore." She smooths down her sweater and gives me a smug smile, as if she is proud of herself.

"What have you done with it?"

"I've ripped it to shreds. It was nothing but a rag, anyway. Perfect for mopping up the floor."

"We're leaving, right now," I say, still gripping Anna's hand.

"Anna," Rianne says, stepping toward us. "You don't want to go with Marissa. She could hurt you."

"I would never harm her," I say, but a voice in my head whispers, *What if she's right?*

Rianne seems to sense my uncertainty. She smiles broadly. "When I move back into the house, Anna will be safe again. Everything will be fine."

"You're delusional," I say. "You don't really believe you'll move back in here, do you?"

She's still standing in our way. "Many couples have separated and then found each other again. Take Elizabeth Taylor and Richard Burton. They were divorced a year before they remarried. Natalie Wood and Robert Wagner. They were married for three years, divorced for ten, and then married again for over eight years until she died. When two people truly care for each other, they find each other again. I know Nathan so well, better than anyone else knows him."

"I'm not arguing," I say. She has lost her mind.

"I only came over to explain this to you. I'm a reasonable person. I saw your umbrella glowing in the dark, and I called your name, but you didn't even reply."

"I wasn't out there. That was Lauren!"

"How was I supposed know?"

"You pushed her off a cliff!"

Rianne grimaces. "She slipped. She lost her balance. She stumbled. It wasn't my fault. If you weren't so—hardheaded. Insistent on pushing your charade with Nathan . . ." Her voice trails off.

"It wasn't a charade," I say softly.

"It was shocking when I realized she wasn't you," she goes on, as if I haven't spoken. "I made a terrible mistake. From a distance, you and Lauren, you look so much alike. Same height, similar hair."

"The scarf was yours, wasn't it?" I'm shaking.

"I didn't realize she had pulled it off until I was already gone. And then you came into the shop . . . I had to think fast."

"You told me Hedra bought the scarf. You forged that receipt?"

She flips her hand through the air. "Piece of cake. The wool item was a different wool item, not the scarf. Big deal."

"You tried to implicate Hedra."

"Well, she is crazy to stay with Keith. Nathan is right. He's psychotic. I've seen the way he talks to her. But you weren't with Nathan long enough to know. Now you're back here again. You should have stayed away."

"When you brought Anna for speech therapy, were you checking up on me? To see if I was with Nathan anymore?"

"The question did pop into my mind, so I asked."

"Unbelievable," I say, shaking my head. "What about Arthur Nguyen? Did you do something to him?"

She makes a clucking sound. "He talks too much. I had no idea he'd seen me that night until his friend came into my shop and told me only this morning. I had to find out what Arthur knew. I found him wading around in that stupid pond. We had a conversation."

"What did you do to him?"

"Me? Nothing at all! As I was leaving, he fell."

A likely story. "You didn't even try to help him."

"What could I do? The poor man had a weak heart."

Anna starts to cry. No wonder she and her mother arrived so quickly. When Rianne argued with Arthur, was Anna waiting in the car? "He was a possible witness," I say. "He's still alive."

"It's unlikely he'll remember what happened to him."

"Did you push him, too? The way you pushed Lauren?"

"How dare you accuse me!"

"You threw her off a cliff! You killed her."

"I told you, she slipped. I didn't kill her!" Rianne lunges at me so fast, I don't have time to react. I barely see her coming. There is no warning, no escalation of anger. She throws me down hard with a guttural shriek. Pain shoots through my head, stabs me behind the eyes. Rianne presses her thumbs into my throat. I try to pry off her fingers, but her steel grip won't budge. I'm gasping. I have to fight. But I can't breathe. Rianne's face swims above me, her eyes wide, spittle forming at the corners of her mouth. *Do you believe in heaven and hell? What if you're good and bad?* Anna's scream echoes in my mind before my vision blurs, images wavering above me, as if I'm underwater.

A voice pierces my brain. Anna shouting "NOOO!" I hear a great cracking sound, and Rianne slumps to the floor. I gasp, grabbing at my throat, and I scramble out from beneath her. Droplets of blood trickle down her forehead. Anna's standing over her, shaking, gripping the neck of the vase she broke against her mother's head. "Mom!" she wails. "Nooooooo!!!"

I feel Rianne's neck—she's got a pulse. "She's alive, Anna," I say, staggering to the kitchen counter for my phone. I dial 911. "We need to go, okay?"

Anna stands there in shock. "No no no no," she says, shaking all over.

The 911 operator comes on the line, asks me where my emergency is. This is the third time I've called emergency in several days. Hedra, Arthur, and now . . . Rianne.

Anna races down the hall to her room. "I need an ambulance," I say. The operator keeps me on the line, asking me more questions about what happened, about Rianne. "She attacked me. It's a long story. Yes. She seems to be breathing. No, she's not conscious. Look, I need to go. I have a child here. I need to check on her." I hang up, hit speed dial for Nathan's number as I rush down the hall to Anna's room. Her window is open, the screen popped out again. Anna is gone.

CHAPTER FORTY

"I'm on my way," Nathan says on the phone. "Get out of there. Go next door!"

"I need to find Anna." I run through the house, calling for her, peering into the guest room. No sign of her.

"You don't have her? You don't have Anna?"

"I'm looking. I think she ran outside again."

"Damn it, Marissa."

I'm pulling on my boots and coat, dashing outside in Nathan's baggy clothes. "Get here as fast as you can." I hang up, sweeping the flashlight beam around the yard. I run to the tree house, climb the ladder. She's not here. I climb down, calling for her. I look to the north, trudge into the wind. A bigger storm creeps in across the sea, blackening the horizon. I jog north, holding up Nathan's pants, which I have secured with a belt, but it's still difficult to move quickly. At the beach stairs, I yell down for Anna, but I can't see her. On a hunch, I keep going toward the trail leading into the wildlife refuge. She's not allowed to come this way on her own. But she did. I'm sure of it. As the meadow gives way to a tunnel of trees, Anna's voice plays in my head. *Go away. Leave me alone.* Her words trembled with fear. She feared her mother. She was scared for me.

"Anna! Anna!" My voice echoes strangely in the forest. I'm trying to run, but Nathan's pant cuffs keep unraveling. I hold the belt with one hand, stop now and then to roll up the cuffs again. She can't have gone far.

Ahead of me, the trail splits into two. The ground is scuffed to the left. A footprint. I take the left branch leading toward the sea. If she's here, does she even know where she's going? The trail abruptly opens and leads to a bluff. I see her, a silhouette bobbing ahead of me. "Anna!" I call out. "Wait!"

She glances over her shoulder, breaks into a run, her backpack bouncing on her back. The wooden railing is gone—it should be there, but now there is only a dangerous bluff. I pick up my pace, my lungs screaming for air. "Don't go near that edge. Anna!" I'm catching up, her knit hat coming into view. She turns to look at me, eyes wide.

She flips the backpack off her back, drops it to the ground.

I stop and hold up my hands. "Anna. What are you doing? Step away. You don't want to—come over here."

She breaks into sobs.

"I'm not going anywhere," I say. "We can talk about this. It's not the end of the world."

She takes a step back toward the cliff, swaying, pebbles falling behind her, crashing down along the rocks to the ocean below.

"Anna, step away! Right now. Honey, right now. Your dad is coming. Everything will be okay. Your mom will be okay. An ambulance will take her to the hospital."

Anna wipes at her eyes. Time slows to the distant ebb and flow of the surf below the cliff. An eternity passes as droplets of rain fall in slow motion.

Nobody's coming. It's up to me. I can do this. I could try to charge after her, wrestle her to the ground, but she could slip, or jump. I could try to talk her down. I think of all the students who repeat their speech exercises, over and over, until one tiny breakthrough occurs. Anna, withdrawing into herself, the words swallowed by her fear, her pain.

"I'm going to sit down," I say. I sit in the grass, in the rain. "Sit with me, Anna. I'm not going to leave you."

She crosses her arms over her chest.

"Let's take a rest." The rain soaks my hair now. I zip my phone into my jacket pocket to keep it dry. I stay seated, resisting every urge to go after her.

She sits slowly next to her backpack. Still too close to the edge.

"I know you don't want to go home; you want to live out here forever."

She nods, looking out to sea. *Don't slip.*

"I don't blame you," I say. "You feel you can't go back. This is so hard."

She nods again.

"All right. I get it. We need to stay warm, then. We could make a fire. I learned how when I was younger, at camp. We'll need food."

She looks at the ground, her face glistening with rain and tears.

"We could pick berries," I say. "Slim pickings this time of year."

She stops crying, sniffs.

"We could find huckleberries," I say. I want to scream at her, *Come away from the edge!* But I sit still, letting the rain soak through me. I don't know how long we've been sitting here, the storm between us. I inch toward her across the wet grass, so slowly I barely notice I'm moving. Nathan shouts in the distance, calling for us.

"Your dad will be here pretty soon," I say. "Want to sit with me? I could use the company."

I'm a few feet away now, so close. I wait, trying not to hold my breath. Forever, I wait. My successes, my failures run through me, and I let them go. An eon passes, the world slowing. Then she picks up her backpack, and head down, she trudges toward me and flops down next to me. I wrap my arms around her and hold her close. "I love you, Anna," I say, and although she doesn't say a word, I know what her reply would be.

CHAPTER FORTY-ONE

"See if you can skip the rocks," Nathan says to Anna. "It has to be flat like this one." He takes a stone and flicks his wrist when he throws. The rock jumps across the water a few times before sinking into the calm sea. I watch his profile, his easy, smooth mannerisms. I thought I knew him, but he's a complicated man.

Anna smiles. Bundled up in her coat and hat and mittens, she looks small and vulnerable. She runs down to the water's edge, delighted to search for another flat stone. It's hard to believe only a week has passed since our traumatic confrontation with her mother. Anna is a resilient child.

Nathan steps back to stand next to me. "I'll go with you to see Hedra."

"I have to go alone. I still have questions."

He sighs. "Okay, but follow the directions I gave you. You won't find the address on a map."

"I know. I'll try not to get lost."

He nods, dejection in his eyes. "I should have done so many things differently. I should have told you about her. I should have fought for full custody of Anna from the beginning. I should have . . . Every damned time she went back to Rianne . . . I'll never be able to live with myself. Why didn't I know? I wish I could go back."

"We can only move forward," I say. "We can't hold on to illusions. Bee Mornay told me that yesterday."

"Bee? Your nosy neighbor?"

"Surprise. She's moving to Hawaii to live with her daughter. The only reason she stayed, she said, was because she believed the spirit of her husband lingered in her house. She talks to him every night. She thinks he has gone to Hawaii to spend time with their daughter, so she's going, too."

"I've heard Brynn outside, talking to her mom," Nathan says.

"I get it," I say. "I still talk to my dad. Sometimes I feel like he's sitting right next to me. I wonder if Brynn feels Lauren close to her."

"Maybe in the backyard. Brynn and her girlfriend planted a memorial dogwood tree back there. Apparently, Lauren loved the white blooms."

"So, Jensen knows about the two of them?"

"I'm guessing so. He was out there with them."

I smile inwardly. A step forward for Brynn.

Nathan bends to pick up another flat rock, sends it skipping across the sea. "I put Anna at risk. And you. I knew Rianne was capable of impulsive, extreme behavior, and I knew what she wanted. The family unit intact no matter what. Borderline personality disorder."

"Is that what your therapist told you?" I say.

"It's a mouthful, but . . . The feeling of abandonment pervaded her life. You're either with her or against her."

"You couldn't have known she would go off the deep end."

"Why didn't my daughter trust me enough to tell me?"

"She's too young to understand that she isn't the selfish, bad kid—that she isn't all of the terrible things her mother told her she was. Maybe she will understand this in time."

"What would I do without you?" He reaches out, but I tuck my hands into my coat pockets. He can't expect more from me. The engagement is on hold, too.

A. J. Banner

"I love you like crazy," Nathan says softly to me.

I smile at him, but I don't answer, not yet. A tall man is striding toward us in a long black coat. The detective. We wave at each other as he approaches. "I'm glad I found you," he says.

"What's the news?" I say, letting out my breath.

"Rianne is under evaluation." He looks toward Anna, crouched on the beach, watching something in the sand.

"What about the scarf? The forensic geologists?" I say.

The detective laughs. "We're piecing together our case. These things take time. How is Anna doing? She started talking?"

"A little," Nathan says. "Mostly to us. She still closes down around strangers."

"Did she tell you any more about what happened that night?"

"She said she was going to delete the video, but her phone got wet. She could see the screen, but it stopped working. She was taking owl videos. She knew she wasn't supposed to be out. But some owls only hunt at night."

"She put the phone in rice," the detective says. "But it would've dried out on its own."

Anna holds up a flat rock and waves it at Nathan. He smiles at her. "If the video came back, someone would see it. She didn't want to let anyone see it."

"She could have destroyed the phone altogether then," the detective says.

"She worried Rianne would get upset, or that it would get her in trouble. Better to bury the phone and give it time to dry out. Then she could retrieve it later and delete the video."

Anna crouches to search for more stones. She looks over toward me, as if to make sure I'm still here. I smile at her and nod while I try to hide my sorrow. I hate that she felt so alone, so vulnerable and scared. I hate that she felt she had to bury her phone inside her jewelry box. I

234

wish I could reach into her mind and remove the memory of her mother pushing another human being off a cliff.

I still feel Lauren close by. Sometimes, when I step into a room, I smell her perfume. When I walk the beach, I see her ahead of me in the distance, always out of reach. But she visits me in dreams. She laughs, raising her wineglass. Once, she apologized. *That day in the apartment. We were young and stupid. I wish I could undo it.* When I woke, her words scattered in the wind.

I've walked to the bluff a few more times, seeking answers that will never come. In the video, she passes the gazebo, strides toward the cliff, although she was afraid of heights. If Rianne had not pushed her that night, would she have jumped? Or would she have turned around and returned to her family? I'll never know.

Anna throws her stone in the water. It skips twice, then sinks. "See what I did, Dad?" she shouts at Nathan.

"Perfect, Sugarplum!" He grins.

We all clap, and she gives us a thumbs-up.

I look at my watch. It's nearly three o'clock. I told Hedra that I would visit her at four, and the drive takes nearly an hour.

"I have to go," I say to the detective. He knows where I'm headed. "Will you keep me in the loop?"

"You know I will," he says as he walks me to the stairs. "Be careful. You don't know what you're going to find when you get there."

CHAPTER FORTY-TWO

His words echo in my mind as I navigate the back roads into the foot-hills of the mountains, civilization growing sparser the farther I drive into the wilderness. I make two wrong turns onto narrow dirt roads before I backtrack and find the house, an unmarked Victorian mansion painted deep green to blend in with the forest. I ring the bell and wave up at a surveillance camera mounted above the door. A minute later, Hedra lets me in. She looks pale and thin, a ghost of herself. She gives me a weak smile, leads me up to the second floor to a large living room. We pass two other women on the way. She gestures to armchairs next to a gas fireplace, and we sit across from each other. Everything here seems run-down—weathered paint on the walls, a threadbare mauve carpet. A slight stale odor.

"It's good to see you," I say, half a lie. "How are you holding up?"

"I'm okay. I've been here only a few days, but it feels like a lifetime. And you? How are things?" She clasps her hands in her lap, looking in my direction, but not at me.

"I'm back at work, taking life day by day."

"I heard about Rianne. Will she be charged with murder?"

"I don't know. There are so many questions. About the video, her muddled confession, what Arthur Nguyen saw."

"How is he?"

"He's still in the hospital recovering. If I had found him any l[...] he might have died."

"I'm glad he didn't," she says, but she's looking toward the window now, shoulders tense, hands twisting in her lap.

"How is your life here? Is your room comfortable?"

"Like a dream." She touches the healing wound on her forehead, from where she hit the nightstand in the hotel. "Nice to have a clear mind for once. Since I got here, all I've felt like taking is an aspirin."

I hear the words she doesn't say, that she meant to take the Sinequan. "Aspirin's a safe bet."

"Over the counter," she says. "My choice, not his, not this time."

"Keith prescribed the Sinequan?" I say.

She heaves a sigh and holds up her hand, looks dispassionately at the fading bruise on her wrist. "He kept telling me to stop complaining and ice it, like it was nothing. Can you believe that?"

"So, Keith was the one who injured you. It didn't happen at a—"

"Photo shoot? No."

"I need to know the truth about what you said. You said, 'Lauren knew.' Did she know about what Keith was doing? Or were you referring to something else? The night she died, she told me she needed to talk to me about Nathan."

Hedra rests her hands in her lap, lightly touches the bruise. "When Keith did this to me, I drove myself to the ER. I waited until he'd left for work. Lauren was on duty. I was surprised to see her all the way out in Bellevue. Shocked, really. She was shocked to see me, too."

I feel something turning over inside me. "What was she doing out there?"

"She had taken some shifts there when Cove Hospital cut back on her hours. The minute she saw my wrist, I could tell she knew."

"What did you two say to each other?" I shift in my chair, looking into the flickering flames of the gas fireplace, then back at her.

"She tried to get me to leave Keith. But I wasn't ready. I mean, I sort of was. But I wasn't. She encouraged me to leave him."

"So, the key card in the closet—"

"Was mine. The hotel manager gave me two keys. I had an extra one."

"Nathan didn't know what was going on."

"Not back then he didn't. But Lauren urged me to talk to him. She said he could help me."

"Why did she think he could help?"

Hedra twirls her hair around her index finger the way she did the morning after Lauren died. "She said she had seen him in action, bringing patients to the ER at Cove Hospital. She said he was a good man, compassionate and discreet. He would keep my secret, she said."

"Even from me," I say dryly. *A good man,* to everyone but his fiancée?

Hedra glares at me. "I don't think that was what she meant."

"I hope it wasn't."

"I think after dinner she was going to tell you . . . about me. But then she had to pick up Brynn from the party. She was going to tell you to talk to Nathan, to get him to help, because I wouldn't. I still had the hotel room, but I had gone back to Keith."

I don't ask why—although the question burns on my tongue. "And at dinner at Nathan's place—"

"She sent me a text, asking how things were going. Keith saw what she wrote. You couldn't tell, but he was furious . . ."

"All of this went over my head. Or under the table."

"I took off to the bathroom . . . I had to keep from falling apart. She texted me again much later that evening, to try to convince me to go back to the hotel. She was going to confront Keith. By then he knew that she knew."

"You could have talked to me. I would have helped . . ."

"I didn't want anyone to know. I still don't." Her words come out dry and brittle, like branches ready to snap. "It took me a while to realize she was right. It was when Keith threatened to break my other wrist. That was when I asked Nathan for help. He extended the hotel rental for me . . ."

"And you and Nathan . . ."

"There wasn't anything going on," she says, but a touch of regret creeps into her voice, and I hear the words she doesn't say. *But I wished there was.*

"Something was beginning. Right?" I still see Nathan burying his face in her hair. "You sent him texts, the ones he said were from Rianne. Late that night, when he got out of bed. Were you the one who texted him?"

"It wasn't me."

"But you texted him the next day."

She shrugs, looks around at the room, at the worn carpeting.

"You did." Another thought dawns on me. "Why did you take those pills?"

"I was feeling down." She refuses to meet my gaze.

"Could it also have been because of Nathan? You wanted to be with him, and he refused you?" I'm only guessing, but I see I've hit a nerve. Her lips tremble, and she focuses on the fading paint on the walls.

"He did, didn't he?" I say.

"I wasn't thinking," she whispers.

"No, you weren't," I say, trying not to sound harsh.

"When I get out of here . . . I need to stand on my own two feet. I need to get my divorce, figure out if I want to press charges . . . You know why I finally came here to the shelter? Keith threatened to break all my bones."

"If he doesn't pay for what he has done to you, he could do it to someone else."

"I know that. I just need time."

"Of course." I get up, feeling my welcome wearing out. "You're brave for leaving him."

The rumble of an engine approaches outside. She gets up, dashes to the window, and pulls back the curtain. Her face pales. Her hand develops a tremor.

"What is it?" I go to stand beside her.

"He must have followed you." Keith's Mercedes creeps up the drive, pulls up in front of the house and comes to a stop. Oh no. Hedra hits a buzzer on the wall, and a woman in a white dress flies up the stairs and rushes to Hedra by the window. Her name tag reads, "Winnifred, Manager."

"That's my husband," Hedra tells Winnifred in a shaky voice.

He gets out of the car in a bespoke black suit. Always impeccably groomed.

"Stay here," Winnifred says. "You're safe right here, inside."

"This is my fault," I say.

"It's all right," Winnifred replies. "It happens. It's happened before."

Keith strides up the walkway and knocks on the door. Rings the bell. Rings and rings.

Winnifred calls out the open window. "Dr. Black. I'm going to have to ask you to leave."

Keith backs up so he can look up at us. "Is my wife in there? Hedra. She needs to come home. Marissa, what are you doing here?"

"She doesn't want to see you," I say, my heart pounding.

Hedra trembles all over. I pull her away from the window. Keith backs up even farther. "Where is she? Tell her to come out."

"She's not coming out," Winnifred says. "Please leave. The police are on their way, and I'm sending out security."

"The police! I'm her husband."

We hear the front door swing open and closed. A large man steps out into view, clad in a blue private security uniform. "Sir, please go on your way."

Keith tries to pass, but the hulking guard holds him back. "Open the damned door. I'm taking her home."

"Sir, please get back into your car," the security guard says.

"I'm not getting into my car! Send her out here."

"Or you'll do what?" Hedra says softly. She draws a deep breath.

"Your wife is not coming with you," the security guard says, gesturing toward Keith's car.

Keith's face contorts into a grimace. He looks up at the window, his hands in fists. A lock of hair falls over his forehead. "Give. Me. My. Wife!" He punches the side mirror of his car, cracking the glass and knocking the mirror askew. He rubs his bloody knuckles. "Give me that fucking bitch whore!"

I recoil at his words. I've never heard him speak this way. Hedra lets go of my hand and crumples to the carpet, breathing fast. Winnifred lifts her from beneath the armpits, helps her to the couch.

The security guard steps closer to Keith. "Sir, leave the premises. Now." Keith hesitates, takes one last look up at the window, his eyes dark, then he gets into his car and drives away. I'm shaking, shot through with adrenaline.

Winnifred kneels in front of Hedra. "He's gone. Can I get you anything, honey? Water? Herbal tea?"

"Tea would be nice," Hedra says weakly.

"I'll stay with her," I say.

Winnifred nods and heads down the stairs. I sit next to Hedra and take her hand. Her fingers are cold and clammy.

"I'll have to move again," she says. "He'll keep coming back."

"You need to tell the police when they get here."

"I know, it's just . . ." She draws a shuddering breath. "I can't believe I protected him. I thought I was doing something good. I thought . . ." Her hand grips mine tightly.

"Protecting him from what?"

She looks up at me, her eyes desperate. "That night, I went out."

"What do you mean, you went out? What night?"

"After dinner at Nathan's place. A noise woke me. I thought Keith had gone out, but he was already back in bed with me. He was still pissed off about Lauren's texts. My wrist hurt so much, I couldn't sleep. So, I went for a walk."

My heart is beating out through the room. "I don't understand what you're saying."

"I didn't bring walking shoes, so I borrowed yours."

My wet shoes, the grass on the soles. The shoeprints on the path the next morning. "You went out in my shoes the night Lauren died. Is that what you're saying?"

She nods, her breathing fast and shallow. She lets go of my hand and crosses her arms over her belly, rocking back and forth. "I went down to the beach," she whispers. "It was early, not even sunrise. It was cold and windy. And dark. I took a flashlight."

My insides are peeling away. "Why didn't you say anything? Why didn't you—?"

"I found her," she says, her face contorting in anguish. "She was on the beach, just . . . lying there."

The walls undulate now. I can't breathe. "But you didn't call 911. You didn't tell anyone. Why not? Why didn't you?" My voice rises.

"I thought Keith had pushed her. I was sure he had. He was so angry that Lauren knew. I thought he was losing his mind."

I stand, nausea surging up through my throat. "You should have woken us. You should have called 911. You should have."

She looks up at me in abject misery. "I thought it must have been an accident. Keith must have argued with her, and she fell. I didn't want him to go to prison. But I should have tried to help her. I know that now."

Her words hammer at me; the room blurs. "What do you mean, you should have tried to help her?" I'm shouting, shaking Hedra's shoulders. Her head flops back and forth like a ragdoll, like she doesn't care.

I feel someone pulling me away from her, and I hear Winnifred's voice yelling, "Stop, stop it! Calm down. The police will be here in a minute."

I whip my cell phone from my coat pocket, but my hands are shaking so much, I can hardly tap in the detective's number. As I wait for him to answer, Hedra gets up and backs away from me, stumbling a little, holding up her hands to ward me off. "It wasn't my fault. I didn't do anything to her. I found her like that."

"Like what?" I shout. The detective's phone is ringing, ringing.

"She was barely alive," Hedra says, breaking into sobs. "By the time I pulled out my phone, she wasn't breathing anymore. I swear, she was already dead."

ACKNOWLEDGMENTS

Deepest thank-you to my brilliant editor, Danielle Marshall; my amazing agent, Paige Wheeler; her associate, Ana Maria Bonner, and their interns; my hardworking author relations manager, Gabriella T. Dumpit; fabulous copyeditor, Rebecca Friedman; wonderful production manager, Nicole Pomeroy; astute proofreaders, Callie Stoker-Graham and Marcus Trower; and the entire Lake Union Publishing team for being awesome in every way. Heartfelt appreciation to the fabulous Tara Parsons, who guided me and believed in me. I'm indebted to my colleagues, experts, and brainstorming crew: Rich Penner, Susan Wiggs, Kate Breslin, Anita LaRae, Christa LaRae, Cynthia Putman Tveit, Patricia Stricklin, Dianne Gardner, Lois Faye Dyer, Sheila Roberts, Elsa Watson, Michael Donnelly, Sherill Leonardi, Elizabeth Wrenn, and Randall Platt. Special thank-you to Glenn Kerns, Leigh Hearon, Anne Clermont, James Hankins, and Yolanda Sibley at Avanti. I'm grateful for keen editorial feedback from Kelli Martin and Shannon O'Neill and to Jennifer Brasch, MD, for information about medications. Special thank-you to Janine Donoho for your perceptive feedback on the manuscript when I asked you to read it in only a few days. Last but never least, I'm deeply appreciative to my readers. You're the reason I write novels. You make this all worthwhile.

ABOUT THE AUTHOR

Photo © 2015 Carol Ann Morris

Born in India and raised in North America, A. J. Banner received degrees from the University of California, Berkeley. Her previous novels of psychological suspense include *The Good Neighbor* and *The Twilight Wife*, a *USA Today* bestseller. She lives in the Pacific Northwest with her husband and six rescued cats. Visit www.ajbanner.com.